William Ellery Channing

Thoreau - The Poet Naturalist

With Memorial Verses

William Ellery Channing

Thoreau - The Poet Naturalist
With Memorial Verses

ISBN/EAN: 9783337280574

Printed in Europe, USA, Canada, Australia, Japan

Cover: Foto ©Andreas Hilbeck / pixelio.de

More available books at **www.hansebooks.com**

THOREAU:

THE POET-NATURALIST.

QUI LEGIT REGIT

Thoreau:

THE POET-NATURALIST.

With Memorial Verses.

BY

WILLIAM ELLERY CHANNING.

"My greatest skill has been to want but little. For joy I could embrace the earth. I shall delight to be buried in it. And then I think of those among men, who will know that I love them, though I tell them not." — H. D. T.

BOSTON:

ROBERTS BROTHERS.

1873.

CAMBRIDGE:

PRESS OF JOHN WILSON AND SON.

DEDICATION.

                                        Silent and **serene,**
The plastic *soul emancipates her kind.*
She leaves the generations **to** *their fate,*
Uncompromised **by grief.   She cannot weep :**
She sheds no tears for us, — **our mother, Nature !**
She is ne'er *rude nor vexed,* **not rough or careless ;**
Out of temper ne'er, patient **as sweet, though winds**
In winter brush her leaves away, and time
To human senses breathes through frost.
                                        My friend !
Learn, from the **joy of Nature, thus to be :**
Not only all resigned to **thy worst fears,**
But, like **herself,** *superior to them all !*
Nor merely *superficial in thy* **smiles ;**
And through the inmost fibres **of thy heart**
May goodness flow, **and fix in** *that*
The **ever-lapsing tides,** *that* **lesser depths**
Deprive of half their *salience.*   **Be, throughout,**
True *as the* **inmost** *life that moves* **the world,**
And in demeanor **show a firm** *content,*
Annihilating **change.**

       Thus Henry *lived,*
Considerate to his kind. **His love bestowed**
Was not a gift in fractions, half-way **done;**
But with some mellow goodness, like **a sun,**
He shone o'er mortal hearts, and taught their **buds**
To blossom early, thence ripe **fruit and seed.**
Forbearing **too oft counsel, yet** *with blows*
By pleasing **reason** *urged he* **touched their thought**
As with a mild **surprise,** *and they were good,*
Even if they knew not whence that motive came;
Nor yet suspected that from Henry's heart —
His warm, confiding heart — the impulse flowed.

" Si tibi pulchra domus, si splendida mensa, quid inde ?
 Si species auri, argenti quoque massa, quid inde ?
 Si tibi sponsa decens, si sit generosa, quid inde ?
 Si tibi sunt nati, si prædia magna, quid inde ?
 Si fueris pulcher, fortis, dives ve, quid inde ?
 Si doceas alios in quolibet arte, quid inde ?
 Si longus servorum inserviat ordo, quid inde ?
 Si faveat mundus, si prospera cuncta, quid inde ?
 Si prior, aut abbas, si dux, si papa, quid inde ?
 Si felix annos regnes per mille, quid inde ?
 Si rota fortunæ se tollit ad astra, quid inde ?
 Tam cito, tamque cito fugiunt hæc ut nihil, inde ?
 Sola manet virtus : nos glorificabimur, inde.
 Ergo Deo pare, bene nam provenit tibi inde."

LAURA BASSI'S
Sonnet on the gate of the Specola at Bologna.

" From sea and mountain, city and wilderness,
 Earth lifts its solemn voice ; but thou art fled,
 Thou canst no longer know or love the shapes
 Of this phantasmal scene, who have to thee
 Been purest ministers, who are, alas !
 Now thou art not.   Art and eloquence,
 And all the shows of the world, are frail and vain
 To weep a loss that turns their light to shade !
 It is a woe too deep for tears when all
 Is reft at once, when some surpassing spirit
 Whose light adorned the world around it leaves
 Those who remain behind nor sobs nor groans,
 But pale despair and cold tranquillity,
 Nature's vast frame, the web of human things,
 Birth and the grave, that are not as they were."

SHELLEY.

" The memory, like a cloudless sky,
 The conscience, like a sea at rest.'

TENNYSON.

" Espérer ou craindre pour un autre est la seule chose qui donne
à l'homme le sentiment complet de sa propre existence."

EUGÉNIE DE GUÉRIN.

"For not a hidden path that to the shades
   Of the beloved Parnassian forest leads
   Lurked undiscovered by him ; not a rill
   There issues from the fount of Hippocrene,
   But he had traced it upward to its source,
   Through open glade, dark glen, and secret dell,
   Knew the gay wild-flowers on its banks, and culled
   Its med'cinable herbs ; yea, oft alone,
   Piercing the long-neglected holy cave,
   The haunt obscure of old Philosophy."

COLERIDGE.

"Such cooling fruit
   As the kind, habitable woods provide."

MILTON.

"My life is but the life of winds and tides,
   No more than winds and tides can I avail."

KEATS.

"Is this the mighty ocean ? — is this all ? "

LANDOR.

"Then bless thy secret growth, nor catch
   At noise, but thrive unseen and dumb ;
   Keep clean, bear fruit, earn life, and watch,
   Till the white-winged reapers come."

VAUGHAN.

"No one hates the sea and danger more than I do ; but I fear
more not to do my duty to the utmost." — SIR ROBERT WILSON.

"The joyous birds shrouded in cheerful shade,
   Their notes unto the voice attempted sweet ;
   Th' angelical soft trembling voices made
   To th' instruments divine respondence meet,
   With the low murmurs of the water's fall ;
   The water's fall with difference discreet,
   Now soft, now loud, unto the wind did call ;
   The gentle warbling wind low answered to all."

SPENSER.

PREFACE.

D R. JOHNSON says that in the dedication to Harris's Hermes, of fourteen lines, there are six grammatical faults. This is as much as we could expect in an English pedant whose work treats of grammar: we trust our prologue will prove more drop-ripe, even if the whole prove dull, — dull as the last new comedy.

In a biographic thesis there can hardly occur very much to amuse, if of one who was reflective and not passionate, and who might have entered like Anthony Wood in his journal, "This day old Joan began to make my bed," — an entry not fine enough for Walpole. At the same time the account of a writer's stock in trade may be set off like the catalogues of George Robins, auctioneer, with illustrations even in Latin or —

> " The learned Greek, rich in fit epithets,
> Blest in the lovely marriage of pure words."

Byron's bath at Newstead Abbey is described as a dark and cellar-like hole. The halos about the brows of authors tarnish with time. Iteration, too, must be respected,— that law of Nature. Authors carry their robes of state not on their backs, but, like the Indians seen

by Wafer, in a basket behind them, — " the times' epitome." But as the cheerful host says : —

> " I give thee all, I can no more,
>   If poor the offering be,"

the best scraps in the larder, like Pip's pork-pie.

A literary life may acquire value by contrast.
"Never mind the world, my dear: you were never in
a pleasanter place in your life. Tenderness is a virtue,
Mr. Twitch." Like the Lady Brilliana Harley, authors
can say of their servants: "I take it as a speciall providence of God, that I have so froward a made aboute
me as Mary is, sence I love peace and quietnes so
well: she has bene extremely froward since I have
bine ill; I did not think that any would have bine so
colericke. I would I could put a little water in her
wine."

Claude Lorraine used to say, "I sell you my landscapes : the figures I give away." So there are patch-
work quilts made by the saints where bits of fine silk
are sewed on pieces of waste paper, that seems, madam,
not that is. But recall the trope that very near to admiration is the wish to admire, and permit the excellence of the subject to defray in a measure the meanness of the treatment : —

> " Stars now vanish without number,
>   Sleepy planets set and slumber."

CONTENTS.

THOREAU.

CHAPTER I.

EARLY LIFE.

" Wit is the Soul's powder."—DAVENANT.

THE subject of this sketch was born in the
town of Concord, Mass., on the twelfth
day of July, 1817. The old-fashioned house on
the Virginia road, its roof nearly reaching to
the ground in the rear, remains as it was when
Henry David Thoreau first saw the light in the
easternmost of its upper chambers. It was the
residence of his grandmother, and a perfect piece
of our New England style of building, with its
gray, unpainted boards, its grassy, unfenced door-
yard. The house is somewhat isolate and remote
from thoroughfares; the Virginia road, an old-
fashioned, winding, at-length-deserted pathway,
the more smiling for its forked orchards, tumbling walls, and mossy banks. About the house
are pleasant, sunny meadows, deep with their
beds of peat, so cheering with its homely, hearth-
like fragrance; and in front runs a constant stream

through the centre of that great tract sometimes called "Bedford levels," — this brook, a source of the Shawsheen River. It was lovely he should draw his first breath in a pure country air, out of crowded towns, amid the pleasant russet fields. His parents were active, vivacious people; his grandfather by the father's side, coming from the Isle of Jersey, a Frenchman and Churchman at home, who married in Boston a Scotch woman called Jeanie Burns. On his mother's side the descent is from the well-known Jones family of Weston, Mass., and from Rev. Asa Dunbar, a graduate of Harvard College, who preached in Salem, and at length settled in Keene, N.H. As variable an ancestry as can well be afforded, with marked family characters on both sides.

About a year and a half from Henry's birth, the family removed to the town of Chelmsford, thence to Boston, coming back however to Concord, when he was of a very tender age. His earliest memory almost of the town was a ride by Walden Pond with his grandmother, when he thought that he should be glad to live there. Henry retained a peculiar pronunciation of the letter *r*, with a decided French accent. He says, "September is the first month with a *burr* in it;" and his speech always had an emphasis, a *burr* in it. His great-grandmother's name was Marie le Galais; and his grandfather,

John Thoreau, was baptized **April 28, 1754, and**
took the Anglican sacrament in **the** parish of **St.**
Helier (Isle of **Jersey), in May, 1773. Thus near
to old France and the Church was our** Yankee
boy.

He drove his cow to pasture, barefoot, like other
village **boys, and was** known among the lads of his
age **as one who did** not fear mud **or** water, **nor
paused to lift** his followers **over** the ditch. **So in
his later journeys, if his companion was** footsore
**and loitered, he steadily pursued the road, making
his strength self-serviceable.**

> " **Who sturdily** could gang,
> Who cared neither for wind nor wet,
> **In lands** where'er he past."

That wildness that **in** him nothing **could** subdue
still lay beneath his culture. **Once when a follower** was done up with headache **and incapable of**
motion, hoping his associate would comfort him
and perhaps afford **him a sip of** tea, he said,
" There **are people who are** sick in that way every
morning, **and go about their** affairs," and then
marched off about his. **In such limits, so** inevita-
ble, was he compacted.

Thoreau was not of those who linger **on the
past: he** had little to **say and less to think of the**
houses or thoughts **in which** he *had* **lived.** They
were, indeed, many mansions. He was entered

of Harvard College in the year 1833, and was a
righteous and-respectable student, having done a
bold reading in English poetry, mastering Chal-
mers's collection, even to some portions or the
whole of Davenant's Gondibert. He made no
college acquaintance which served him practically
in after life, and partially escaped " his class,"
admiring the memory of the class secretary. No
doubt, the important event to him in early man-
hood was his journey to the White Mountains
with his only brother John, who was the elder,
and to whom he was greatly attached. With this
brother he kept the Academy in Concord for a
year or two directly after leaving college. This
piece of travel by boat and afoot was one of the
excursions which furnish dates to his life. The
next important business outwardly was building
for himself a small house close by the shore of
Walden Pond in Concord, the result of economic
forethought. It was a durable garment, an over-
coat, he had contrived and left by Walden, convenient for shelter, sleep, or meditation. It had
no lock to the door, no curtain to the window, and
belonged to nature nearly as much as to man.
His business taught him expedients to husband
time : in our victimizing climate he was fitted for
storms or bad walking ; his coat must contain
special convenience for a walker, with a note-book

and spy glass, — a soldier in his outfits. For shoddy he had an aversion: a pattern of solid Vermont gray gave him genuine satisfaction, and he could think of corduroy. His life was of one fabric. He spared the outfitters no trouble; he wished the material cut to suit *him*, as he was to wear it, not worshipping "the fashion" in cloth or opinion. He bought but few things, and "those not till long after he began to want them, so that when he did get them he was prepared to make a perfect use of them and extract their whole sweet. For if he was a mystic or transcendentalist, he was also a natural philosopher to boot." He did not live to health or exercise or dissipation, but work; his diet spare, his vigor supreme, his toil incessant. Not one man in a million loses so few of the hours of life; and he found soon what were "the best things in his composition, and then shaped the rest to fit them. The former were the midrib and veins of the leaf." Few were better fitted. He had an unusual degree of mechanic skill, and the hand that wrote "Walden" and "The Week" could build a boat or a house.

Sometimes he picked a scanty drift-wood from his native stream, and made good book-cases, chests, and cabinets for his study. I have seen the friendly "wreck" drying by his little air-tight stove for those homely purposes. He bound his own books, and measured the farmers' fields in his village by chain or compass. In more than one the bounds were detected by the surveyor, who was fond of metes and bounds in morals and deeds. Thus he came to see the inside of almost every farmer's house and head, his "pot of beans" and mug of hard cider. Never in too much hurry for a dish of gossip, he could "sit out the oldest frequenter of the bar-room," as he believed, and was alive from top to toe with curiosity, — a process, it is true, not latent in our people. But if he learned, so he taught; and says he "could take one or twenty into partnership, gladly share his gains." On his return from a journey, he not only emptied his pack of flowers, shells, seeds, and other treasures, but liberally contributed every fine or pleasant or desirable experience to those who needed, as the milkweed distributes its lustrous, silken seeds.

He was a natural Stoic, not taught from Epictetus nor the trail of Indians. Not only made he no complaint, but in him was no background of complaint, as in some, where a lifelong tragedy dances in polished fetters. He *enjoyed* what sadness he could find. He would be as melancholy as he could and rejoice with fate. "Who knows but he is dead already?" He voyaged about his river in December, the drops freezing on the oar, with a cheering song; pleased with the silvery chime of icicles against the stems of the button-bushes, toys of "immortal water, alive even to the superficies." The blaze of July and the zero of January came to him as wholesome experiences, — the gifts of Nature, as he deemed them. He desired to improve every opportunity, to find a good in each moment, not choosing alone the blissful. He said that he could not always eat his pound cake; while corn meal lasted he had resource against hunger, nor did he expect or wish for luxuries, and would have been glad of that Indian delicacy, acorn oil. "It was from out the shadow of his toil he looked into the light."

Thoreau says that he knew he loved some things, and could *fall back* on them; and that he "never chanced to meet with any man so cheering and elevating and encouraging, so infinitely suggestive, as the stillness and solitude of the Wellmeadow field." His interest in swamps and bogs was familiar: it grew out of his love for the wild. He thought that he enjoyed himself in Gowing's Swamp, where the hairy huckleberry grows, equal to a domain secured to him and reaching to the South Sea; and, for a moment, experienced there the same sensation as if he were alone in a bog in Rupert's Land, thus, also, saved the trouble of going there. The small cranberries (not the common species) looked to him "just like some kind of swamp-sparrow's eggs in their nest; like jewels worn or set in those sphagneous breasts of the swamp,—swamp pearls we might call them." It was the bog in our brain and bowels, the primitive vigor of nature in us, that inspired that dream; for Rupert's Land is recognized as surely by one sense as another. "Where was that strain mixed into which the world was dropped but as a lump of sugar to sweeten the draught? I would be drunk, drunk, drunk,—dead-drunk to this world with it for ever!"

> "Kings unborn shall walk with me;
> And the poor grass shall plot and plan
> What it will do when it is man."

This tone of mind grew out of no insensibility; or, if he sometimes looked coldly on the suffering of more tender natures, he sympathized with their afflictions, but could do nothing to admire them. He would not injure a plant unnecessarily. And once meeting two scoundrels who had been rude to a young girl near Walden Pond, he took instant means for their arrest, and taught them not to repeat that offence. One who is greatly affected by the commission of an ignoble act cannot want sentiment. At the time of the John Brown tragedy, Thoreau was driven sick. So the country's misfortunes in the Union war acted on his feelings with great force: he used to say he "could never recover while the war lasted."

The high moral impulse never deserted him, and he resolved early " to read no book, take no walk, undertake no enterprise, but such as he could endure to give an account of to himself; and live thus deliberately for the most part." In our estimate of his character, the moral qualities form the basis: for himself, rigidly enjoined; if in another, he could overlook delinquency. Truth before all things; in your daily life, integrity before all things; in all your thoughts, your faintest breath, the austerest purity, the utmost fulfilling of the interior law; faith in friends, and an iron and flinty pursuit of right, which nothing can tease or purchase out of us. If he made an engagement, he was certain to fulfil his part of the contract; and if the other contractor failed, then his rigor of opinion prevailed, and he never more dealt with that particular bankrupt.

> "Merchants, arise
> And mingle conscience with your merchandise."

Thus, too, when an editor left out this sentence from one of his pieces, about the pine-tree, — " It is as immortal as I am, and perchance will go to as high a heaven, there to tower above me still," — Thoreau, having given no authority, considered the bounds of right were passed, and no more

1*

indulged in that editor. His opinion of publishers was not flattering. For several of his best papers he received nothing in cash, his pay coming in promises. When it was found that his writing was like to be popular, merchants were ready to run and pay for it. Soap-grease is not diamond; to use a saying of his, " Thank God, they cannot cut down the clouds." To the work of every man justice will be measured, after the individual is forgotten. So long as our plain country is admired, the books of our author should give pleasure, pictures as they are of the great natural features, illustrated faithfully with details of smaller beauties, and having the pleasant, nutty flavor of New England.

The chief attraction of " The Week " and " Walden " to pure and aspiring natures consists in their lofty and practical morality. To live rightly, never to swerve, and to believe that we have in ourselves a drop of the Original Goodness besides the well-known deluge of original sin, — these strains sing through Thoreau's writings. Yet he seemed to some as the winter he once describes, — " hard and bound-out like a bone thrown to a famishing dog." The intensity of his mind, like Dante's, conveyed the breathing of aloofness, — his eyes bent on the ground, his long, swinging gait, his hands perhaps clasped behind him or held

closely at his side, the fingers made into a fist.
Yet, like the lock-tender at Middlesex, "he was
meditating some **vast** and sunny problem," or giving
its date to a humble flower. He did, in one manner, live in himself, as the poet **says,** —

" Be thy own palace, or the world 's thy jail; "

or as Antoninus, "Do but few things **at** a time,
it has been said, if thou would'st preserve thy
peace."

A pleasing trait **of his warm** feeling **is** remem-
bered, when he asked **his mother, before** leaving
college, what profession **to choose, and she replied**
pleasantly, " You can **buckle on your** knapsack,
and roam abroad to seek **your fortune." The**
tears **came** in his eyes **and rolled down his cheeks,**
when **his** sister Helen, who **was standing by, ten-**
derly put her **arm** around him and **kissed him, say-**
ing, " **No,** Henry, you shall not **go: you shall** stay
at home and live with **us." He** also **had** the firm-
ness of the Indian, **and** could repress his pathos;
as when he carried **(about the age of** ten) his pet
chickens to an **innkeeper for sale in a** basket, **who**
thereupon **told him "** *to stop*," **and** for convenience'
sake took them **out one by one** and wrung their
several pretty necks before **the poor** boy's eyes, who
did not budge. **He** had such seriousness at the
same age that **he was called** "judge." His habit

of attending strictly to his own affairs appears from this, that being complained of for taking a knife belonging to another boy, Henry said, "I did not take it," — and was believed. In a few days the culprit was found, and Henry then said, "I knew all the time who it was, and the day it was taken I went to Newton with father." " Well, then," of course, was the question, " why did you not say so at the time?" " I did not take it," was his reply. This little anecdote is a key to many traits in his character. A school-fellow complained of him because he would not make him a bow and arrow, his skill at whittling being superior. It seems he refused, but it came out after that he had no knife. So, through life, he steadily declined trying or pretending to do what he had no means to execute, yet forbore explanations; and some have thought his refusals were unwillingness. When he had grown to an age suitable for company, and not very fond of visiting, he could not give the common refusal, — that it was not convenient, or not in his power, or he regretted, — but said the truth, — " I do not want to go." An early anecdote remains of his being told at three years that he must die, as well as the men in the catechism. He said he did not want to die, but was reconciled; yet, coming in from coasting, he said he " did not want to die and go to heaven, because he could not carry his sled with him ; for the boys said, as it was not shod with iron, it was not worth a cent." This answer prophesied the future man, who never could, nor did, believe in a heaven to which he could not carry his views and principles, some of which were not shod with the vanity of this world, and pronounced worthless. In his later life, on being conversed with about leaving here as a finality, he replied that "he thought he should not go away from here."

With his peculiarities, he did not fail to be set down by some as an original, — one of those who devise needlessly new ways to think or act. His retreat from the domestic camp to picket duty at Walden gave rise to sinister criticism, and the common question he was asked while there, " What do you live here for ? " as the man wished to know who lost his hound, but was so astonished at finding *Henry* in the woods, as quite to forget the stray dog. He had lost his hound, but he had found a man. As we learn from the verse, —

" He that believes himself doth never lie,"

so Thoreau lived a true life in having his own belief in it. We may profitably distinguish between that sham egotism which sets itself above all other values, and that loyal faith in our instincts on which all sincere living rests. His life was a healthy utterance, **a free** and vital progress, joyous and serene, **and thus** proving its **value. If he** passed by forms that **others hold, it was because his** time and **means were invested elsewhere. To do one** thing well, to **persevere, and accomplish one** thing perfectly, was **his faith; and he said that** fame **was sweet, " as the evidence that the effort was a** success."

Henry, from his childhood, **had** quite a peculiar **interest in the place of** his birth, — Concord. **He lived** nowhere else for any length **of** time, and **Staten Island, or the White** Hills, **or New** Bedford, seemed little to him contrasted with that. **I think he** loved Cape Cod. The phrase *local associations*, or the delightful word ***home*, do not** explain his absorbing love **for a town with few picturesque** attractions beside **its river. Concord is mostly** plain land, with **a** sandy **soil; or,** on the river, **wide** meadows, covered with wild grass, and apt to **be flooded twice a year and** changed to shallow **ponds. The absence of** striking scenery, unpleasing to the tourist, is an **advantage** to the naturalist : **too** much farming **and** gentlemen's estates **are in** his **way.** Concord contains an unusual extent of wood and meadow ; and the wood-lots, **when** cut off, are usually continued for the same purpose. So it is a village surrounded by tracts of woodland and meadow, abounding in convenient yet retired paths for walking.

No better place for his business. He enjoyed its use because he found there his materials for work. Perhaps the river was his great blessing in the landscape. No better stream for boating in New England, — " the sluggish artery of the Concord," as he names it. By this, he could go to other points; as a trip up the river rarely ended with the water, but the shore was sought for some special purpose, to examine an animal or a plant, or get a wider view, or collect some novelty or crop. The study of the river-plants never ended, and like themselves floated for ever with the sweet waves; the birds and insects peculiarly attracted to the shores; the fish and musquash, sun and wind, were interesting. The first spring days smile softest on the river, and the fleet of withered leaves sailing down the stream in autumn give a stately finish to the commerce of the seasons.

The hills, Anursnac, Nashawtuc, Fairhaven, are not lofty. Yet they have sufficient outlook, and carry the eye to Monadnock and the Peterboro' Hills, while nearer blue Wachusett stands alone.

Thoreau visited more than once the principal mountains in his prospect. It was like looking off on a series of old homes. He went in the choice August or September days, and picked berries on Monadnock's stony plateau, took his roomy walk over the Mason Hills, or explored the great Wachusett pasture, — the fairest sight eye ever saw. For daily talk, Fairhaven *answered* very well. From this may be seen that inexhaustible expanse, Conantum, with its homely slopes; thence Blue Hill, Nobscot, the great elm of Weston, and Prospect Hill. From the hills, always the stream, the bridges, the meadows: the latter, when flowed, the finest place for ducks and gulls; whilst in their dry dress they furnish opportunities, from Copan down to Carlisle Bridge, or from Lee's to the causey in Wayland, for exploration in the mines of natural history. As the life of a hunter furnishes an endless story of wood and field, though pursued alone, so Nature has this inevitable abundance to the naturalist; to the docile eye, a meadow-spring can furnish a tide of discourse.

Three spacious tracts, uncultivated, where the patches of scrub-oak, wild apples, barberries, and other plants grew, which Mr. Thoreau admired, were Walden woods, the Estabrook country, and the old Marlboro' road. A poem on the latter crops out of his strictures on " Walking." They represent the fact as botanists, naturalists, or walkers would have it, — in a russet suit for field sports, not too much ploughed and furrowed out, with an eye looking to the sky. (Thoreau said that his heaven was south or south-west, in the neighborhood of the old Marlboro' road.) They have their ponds, choice fields or plants, in many cases carefully hid away. He was compelled to name places for himself, like all fresh explorers. His Utricularia Bay, Mount Misery, Cohosh Swamp, Blue Heron Rock, Pleasant Meadow, Scrub-oak Plain, denote localities near Fairhaven. He held to the old titles; thus, — the Holt (in old English, a small, wooded tongue of land in a river), Beck Stow's Hole, Seven-star Lane, and the " Price Road." He knew the woods as a poet and engineer, and studied their successions, the growth and age of each patch, from year to year, with the chiefs of the forest, the white-pine, the pitch-pine, and the oak. Single localities of plants occur: in Mason's pasture is, or was, a bayberry; on Fairhaven, a patch of yew. Some warm side hills afford a natural greenhouse. Thus Lee's Cliff, on Fairhaven Pond, shelters early cress and tower mustard, as well as pewees. If the poet's faculty be naming, he can find applications for it in the country. Thoreau had his Thrush Alley and Stachys Shore.

A notice of him would be incomplete which did not refer to his fine social qualities. He served his friends sincerely and practically. In his own home he was one of those characters who may be called household treasures: always on the spot with skilful eye and hand to raise the best melons in the garden, plant the orchard with the choicest trees, act as extempore mechanic; fond of the **pets, the** sister's flowers, or sacred **Tabby, kittens being his** favorites, — he would play **with** them **by the half-** hour.

Some have fancied because he moved to **W**alden he left his family. He bivouacked there, and really lived **at home,** where he went every day. It is needless to **dwell on** the genial and hospitable enter- **tainer he always was. His** readers came many miles to see him, attracted by his writings. Those **who** could **not** come sent their letters. Those who **came** when they could no more see him, as strangers on a pilgrimage, **seemed as if they had been his** intimates, **so** warm **and cordial was the sympathy** they received **from his letters. If he also** did **the** duties that **lay nearest and** satisfied those **in his** immediate circle, certainly **he did a** good **work; and** whatever the impressions **from** the theoretical part . of his writings, **when the** matter **is** probed to the **bottom,** good **sense and** good feeling will be detected **in it. A great comfort in him, he** was eminently **reliable. No** whim **of** coldness, **no.absorption** of **his time by** public or private business, deprived those **to whom he** belonged **of** his kindness **and** affection. He was **at the mercy of no caprice : of** a reliable will and uncompromising sternness **in** his moral nature, he carried **the same** qualities into his relation with others, and gave them **the** best he had,

without stint. He loved firmly, acted up to his
love, was a believer in it, took pleasure and satisfaction in abiding by it. As Thomas Froysell says of
Sir Robert Harley, — " My language is not a match
for his excellent virtues ; his spirituall lineaments
and beauties are above my pencil. I want art to
draw his picture. I know he had his humanities.
. . . He was a friend to God's friends. They that
did love God had his love. God's people were his
darlings; they had the cream of his affection. If
any poor Christian were crushed by malice or
wrong, whither would they fly but to Sir Robert
Harley ? "

CHAPTER II.

MANNERS AND READING.

"Since they can only judge, who can confer." — BEN JONSON.

WE hear complaint that he set up for a reformer; and what capital, then, had he to embark in that line? How was it he knew so much more than the rest, as to correct abuses, to make over church and state? He had no reform theories, but used his opinions in literature for the benefit of man and the glory of God. Advice he did not give. His exhortations to young students and poor Christians who desired to know his economy never meant to exclude the reasonable charities. Critics have eagerly rushed and made the modest citizen and "home-body" one of the travelling conversational Shylocks, who seek their pound of flesh in swallowing humanity, each the special saviour on his own responsibility. As he says of reformers, "They addressed each other continually by their Christian names, and rubbed you continually with the greasy cheek of their kindness. They would not keep their distance, but cuddle up and lie spoon-fashion with you, no matter how hot the weather or how narrow the bed. . . . It was difficult to keep clear of the slimy benignity with which he sought to cover you, before he took you fairly into his bowels. He addressed me as Henry, within one minute from the time I first laid eyes on him; and when I spoke, he said, with drawling, sultry sympathy: 'Henry, I know all you would say, I understand you perfectly: you need not explain any thing to me.'" Neither did he belong to the "Mutual Admiration" society, where the dunce passes for gold by rubbing his fractional currency on pure metal. His was not an admiring character.

The opinion of some of his readers and lovers has been that in his "Week" the best is the discourse of Friendship. It is certainly a good specimen of his peculiar style, but it should never be forgot that the treatment is poetical and romantic. No writer more demands that his reader, his critic, should look at his writing as a work of art. Because Michel Angelo painted the Last Judgment, we do not accuse him of being a judge: he is working as artist. So our author, in his writing on Friendship, treats the topic in a too distant fashion. Some might call it a lampoon: others say, "Why, this watery, moonlit glance and glimpse contains no more of the flesh and blood of friendship than so much lay-figure; if this was all the writer knew of Friendship, he had better have sheared off and let this craft go free." As when he says, " One goes forth prepared to say 'Sweet friends!' and the salutation is, ' Damn your eyes!'" — to read this literally would be to accuse him of stupidity. The meaning is plain: he was romancing with his subject, playing a strain on his "theorbo" like the bobolink. The living, actual friendship and affection which makes time a reality, no one knew better. He gossips of a high, imaginary world, giving a glance to the inhabitants of this world of that; bringing a few mother-of-pearl tints from the skies to refresh us in our native place. He did not wish for a set of cheap friends to eat up his time; was rich enough to go without a train of poor relations, — the menagerie of dunces with open mouths. In the best and practical sense, no one had more friends or was better loved. He drew near him simple, unlettered Christians, who had questions they wished to discuss; for, though nothing was less to his mind than chopped logic, he was ready to *accommodate* those who differed from him with his opinion, and never too much convinced by opposition. And to those in need of information — to the farmer-botanist naming the new flower, the boy with his puzzle of birds or roads, or the young woman seeking for books — he was always ready to give what he had.

Literally, his views of friendship were high and

noble. Those who loved him never had the least
reason to regret it. He made no useless profes-
sions, never asked one of those questions which
destroy all relation ; but he was on the spot at the
time, and had so much of human life in his keeping, to the last, that he could spare a breathing
place for a friend. When one said that a change
had come over the dream of life, and that solitude
began to peer out curiously from the dells and wood-
roads, he whispered, with his foot on the step of
the other world, "It is better some things should
end." Having this unfaltering faith, and looking
thus on life and death, after which, the poet says,
a man has nothing to fear, let it be said for ever
that there was no affectation or hesitancy in his
dealing with his friends. He meant friendship, and
meant nothing else, and stood by it without the
slightest abatement ; not veering as a weathercock
with each shift of a friend's fortune, or like those
who bury their early friendships in order to gain
room for fresh corpses. If he was of a Spartan
mould, in a manner austere, if his fortune was not
vast, and his learning somewhat special, he yet had
what is better, — the old Roman belief which con-
fided there was more in this life than applause and
the best seat at the dinner-table : to have a moment
to spare to thought and imagination, and to the *res
rusticæ* and those who need you ;

" That hath no side at all
But of himself."

A pleasant account of his easy assimilation is given of his visit to Canton, where in his Sophomore year he kept a school of seventy pupils, and where he was consigned to the care of Rev. O. A. Brownson, then a Unitarian clergyman, for examination. The two sat up talking till midnight, and Mr. Brownson informed the " School Committee " that Mr. Thoreau was examined, and would do, and board with him. So they struck heartily to studying German, and getting all they could of the time together like old friends. Another school experience was the town school in Concord, which he took after leaving college, announcing that he should not flog, but would talk morals as a punishment instead. A fortnight sped glibly along, when a knowing deacon, one of the School Committee, walked in and told Mr. Thoreau that he must flog and use the ferule, or the school would spoil. So he did, by feruling six of his pupils after school, one of whom was the maid-servant in his own house. But it did not suit well with his conscience, and he reported to the committee that he should no longer keep their school, as they interfered with his arrangements ; and they could keep it.

A moment may be spent on a few traits of

Thoreau, of a personal kind. In height, he was about the average; in his build, spare, with limbs that were rather longer than usual, or of which he made a longer use. His face, once seen, could not be forgotten. The features were quite marked: the nose aquiline or very Roman, like one of the portraits of Cæsar (more like a beak, as was said); large, overhanging brows above the deepest set blue eyes that could be seen, in certain lights, and in others gray, — eyes expressive of all shades of feeling, but never weak or near-sighted; the forehead not unusually broad or high, full of concentrated energy and purpose; the mouth with prominent lips, pursed up with meaning and thought when silent, and giving out when open a stream of the most varied and unusual and instructive sayings. His hair was a dark brown, exceedingly abundant, fine and soft; and for several years he wore a comely beard. His whole figure had an active earnestness, as if he had no moment to waste. The clenched hand betokened purpose. In walking, he made a short cut if he could, and when sitting in the shade or by the wall-side seemed merely the clearer to look forward into the next piece of activity. Even in the boat he had a wary, transitory air, his eyes on the outlook, — perhaps there might be ducks, or the Blondin turtle, or an otter, or sparrow.

2

Thoreau **was a plain man in his features and**
dress, one who could **not be mistaken. This kind**
of plainness is not out of keeping with beauty.
He sometimes **went as far as homeliness, which**
again, **even if there be a** prejudice against it, shines
out at times **beyond a** vulgar **sense.** Thus, he
alludes to **those who** pass the night on the steamer's
deck, and see the mountains in **moonlight;** and he
did **this himself once on the Hudson at** the prow,
when, after a "hem" or two, the passenger who
stood next inquired in **good faith: "Come, now,**
can't ye lend me a chaw o' **baccy?" He** looked
like a shipmate. **It was on another** Albany steam-
boat that he walked the deck hungrily among **the**
fine gentlemen and **ladies, eating, upon a half-loaf**
of bread, his dinner **for the day, and very late. A**
plain **man could do this** heartily: **an** ornamental,
scented **thing** looks affected. That was before the
pedestrian disease. And once, **as** he came late into
a town devoid **of a tavern, on going** to the best-
looking house **in the** place **for a bed, he** got one in
the entry, within range **of the family,** his speech
and manners being **those** of polite society; but in
some **of** our retired towns there **are** traditions of
lodgers who arise before light and **depart** with the
feather bed, **or** the origin **of** feathers in the hen-
coop. **Once walking in old** Dunstable, he much
desired **the town history by C. J.** Fox; and, knock-

ing as usual at the best house, went in and asked a young lady who made her appearance whether she had the book in question : she had, — it was produced. After consulting it somewhat, Thoreau in his sincere way inquired very modestly whether she " would not *sell* it to him." I think the plan surprised her, and have heard that she smiled ; but he produced his wallet, gave her the pistareen, and went his way rejoicing with the book.

He did his stint of walking on Cape Cod, where a stranger attracts a partial share of criticism, and "looked despairingly at the sandy village whose street he must run the gauntlet of; there only by sufferance, and feeling as strange as if he were in a town in China." One of the old Cod could not believe that Thoreau was not a pedler; but said, after explanations failed, "Well, it makes no odds what it is you carry, so long as you carry truth along with you." One of those idiots who may be found in some of the houses, grim and silent, one night mumbled he would get his gun "and shoot that damned pedler." And, indeed, he might have followed in the wake of a spectacle pedler who started from the inn of *Meg Dods* in Wellfleet, the same morning, both of them looking after and selling spectacles. He once appeared in a mist, in a remote part of the Cape,

with a bird **tied to the top of his umbrella, which**
he shouldered like **a gun :** the **inhabitants of the**
cottage, **one of** whom **was a man with a sore leg,**
set the traveller **down for a** " crazy **fellow."   At**
Orleans **he was** comforted **by two** Italian organ-
boys who had ground their harmonies **from** Provincetown, **for two score miles in the sand,** fresh
and gay.

' **He once stopped at** a hedge-tavern where **a**
large **white** bull-dog was kept **in** the entry **:** on
asking the bar-tender what Cerberus would do to an
early riser, **he** replied, **" Do ?** — why, **he** would
tear out the substance **of your** pantaloons."   This
was a **good notice not to quit the premises with-**
out meeting **the rent.   Whatever was suitable he**
did **: as lecturing in the basement of an** Ortho-
dox church **in** Amherst, when he **hoped facetiously**
he " contributed something to upheave an**d demol-**
ish the structure."   **He** lectured in a Boston read-
ing-room, the subscribers snuffing their chloroform
of journals, not awoke by **the** lecture.   **A** simple
person can thus find easy paths.

In the course **of** his travels, he sometimes met
with a character that inspired him to describe it.
He drew a Flemish sketch **of a** citizen **of** New
York.

" Getting into Patchogue **late one** night, there
was a drunken Dutchman **on board,** whose wit

reminded me of Shakespeare. When we came to
leave the beach our boat was aground, and we
were detained waiting for the tide. In the mean
while, two of the fishermen took an extra dram at
the Beach House. Then they stretched themselves on the seaweed by the shore in the sun, to
sleep off the effects of their debauch. One was
an inconceivably broad-faced young Dutchman,
but oh! of such a peculiar breadth and heavy look
I should not know whether to call it more ridiculous or sublime. You would say that he had
humbled himself so much that he was beginning to
be exalted. An indescribable Mynheerish stupidity.
I was less disgusted by their filthiness and vulgar-
ity, because I was compelled to look on them as
animals, as swine in their stye. For the whole
voyage they lay flat on their backs in the bottom
of the boat in the bilge-water, and wet with each
bailing, half-insensible and wallowing in their filth.
But ever and anon, when aroused by the rude
kicks of the skipper, the Dutchman, who never
lost his wits nor equanimity, though snoring and
rolling in the reek produced by his debauch, blurted
forth some happy repartee like an illuminated
swine. It was the earthliest, slimiest wit I ever
heard. The countenance was one of a million.
It was unmistakable Dutch. In the midst of a
million faces of other races it could not be mis-

taken. It told of Amsterdam. I kept racking my brains to conceive how he had been born in America, how lonely he must feel, what he did for fellowship. When we were groping up the narrow creek of Patchogue at ten o'clock at night, keeping our boat now from this bank, now from that, with a pole, the two inebriates roused themselves betimes. For in spite of their low estate they seemed to have all their wits as much about them as ever, ay, and all the self-respect they ever had. And the Dutchman gave wise directions to the steerer, which were not heeded (told where eels were plenty in the dark, &c.). At last he suddenly stepped on to another boat which was moored to the shore, with a divine ease and sureness, saying, 'Well, good-night, take care of yourselves, I can't be with you any longer.' He was one of the few remarkable men I have met. I have been inspired by one or two men in their cups. There was really a divinity stirred within them, so that in their case I have reverenced the drunken, as savages the insane man. So stupid that he could never be intoxicated; when I said, 'You have had a hard time of it to-day,' he answered with indescribable good-humor out of the very midst of his debauch, with watery eyes, 'It doesn't happen every day.' It was happening then."

With these plain ways, no person was usually easier misapplied by the cultivated class than Thoreau. Some of those afflicted about him have started with the falsetto of **humming a void esti-mate** on his life, his manners, sentiments, and all that in **him was.** His two books, " Walden " and the " Week," **are** so excellent and generally read, that a commendation of their easy, graceful, yet vigorous style and matter is superfluous. Singular traits run through his writing. **His** sentences will bear study ; meanings not detected at the first glance, subtle hints which the writer himself may not have foreseen, appear. It is a good English style, growing out of choice reading and familiarity with the classic writers, with the originality adding a piquant humor and unstudied felicities of diction. He was not in the least degree an imitator of any writer, old or new, and with little of his times or their opinions in his books. Never eager, with a pensive hesitancy he steps about his native fields, singing the praises of music and spring and morning, forgetful of himself. No matter where he might have lived, or in what circumstance, he would have been a writer: he was made for this by all his tendencies of mind and temperament ; a writer because a thinker and even a philosopher, a lover of wisdom. No bribe could have drawn him from his native fields, where his ambition was — a very honorable **one** — **to** fairly represent himself in his works, accomplishing as perfectly as lay in his power what he conceived his business. More society would have impaired his designs; **and a story from a** fisher or hunter was better to him than an evening of triviality in shining parlors where he was misunderstood. His eye and ear **and hand** fitted in with the special task he **undertook, — certainly as** manifest a destiny as any man's ever was.

The best test of the worth **of** character, — whether **the** person **lived a contented,** joyous life, filled his hours agreeably, **was useful in his way,** and on the whole achieved his purposes, — this **he** possessed. **The** excellence of his books and style is identical **with** the excellence **of his** private life. He wished to **write** living books that spoke of out-of-door things, as **if** written **by an** out-of-door man; and thinks his "Week" **had that** *hypæthral* **character he hoped for. In this he** was an artist. **The impression of the** "Week" and "Walden" is single, **as of a living product;** a perfectly jointed building, **yet no** more composite productions could be cited. The same applies to the lectures on "Wild Apples" **or** "Autumnal **Tints,"** which possess this unity **of** treatment; **yet** the materials were drawn from **the** utmost **variety** of resources, observations **made** years apart, so skilfully woven as to appear a seamless garment of thought. **This** constructive, combining talent belongs with the adaptedness to the pursuit. Other gifts were **sub-**sidiary to his literary gift. **He observed** nature; **but who would** have known or **heard of** that except through his literary effort? He observed nature, yet not for **the sake of** nature, but of man; **and says, "If it** is possible to conceive of **an** event **outside to humanity, it is not of** the slightest **importance, though it were the** explosion of the **planet."**

Success is his rule. He had practised a variety of arts with many tools. **Both he and his father** were ingenious persons (the **latter a pencil-maker) and** fond **of** experimenting. **To show the excel-**lence of their work, they resolved to make **as good a** pencil out of paste as those sawed **from black** lead in London. The result was accomplished and **the** certificate obtained, Thoreau himself claim-ing **a good** share **of** the success, as he found the means **to cut** the plates. After his father's death he carried **on** the pencil **and** plumbago business; had his own **mill, and used** the same punctuality and **prudence in these** affairs **as** ever distinguished **him.**

In **one or two of** his **later** articles, expressions crept **in** which might lead the reader to suspect **him of** moroseness, or that **his** old trade of schoolmaster stuck **to him.** He rubbed out as perfectly as he could the more humorous part of those articles, originally **a relief to their sterner features,** and said, " I cannot **bear the levity I find."** To which **it was replied, that it was** hoped he would spare **them, even to** the puns; for he sometimes indulged. **As** when a farmer **drove** up with a **strange pair of** long-tailed ponies, his companion **asked whether such a** person would not carry a **Colt's revolver to protect him in the** solitude, Thoreau replied **that " he did not know about that,** but he saw he had **a pair of revolving colts before** him." A lady once asked whether he ever laughed, — and she was well acquainted with **him** halfway, but did not see him, unless **as a visitor. He never** became versed in making formal visits, and had not much success with first acquaintance. As to his laughing, no one did that more **or** better. One was surprised to see him dance, — he had been well taught, **and** was a vigorous dancer; and any one **who ever** heard him sing **" Tom** Bowlin" will agree that, **in tune and in tone,** he answered, and went far beyond, all expectation. His favorite songs were Mrs. Hemans's " Pilgrim Fathers," Moore's " Evening Bells **" and " Canadian Boat** Song," and Wolfe's " Burial of **Sir John Moore,"** — precisely the most tender and popular songs. And oh, how sweetly he played upon his flute! Not unfre-

quently he sang **that brave catch of Izaak Wal-**
ton's, —

> **"In** the morning when we rise,
> **Take a cup to wash our eyes,"**

his **cup of** cold water. The Indians **loved to**
drink at running brooks which were warm, but he
loved ice-cold water. Summer or winter **he drank**
very little, and would sometimes try to recollect
when he drank last.

Before he set out **on a foot journey, he collected**
every information as to **the routes and the place to**
which he was going, through the maps **and guide-**
books. **For this State he had the large State map**
divided **in portions convenient, and carried in a**
cover such **parts as he wanted: he deemed this**
map, for his purposes, excellent. **Once he made**
for himself a knapsack, with partitions for his books
and papers, — india-rubber cloth, strong **and large**
and spaced, the common knapsacks being unspaced.
The partitions were **made of** stout book-paper.
His route being known, **he made** a list of all he
should carry, — the sewing materials never forgot-
ten (as he was a vigorous walker, and did not stick
at a hedge **more than an** English **racer),** the pounds
of bread, the sugar, salt, **and tea carefully decided**
on. After trying **the merit of cocoa,** coffee, **water,**
and the like, tea **was put down as the felicity of**
a walking "*travail*," —tea plenty, strong, with

enough sugar, made **in a tin pint** cup; **when it
may be said the** walker will be refreshed and grow
intimate with **tea-leaves.** With **him the botany
must go** too, and the **book** for pressing flowers (an
old " Primo Flauto " of his father's), and the guide-
book, spy-glass, and **measuring-tape;** and every
one **who has** carried **a pack up a** mountain knows
how every fresh **ounce tells.** He would run **up
the steepest place as swiftly as if he were** on dry
land, and his breath never failed. **He** commended
every party to carry " a junk **of** heavy cake " with
plums in it, having found by long experience that
after toil it was a capital refreshment.

He made three journeys into **the** Maine wilderness, two from **Moosehead Lake** in canoes, accompanied by Indians, another to Katahdin Mountain.
These taught him **the art** of camping out; **and he**
could construct in a short time a convenient camp
sufficient for permanent occupancy. His last excursion of this kind was **to** Monadnock Mountain
in August, 1859. **He spent five** nights in camp,
having built **two huts to** get varied views. On a
walk like **this he always** carried his umbrella; and
on this Monadnock trip, when about one mile from
the station, a torrent of rain came down, the day
being previously fine, when without his well-used
aid his books, **blankets,** maps, and provisions
would **all** have been spoiled, or the morning lost

by delay.   **On the** mountain, the first plateau being reached perhaps at about **three,** there being a thick, rather soaking fog, the first object was **to** camp and make tea.   Flowers, birds, lichens, and the rocks were carefully examined, **all parts** of the mountain being visited; and as accurate **a map as** could be made by pocket-compass carefully sketched and drawn **out, in the five days** spent there, with notes of the striking aerial phenomena, incidents of travel and natural history.

Doubtless he directed **his work with the view to** writing **on** this and other mountains, and **his collec**tions were **of** course in his mind.   **Yet all this was** incidental **to the excursion itself, the other things** collateral.   **The capital in use,** the opportunity **of the** wild, free life, the open air, the new and strange sounds by night and day, the **odd and** bewildering rocks among which **a** person can **be** lost within **a rod of** camp; the strange cries of visitors to the summit; the great valley over **to** Wachusett with its thunder-storms and battles in the cloud, to look **at,** not fear; **the** farmers' back-yards in Jaffrey, where the family cotton can be **seen** bleaching **on** the grass, **but no** trace of the pygmy family; **the** rip of night-hawks after twilight **putting up dor**bugs, and **the** dry, soft air all the night; **the** lack **of** dew in the morning; the **want of water,** a pint being a good **deal, — these and similar** things

make up some part of such an excursion. It is
all different from any thing, and would be so if
you went a hundred times. The fatigue, the blazing sun, the face getting broiled; the pint cup
never scoured; shaving unutterable; your stock-
ings dreary, having taken to peat, — not all the
books in the world, as Sancho says, could contain
the adventures of a week in camping.

A friendly coincidence happened on his last
excursion, July, 1858, to the White Mountains.
Two of his friends thought they might chance
upon him there; and, though he dreamed little of
seeing them, he left a note at the Mountain House
which said where he was going, and told them if
they looked "they would see the smoke of his
fire." This came to be true, the brush taking
the flame, and a smoke rising to be seen over
all the valley. Meantime, Thoreau, in leaping
from one mossy rock to another (after nearly sliding down the snow-crust on the side of Tucker-
man's Ravine, and saved by digging his nails into
the snow), had fallen and severely sprained his
foot. Before this, he had found the *Arnica mollis*,
a plant famous for its healing properties; but he
preferred the ice-cold water of the mountain
stream, into which he boldly plunged his tortured
limb to reduce the swelling, had the tent spread,
and then, the rain beginning to come down, so

came his two friends down the mountain as well, their outer integuments decimated with their tramp in the scrub. They had seen the smoke; and here they were in his little tent made for two, the rain falling all the while, and five full-grown men to be packed in for five days and nights, Thoreau unable to move on, but he sat and entertained them heartily. He admired the rose-colored linnæas lining the side of the narrow horse-track through the fir-scrub, and the leopard-spotted land below the mountains. He had seen the pines in Fitzwilliam in a primeval wood-lot, and "their singular beauty made such an impression that I was forced to turn aside and contemplate them. They were so round and perpendicular that my eyes slid off." The rose-breasted grosbeaks sang in a wonderful strain on Mount Lafayette. He ascended such hills as Monadnock or Saddle-back Mountains by his own path, and would lay down his map on the summit and draw a line to the point he proposed to visit below, perhaps forty miles away in the landscape, and set off bravely to make "the short-cut." The lowland people wondered to see him scaling the heights as if he had lost his way, or at his "jumping over their cow-yard fences," asking if he had fallen from the clouds.

Allusion has been made to his faithful reading of English poetry at college. That he was familiar with the classics and kept up the acquaintance, is shown by his translations from Persius, Æschylus, Homer, Cato, **Aristotle**, Pindar, Anacreon, Pliny, and other old writers. His "Prometheus Bound" was reprinted and **used as a** "**pony**" at Harvard College. Homer and Virgil **were** his favorites, like the world's. In English, Chaucer, Milton, Ossian, the **Robin Hood** Ballads; **the** "Lycidas" **never out of his mind, for he** had the habit, more **than usual among** scholars, of thinking in the language **of another, in an unstudied way.** Of his favorites, he **has written a pleasant account in his** "Week." But **he used these and all** literature **as** aids, and did **not stop in a book; rarely or never** read them **over.** His reading was done **with a** pen in his hand: he made what he calls "Fact-books," —citations which concerned his studies. **He** had **no favorite** among modern writers **save** Carlyle. **Stories,** novels (excepting the **History of** Froissart **and** the grand **old Pelion on** Ossa of the Hindoo Mythology), **he did not** read. His East Indian studies **never went deep, technically:** into the philological **discussion as to** whether **ab, ab, is** Sanscrit, or "**what is** Om?" **he** entered **not.** But no one **relished the** Bhagvat **Geeta better, or** the **good sentences from** the **Vishnu Purana.** He **loved the Laws of Menu, the** Vishnu Sarma, Saadi, and similar books. After he had ceased to read these works, he received a collection of them as a present, from England. Plato and Montaigne and Goethe were all too slow for him: the hobbies he rode dealt with realities, not shadows, and he philosophized *ab initio.* Metaphysics was his aversion. He believed and lived in his senses loftily. Speculations on the special faculties of the mind, or whether the Not Me comes out of the "I," or the All out of the infinite Nothing, he could not entertain. Like the Queen of Prussia, he had heard of *les infiniments petits.* In his way, he was a great reader and eagerly perused books of adventure, travel, or fact; and never could frame a dearer wish than spending the winter at the North pole: "could eat a fried rat with a relish," if opportunity commanded.

The " Week " is a mine of quotations from good authors, the proof of careful reading and right selection. Such knotty writers as Quarles and Donne here find a place in lines as fresh and sententious as the fleetest wits. What so subtle as these lines from Quarles, — his " Divine Fancies " ?

> " He that wants faith, and apprehends a grief,
> Because he wants it, hath a true belief;
> And he that grieves because his grief 's so small,
> Has a true grief, and the best Faith of all."

> " The laws of Nature break the rules of art,"

is from **the** same; and the Emblems, **Book IV.,**
II., give the lines: —

> " I asked the schoolman, his advice was free,
> . **But** scored me **out too** intricate a way."

Also his favorites, —

> " Be wisely worldly, but not worldly wise."

> "**The ill that 's** wisely feared is half withstood."

> "**An unrequested star did** gently slide
> Before the wise men to a greater light."

> " Lord, **if** my cards be bad, yet grant me skill
> To play them wisely and make **the** best of ill."

The famous Dean **of St. Paul's, the learned Dr.**
Donne, was **not less his** favorite. He **might have**
quoted, as **an example of** his own prevailing **mag-
nanimity, the** stanza, —

> "**For me** (if there **be such a** thing **as I**),
> Fortune (if there be such **a** thing as she),
> Spies that I bear so well her tyranny,
> **That** she thinks nothing else so fit **for me.**"

He **had put this** wise verse in his note-book **as**
early as **1837,** from the same: —

> " **Oh, how feeble** is man's power,
> That if good Fortune fall,
> Cannot add another hour,
> Nor a lost hour recall;
> But come bad chance,
> And we join to 't our strength,
> And we teach it art and length,
> Itself **o'er us t' advance.**"

> " Only **he who knows**
> Himself knows more."

The " Musophilus [of Samuel Daniel] ; containing a general defence of learning, to the Right worthy and Judicious Favorer of Virtue, Mr. Fulke Grevill," was a special gift to him from the age of Elizabeth. Daniel has other good backers; but they have never found the best lines, as it was Thoreau's enviable privilege to do. This precious stanza is from the poem above-named: —

> " Men find that action **is another** thing
> Than what they in discoursing papers read;
> The world's affairs require in managing
> More arts than those wherein you clerks **proceed.**"

And this, too, **a verse very often repeated by** him, is from Daniel's " Epistle **to the Lady Margaret, Countess of Cumberland : "** —

> " Unless above himself **he can**
> Erect himself, **how** poor a thing **is man.**"

So Daniel has his **say on** learning in the verse, —

> " **How** many thousand never heard the name
> **Of** Sidney or of Spenser, or their books?
> **And yet** brave **fellows,** and presume of fame,
> **And seem to bear down** all the world with looks."

Charles **Cotton, the friend of Izaak Walton, gave him** a motto for morning: —

> " And round about good morrows fly,
> **As if** day taught humanity."

And one for evening, which **Virgil, or Turner**

the English painter, would have appreciated (*Et jam summa procul*, etc.) : —

> " A very little, little flock
>   Shades thrice the ground that it would stock,
>   Whilst the small stripling following them
>   Appears a mighty Polypheme."

Cotton also afforded the fine definition of " Contentment : " —

> " Thou bravest soul's terrestrial paradise."

And that great lament for the death of Thomas, Earl of Ossory : —

> " The English infantry are orphans now."

He refers to Michael Drayton's Elegy, " To my dearly beloved friend, Henry Reynolds, of Poets and Poesy," where he says : —

> " Next Marlowe bathed in the Thespian springs
>   Had in him those brave translunary things
>   That your first poets had : his raptures were
>   All air and fire, which made his verses clear ;
>   For that fine madness still he did retain
>   Which rightly should possess a poet's brain."

So Drummond's sonnet, " Icarus," pleased him with its stirring line : —

> " For still the shore my brave attempt resounds."

Spenser's " Ruines of Rome " gave him those lines, —

> " Rome living was the world's **sole ornament ;**
> And dead, **is now the** world's **sole** monument. . . .
> With **her own** weight down pressèd now she lies,
> And by **her heaps** her hugeness testifies."

Ever alive to distinction, he admired that **verse** of Habington's, —

> "**Let us set so just**
> A rate **on** Knowledge, that the world may trust
> The **poet's** sentence, and not still aver
> **Each art is to itself a flatterer."**

While the poem **of the** same author, with that nonpareil title, " *Nox nocti indicat scientiam*," **drew** the Esquimaux **race, —**

> "**Some nation yet shut in**
> With **hills of ice."**

As for Giles and Phineas Fletcher, he **exhumed** from them certain of **the** best lines **in his** " Week," **such as the** passage from the **former's** " **Christ's Victory and** Triumph," beginning, —

> " How may a worm that crawls along the dust
> Clamber the azure mountains, thrown so high."

As well as this : —

> " And now **the taller sons whom Titan warms,**
> Of unshorn **mountains** blown with **easy winds,**
> Dandle **the morning's** childhood **in their arms ;**
> **And, if they** chanced **to slip the** prouder **pines,**
> The under corylets did catch their **shines,**
> **To gild** their leaves."

The two splendid stanzas from the " Purple

Island " of Phineas Fletcher are unsurpassed in Elizabethan or later verse, beginning with, —

> " By them went Fido, marshal of the field."

George Peele's mighty lines he knew, —

> " When Fame's great double-doors fall to and shut;"

and John Birkenhead's tribute to Beaumont, the dramatist, —

> " Thy ocean fancy knew nor banks nor dams,
> We ebb down dry to pebble anagrams." .

CHAPTER III.

NATURE.

" For this present, hard
Is the fortune of the bard
Born out of time." —**EMERSON.**

HIS habit was to go abroad a portion of each
day to fields or woods, or the river: "I go
out to see what I have caught in my traps, which I
set for facts." He looked to fabricate an epitome
of creation, and give us a homœopathy of nature.
All must get included. "No fruit grows in vain.
The red squirrel harvests the fruit of the pitch-
pine." He wanted names. "I never felt easy till
I got the name for the *Andropogon scoparius* (a
grass): I was not acquainted with my beautiful
neighbor, but since I knew it was the Andropogon
I have felt more at home in my native fields." He
had no trace of that want of memory which
infests amiable beings. He loved the world and
could not pass a berry, nor fail to ask his question,
I fear — leading. Men who had seen the partridge
drum, caught the largest pickerel, and eaten the
most swamp apples, did him service; and he long
frequented one who, if not a sinner, was no saint,

whose destiny carried him for ever to field or
stream, — not too bad for Nature. "Surely he is
tenacious of life ; hard to scale." The Farmer who
could find him a hawk's egg or give him a fisher's
foot, he would wear in his heart of hearts, whether
called Jacob or not. He admired our toil-crucified
farmers, conditioned like granite and pine, slow
and silent as the Seasons, — "like the sweetness of
a nut, like the toughness of hickory. He, too, is
a redeemer for me. How superior actually to the
faith he professes! He is not an office-seeker.
What an institution, what a revelation is a man!
We want foolishly to think the creed a man professes a more significant fact than the man he is.
It matters not how hard the conditions seemed,
how mean the world, for a man is a prevalent
force and a new law himself. He is a system
whose law is to be observed. The old farmer still
condescends to countenance this nature and order
of things. It is a great encouragement that an
honest man makes this world his abode. He rides
on the sled drawn by oxen, world-wise, yet comparatively so young as if he had not seen scores
of winters. The farmer spoke to me, I can swear,
clear, cold, moderate as the snow where he treads.
Yet what a faint impression that encounter may
make on me after all. Moderate, natural, true, as
if he were made of stone, wood, snow. I thus meet

in this universe kindred of mine composed of these elements. I see men like frogs: their peeping I partially understand."

For cities, he felt like the camels and Arab camel-drivers who accompany caravans across the desert. The books and Dr. Harris, the college librarian, he saw in Cambridge, and in Boston the books and the end of Long Wharf, where he went to snuff the sea. The rest, as he phrased it, " was barrels." In books, he found matters that transcend legislatures: " One wise sentence is worth the State of Massachusetts many times over." I never heard him complain that the plants were too many, the hours too long. As he said of the crow, " If he has voice, I have ears." The flowers are furnished, and he can bring his note-book.

> " As if by secret sight, he knew
> Where, in far fields, the orchis grew."

He obeyed the plain rule, —

> " Take the goods the gods provide thee,"

and having neither ship nor magazine, gun or javelin, horse or hound, had conveyed to him a property in many things equal to the height of all his ambition. What he did not covet was not forced on his attention. What he desired lay at his feet. The breath of morning skies with the saffron of Aurora beautifully dight; children of the air waft-

ing the smiles of spring from **the vexed Bermoothes ;**
fragrant life-everlasting in **the dry pastures ;** blue
forget-me-nots along the brook, — were **his : ice**
piled its shaggy enamel **for him, where coral cran-**
berries yesterday glowed in the grass ; and forests
whispered loving secrets **in his ear.** For is not the
earth kind ?

" **We are rained and snowed on** with gems. I
confess **that I** was a little **encouraged, for I was**
beginning **to believe** that Nature **was** poor and
mean, and I now was convinced that she turned off
as good work as **ever.** What a world **we live in !**
Where are the jeweller's shops ? There **is nothing**
handsomer **than a** snow-flake and a dew-drop. I
may say that the Maker of **the** world exhausts **his**
skill with **each** snow-flake and dew-drop that He
sends down. **We think** that **the** one mechanically
coheres, and that the other simply flows together
and falls ; **but in truth** they are **the** product **of**
enthusiasm, **the children of an ecstasy,** finished
with the artist's utmost skill."

He dreamed, for such **a space as** that filled **by**
the town **of** Concord, he might construct **a** cal-
endar, — the out-of-door performances **in order ;**
and paint **a** sufficient panorama of the **year,** which
multiplied the image of a **day.** It embraced cold
and heat. He had gauges for **the river,** constantly
consulted **; he** noted the temperatures of springs

and ponds; set down each novel **sky**; the flowering of plants, their blossom and fruit; the fall of leaves; the arrivals and departures of the migrating birds; the habits of animals; **and** made **new** seasons. No hour tolled on the great world-horologe must be omitted, no movement of the second-hand of this patent lever that is so full-jewelled.

> "Behold these flowers, let us **be** up with time,
> Not dreaming of three thousand years ago."

No description can be given of **the labor** necessary for this undertaking, — **labor and time** and perseverance. He drinks in the meadow, **at Second Division Brook**; "then sits awhile **to** watch **its** yellowish pebbles, **and** the **cress in it and the weeds.** The ripples cover its surface as a **network,** and are faithfully reflected **on the** bottom. **In** some places, the sun reflected from ripples on **a** flat stone looks like **a** golden comb. The whole brook seems as busy as a loom: it is a woof and warp **of** ripples; fairy fingers are throwing the shuttle **at** every step, and the long, waving brook is the fine product. The water is so wonderfully clear, — to have a hut here and **a** foot-path to the brook. **For** roads, I think that **a poet cannot** tolerate more than a foot-path through **the** field. That is wide enough, **and** for purposes **of** winged poesy suffices. **I** would fain travel by a foot-path **round the** world."

So might he say in that mood, yet think the wider wood-path was not bad, as two could walk side by side in it in the ruts, — ay, and one more in the horse-track.   He loved in the summer to lay up a stock of these experiences "for the winter, as the squirrel, of nuts, — something for conversation in winter evenings.   I love to think then of the more distant walks I took in summer. Might I not walk further till I hear new crickets, till their creak has acquired some novelty as if they were a new species whose habitat I had discovered?"

Night and her stars were not neglected friends. He saw

" The wandering moon
Riding near her highest noon,"

and sings in this strain : —

" My dear, my dewy sister, let thy rain descend on me.   I not only love thee, but I love the best of thee; that is to love thee rarely.   I do not love thee every day, commonly I love those who are less than thee; I love thee only on great days.   Thy dewy words feed me like the manna of the morning. I am as much thy sister as thy brother; thou art as much my brother as my sister.   It is a portion of thee and a portion of me which are of kin. Thou dost not have to woo me.   I do not have to woo thee.   O my sister!   O Diana!   thy tracks are on the eastern hill. Thou merely passed that way. I, the hunter, saw them in the morning dew. My eyes are the hounds that pursued thee. Ah, my friend, what if I do not know thee? I hear thee. Thou canst speak; I cannot; I fear and forget to answer; I am occupied with hearing. I awoke and thought of thee, thou wast present to my mind. How cam'st thou there? Was I not present to thee likewise?"

Thou couldst look down with pity on that mound. Some silver beams faintly raining through the old locust boughs, for thy lover, thy Endymion, is watching there. He was abroad with thee after the midnight mass had tolled, and the consecrated dust of yesterdays each in its narrow cell for ever laid, which he lived to hive in precious vases for immortality, — tales of natural piety, bound each to each.

> "Now chiefly is my natal hour,
> And only now my prime of life.
> I will not doubt the love untold,
> Which not my worth nor want hath bought,
> Which wooed me young and wooes me old,
> And to this evening hath me brought."

Thus conversant was he with great Nature. Perchance he reached the wildness for which he longed.

"A nature which I cannot put my foot through,

woods where the wood-thrush **for ever sings, where** the hours are early morning ones **and the** day **is for** ever improved, where **I** might **have a fertile** unknown for **a** soil **about me."**

Always suggestive (possibly **to some unattractive)** themes lay **about** him in this **Nature.** Even "along the wood-paths, **wines of all** kinds and **qualities, of** noblest vintages, are **bottled up** in the **skins of countless berries,** for the taste **of** men and **animals. To men** they seem offered, not so much **for food as for sociality, that they may** picnic with **Nature. Diet drinks, cordial wines, we** pluck and eat in remembrance of **her. It** is a sacrament, a communion. **The** *not* Forbidden Fruits, which **no** Serpent tempts **us to** taste."

We will not forget the **apothegm, — "A** writer, a man writing, is the scribe **of all** nature ; **he is the corn and** the grass and the atmosphere writing," **—or that he says, "** My business **was** writing." **To this** he neglected no **culture from facts** or men, **or travel or** books, neither did he gallop his ideas, and **race for** oblivion. "Whatever wit has **been** produced **on the spur of the** moment will bear to be reconsidered **and reformed with** phlegm. The arrow had best **not be loosely shot. The** most transient and passing **remark must be** reconsidered by the writer, made **sure and warranted as** if the earth had rested on its axle to **back** it, and all the

natural **forces lay behind** it. **The** writer must
direct his **sentences as** carefully as **the** marksman
his rifle, who shoots sitting and **with** a rest, with
patent **sights and** conical **balls besides. If** you
foresee **that a** part of your essay **will** topple down
after the lapse of time, throw it **down** yourself."
This was his sure and central fire, — the impulse to
faithfully **account for himself.** " **Facts** collected
by a poet are set down at last as winged seeds **of
truth, —** *samaræ,* **tinged with** his expectation. **Oh,
may my words be** verdurous **and sempiternal as
the** hills ! "

No labor too onerous, **no** material too costly, **if**
outlaid **on the** right enterprise. **Every thing has
its price. His** working up the **Indians corroborates
this. These** books form a library by themselves.
Extracts from reliable **authorities from DeBry to
poor** Schoolcraft, with the early **plates and** maps
accurately copied, and selections from travellers the
world **over;** for his notes embraced **all** that bears
on his " **list** of subjects," — wherever scalps, wam-
pum, **and the Great Spirit prevail,—in** all uncivilized people. Indian customs in **Natick are savage**
customs in **Brazil, the** Sandwich **Islands, or Tim-
buctoo.** With **the Indian vocabularies he was**
familiar, and in his Maine **excursions** tested **his**
knowledge by all the **words** he could get from the
savages *in puris* naturalibus. Personally these liv-

ing red men **were not charming;** and he would creep **out of camp at** night **to refresh his olfac-** tories, damped **with uncivilized perfumes, which it** seems, **like musquash and other animals, they** **enjoy.** After **the** toughest day's work, when even *his* **bones ached, the Indians would keep awake** till midnight, **talking eternally all the** while. **They** **performed valiant feats as trencher-men, "licked** **the** platter clean," **and for all answer to many of** **his questions grunted;** which **did not discourage** **him, as he could grunt** himself. **Their knowledge** **of the woods, the absolutisms of their scent, sight,** and appetite, **amazed him.** He says, **"There is** always **a** slight **haze or mist in the brow of the** Indian." **He read** and translated **the Jesuit rela-** tions **of the first Canadian** missions, containing **"**the commodities and discommodities **" of the** **Indian** life, such **as** the roasting of a fresh parson. He read that romantic book, " Faite par le Sieur de la Borde," upon **the** origin, manners, customs, **wars, and** voyages **of the** Caribs, **who** were the Indians **of the** Antilles **of America; how these** patriots **will sell their** beds **in** the morning (their memories too short **for** night), and **in** their heaven, *Ouicou,* **the Carib beer runs all the while. The** children eat **dirt and** the mothers work. **If** the dead man own **a negro,** they bury him with his master to wait on **him** in paradise, **and** despatch the doctor to be sure of one in the other state. The men and women dress alike, and they have no police or civility; everybody does what he pleases.

> " Lo, the poor Indian, whose untutored mind
>   **Brews beer** in heaven, and drinks it for mankind."

CHAPTER IV.

ANIMALS AND SEASONS.

" Lus aguas van con los cielos." — COLUMBUS.
" It snewed in his house of mete and drinke." — CHAUCER.

ANOTHER faithful reading was those old Roman farmers, Cato and Varro, and musically named Columella, for whom he had a liking. He is reminded of them by seeing the farmers so busy in the fall carting out their compost. "I see the farmer now on every side carting out his manure, and sedulously making his compost-heap, or scattering it over his grass-ground and breaking it up with a mallet, and it reminds me of Cato's advice. He died 150 years before Christ. Indeed, the farmer's was pretty much the same routine then as now. 'Sterquilinium magnum stude ut habeas. Stercus sedulo conserva, cum exportatis purgato et comminuito. Per autumnum evehito.' Study to have a great dungheap. Carefully preserve your dung. When you carry it out, make clean work of it, and break it up fine. Carry it out during the autumn." Just such directions as you find in the Farmers' Almanac to-day. As if the farmers of Concord were obeying Cato's directions, who but repeated **the** maxims **of** a remote antiquity. Nothing **can be more homely** and suggestive **of the** every-day **life of the Roman** agriculturists, thus supplying **the usual deficiencies in what is technically** called Roman history ; *i.e.*, revealing to us **the** actual life **of the** Romans, the " how they **got** their **living," and** " what they did from day to day." **Rome and** the Romans commonly are a piece of rhetoric, but **we** have here their "New England Farmer," or the very manual those Roman farmers read, as fresh as a dripping dishcloth from a Roman kitchen.

His study of old writers on Natural **History was** careful: Aristotle, Ælian, and Theophrastus **he** sincerely entertained, and found from the latter that neither the weather nor its signs had altered since his **day.** Pliny's *magnum opus* was his **last** reading in **this** direction, a work so **valuable to** him, **with the** authors just named, **that** he meant probably **to** translate and write **on** the subject as viewed **by the** ancients. As illustrations, he carefully noted many facts from modern travellers, whose writing hatches Jack-the-Giant-Killers **as** large as Pliny's. He observed that Aristotle **was** furnished by the king **with** elephants **and** other creatures for dissection and study: his observations on the habits of fish and their nests especially interested Thoreau, an expert in **spawn.** In continuing this line of study, he was aided by the perusal of St. Pierre, Gerard, Linnæus, and early writers. The "Studies of Nature" he admired, as written with enthusiasm and spirit, — qualities in his view essential to all good writing. The old English botanist pleased him by his affectionate interest in plants, with something quaint, like Evelyn, Tusser, and Walton. Recent scientific *pâté-de-foie-gras* — a surfeit of microscope and "dead words with a tail" — he valued for what it is worth, — the stuffing. For the Swede, his respect was transcendent. There is no better explanation of his love for botany than the old — "Consider the lilies of the field how they grow; they toil not, neither do they spin: and yet I say unto you, that even Solomon in all his glory was not arrayed like one of these." His pleasant company, during so many days of every year, he wished he was better acquainted with. The names and classes change, the study of the lovely flower persists. He wished to know willow and grass and sedge, and there came always with the new year the old wish renewed: a carex, a salix, kept the family secret.

" For years my appetite was so strong that I fed, I browsed on the pine-forest's edge seen against the winter horizon, — the silvery needles of the pine straining the light; the young aspen-leaves like light green fires. The young birch-leaves very neatly plaited, small, triangular, light green leaves, yield an agreeable, sweet fragrance, just expanded and sticky, sweet-scented as innocence. . . . The first humble-bee, that prince of hummers, — he follows after flowers. To have your existence depend on flowers, like the bee and humming-birds. . . . I expect that the lichenist will have the keenest relish for Nature in her every-day mood and dress. He will have the appetite of the worm that never dies, of the grub. This product of the bark is the essence of all times. The lichenist loves the tripe of the rock, that which eats and digests the rock: he eats the eater. A rail is the fattest and sleekest of coursers for him. . . . The blue curls and fragrant everlasting, with their ripening aroma, show themselves now pushing up on dry fields, bracing to the thought; I need not smell the calamint, — it is a balm to my mind to remember its fragrance. The pontederia is in its prime, alive with butterflies, — yellow and others. I see its tall blue spikes reflected beneath the edge of the pads on each side, pointing down to a heaven beneath as well as above. Earth appears but a thin crust or pellicle.

"It is a leaf — that of the green-briar — for poets to sing about: it excites me to a sort of autumnal madness. They are leaves for satyrs and fawns to make their garlands of. My thoughts

break **out** like them, spotted **all over, yellow and
green and** brown, — the freckled leaf. Perhaps
they should be poison to be thus spotted. **I** have
now found all the Hawk-weeds. Singular **are
these** genera of plants, — plants manifestly related,
yet distinct. They suggest **a** history to nature, a
natural history in a new sense. . . . Any anomaly
in vegetation makes Nature seem more **real** and
present in **her** working, as the various red and
yellow excrescences on young oaks. I am affected
as if it were a different nature that produced them.
As if **a poet** were born, who had **designs in his**
head. . . . I perceive in the **Norway cinque-foil**
(*Potentilla Norvegica*), **now nearly out of blossom,**
that **the alternate six leaves of the** calyx **are clos-**
ing over **the seeds to** protect them. This evidence
of forethought, this simple *reflection* **in** a double
sense of the term, in this flower is affecting to me,
as if it said to me, 'Not even when I have blos-
somed and have lost my painted petals, and am
preparing to die down to its root, do I forget to
fall **with my** arms around my babe, faithful to the
last, that **the** infant may be found preserved **in** the
arms **of the** frozen mother.' There **is one** door
closed of the closing year. **I am** not ashamed to
be contemporary with the cinque-foil. May **I** per-
form my part as well. **We love to see** Nature
fruitful in whatever kind. I love to see the acorns

plenty on the scrub-oaks, ay, and the night-shade berries. It assures us of her vigor, and that she may equally bring forth fruits which we prize. I love to see the potato-balls numerous and large, as I go through a low field, the plant thus bearing fruit at both ends, saying ever and anon, 'Not only these tubers I offer you for the present, but if you will have new varieties (if these do not satisfy you), plant these seeds, fruit of the strong soil, containing potash; the vintage is come, the olive is ripe. Why not for my coat-of-arms, for device, a drooping cluster of potato-balls in a potato field?

> "I come to pluck your berries harsh and crude,
> And with forced fingers rude,
> Shatter your leaves before the mellowing year."

These glimpses at the life of the lover of nature admonish us of the richness, the satisfactions in his unimpoverished districts. Man needs an open mind and a pure purpose, to become receptive. His interest in animals equalled that in flowers. At one time he carried his spade, digging in the galleries and burrows of field-mice. "They run into their holes, as if they had exploded before your eyes." Many voyages he made in cold autumn days and winter walks on the ice, to examine the cabins of the muskrat and discover precisely how and of what they were built, — the suite of rooms always damp, yet comfortable for the household, dressed in their old-fashioned waterproofs. He respected the skunk as a human being in a very humble sphere.

In his western tour of 1860, when he went to Minnesota and found the crab-apple and native Indians, he pleased himself with a new friend, — the gopher with thirteen stripes. Rabbits, woodchucks, red, gray, and "chipmunk" squirrels, he knew by heart; the fox never came amiss. A Canada lynx was killed in Concord, whose skin he eagerly obtained and preserved. It furnished a proof of wildness intact, and the nine lives of a wildcat. He mused on the change of habit in domestic animals, and recites a porcine epic, — the adventures of a fanatic pig. He was a debtor to the cows like other walkers.

"When you approach to observe them, they mind you just enough. How wholesome and clean their clear brick red! No doubt man impresses his own character on the beasts which he tames and employs. They are not only humanized, but they acquire his particular human nature. . . . The farmer acts on the ox, and the ox reacts on the farmer. They do not meet half way, it is true; but they do meet at a distance from the centre of each, proportionate to each one's intellectual power."

Let us hasten to his lovely idyl of the "Beautiful Heifer:" —

"One more confiding heifer, the fairest of the herd, did by degrees approach as if to take some morsel from our hands, while our hearts leaped to our mouths with expectation and delight. She by degrees drew near with her fair limbs (progressive), making pretence of browsing; nearer and nearer, till there was wafted to us the bovine fragrance, — cream of all the dairies that ever were or will be: and then she raised her gentle muzzle towards us, and snuffed an honest recognition within hand's reach. I saw it was possible for his herd to inspire with love the herdsman. She was as delicately featured as a hind. Her hide was mingled white and fawn color, and on her muzzle's tip there was a white spot not bigger than a daisy; and on her side turned toward me, the map of Asia plain to see.

"Farewell, dear heifer! Though thou forgettest me, my prayer to heaven shall be that thou mayst not forget thyself. There was a whole bucolic in her snuff. I saw her name was Sumac. And by the kindred spots I knew her mother, more sedate and matronly with full-grown bag, and on her sides was Asia great and small, the plains of Tartary, even to the pole; while on her daughter's was Asia Minor. She was not disposed to wanton with the herdsman. And as I walked she followed me, and took an apple from my hand,

and seemed to care more for the hand than the apple. So innocent a face as I have rarely seen on any creature, and I have looked in the face of many heifers. And as she took the apple from my hand I caught the apple of her eye. She smelled as sweet as the clethra blossom. There was no sinister expression. And for horns, though she had them, they were so well disposed in the right place, but neither up nor down, I do not now remember she had any. No horn was held towards me."

Seeing a flock of turkeys, the old faintly gobbling, the half-grown young peeping, they suggest a company of "turkey-men." He loves a cricket or a bee:—

" As I went through the deep cut before sunrise, I heard one or two early humble-bees come out on the deep, sandy bank: their low hum sounds like distant horns far in the horizon, over the woods. It was long before I detected the bees that made it, so far away musical it sounded, like the shepherds in some distant vale greeting the king of day. Why was there never a poem on the cricket? so serene and cool,—the iced-cream of song. It is modulated shade; heard in the grass chirping from everlasting to everlasting, the incessant cricket of the fall; no transient love-strain hushed when the incubating season is past. They creak hard now after sunset, no word will spell it; and the humming of a dorbug drowns all the noise of the village. So roomy is the universe. The moon comes out of the mackerel-cloud, and the traveller rejoices."

No class of creatures he found better than birds. With these mingled his love for sound: "Listen to music religiously, as if it were the last strain you might hear. Sugar is not as sweet to the palate as sound to the healthy ear. Is not all music a hum more or less divine?" His concert was the blue-bird, the robin, and song-sparrow, melting into joy after the silent winter. "Do you know on what bushes a little peace, faith, and contentment grow? Go a-berrying early and late after them." The color of the bluebird seemed to him "as if he carried the sky on his back. And where are gone the bluebirds whose warble was wafted to me so lately like a blue wavelet through the air, warbling so innocently to inquire if any of its mates are within call? The very grain of the air seems to have undergone a change, and is ready to split into the form of the bluebird's warble. The air over these fields is a foundry full of moulds for casting bluebirds' warbles. Methinks if it were visible or I could cast up some fine dust which would betray it, it would take a corresponding shape."

CHAPTER V.

LITERARY THEMES.

> No tidings come to thee
> Not of thy. very neighbors,
> That dwellen almost at thy doors,
> Thou hearest neither **that nor this;**
> For when thy labor all done is,
> And hast made all thy reckonings,
> **Instead of** rest and of new **things,**
> Thou goest home to thy house anon.
>   CHAUCER.

> To hill and cloud his face was known, —
> It seemed the likeness of their own.   .
>   EMERSON.

> **His** short parenthesis of life was sweet.
>   STORER'S LIFE OF WOLSEY.

"MEN commonly exaggerate the theme. Some themes they think are significant, and others insignificant. I feel that my life is very homely, my pleasures very cheap. Joy and sorrow, success and failure, grandeur and meanness, and indeed most words in the English language, do not mean for me what they do for my neighbors. I see that my neighbors look with compassion on me, that they think it is a mean and unfortunate destiny which makes me to walk in these fields and woods so much, and sail on this river alone. But so long as I find here the only real elysium, I cannot hesitate in my choice. My work is writing, and I do not hesitate though I know that no subject is too trivial for me, tried by ordinary standards; for, ye fools, the theme is nothing, the life is every thing. All that interests the reader is the depth and intensity of the life exerted. We touch our subject but by a point which has no breadth; but the pyramid of our experience, or our interest in it, rests on us by a broader or narrower base. What is man is all in all, Nature nothing but as she draws him out and reflects him. Give me simple, cheap, and homely themes."

These words from Thoreau partially illustrate his views upon the subjects he proposed to treat and how they should be treated, with that poetic wealth he enjoyed, and no one need look for prose. He never thought or spoke or wrote that.

In the same spirit he says of his first book, which had a slow sale: " I believe that this result is more inspiring and better for me than if a thousand had bought my wares. It affects my privacy less, and leaves me freer. Men generally over-estimate their praises." Of these themes, the following is one view among others: —

" As I walked I was intoxicated with the slight, spicy odor of the hickory-buds and the bruised bark of the black-birch, and in the fall with the pennyroyal. The sight of budding woods intoxicates me like diet-drink. I feel my Maker blessing me. To the sane man the world is a musical instrument. Formerly methought Nature developed as I developed, and grew up with me. My life was ecstasy. In youth, before I lost any of my senses, I can remember that I was all alive and inhabited my body with inexpressible satisfaction; both its weariness and its refreshment were sweet to me. This earth was the most glorious musical instrument, and I was audience to its strains. To have such sweet impressions made on us, such ecstasies begotten of the breezes, I can remember I was astonished. I said to myself, I said to others, there comes into my mind such an indescribable, infinite, all-absorbing, divine, heavenly pleasure, a sense of salvation and expansion. And I have had naught to do with it; I perceive that I am dealt with by superior powers. By all manner of bounds and traps threatening the extreme penalty of the divine law, it behooves us to preserve the purity and sanctity of the mind. That I am innocent to myself, that I love and reverence my life."

To make these themes into activities, he considered, —

" The moods and thoughts of man are revolving just as steadily and incessantly as Nature's. Nothing must be postponed; take time by the forelock, now or never. You must live in the present, launch yourself on any wave, find your eternity in each moment. Fools stand on their island opportunities, and look toward another land. There is no other land, there is no other life but this or the like of this. Where the good husbandman is, there is the good soil. Take any other course, and life will be a succession of regrets."

If writing is his business, to do this well must be sought.

" What a faculty must that be which can paint the most barren landscape and humblest life in glorious colors. It is pure and invigorated sense reacting on a sound and strong imagination. Is not this the poet's case? The intellect of most men is barren. It is the marriage of the soul with Nature that makes the intellect fruitful, that gives birth to imagination. When we were dead and dry as the highway, some sense which has been healthily fed will put us in relation with Nature, in sympathy with her, some grains of fertilizing pollen floating in the air fall on us, and suddenly the sky is all one rainbow, is full of music and fragrance and flavor. The man of intellect only, the prosaic man, is a barren and staminiferous flower; the poet is a fertile and perfect flower. The poet must keep himself unstained and aloof. Let him perambulate the bounds of Imagination's provinces, the realms of poesy and not the insignificant boundaries of towns. How many faculties there are

which we have never found. Some men methinks
have found only their hands and feet.

" It is wise to write on many subjects, to try many
themes, that so you may find the right and inspiring one. Be greedy of occasions to express your
thoughts ; improve the opportunity to draw anal-
ogies ; there are innumerable avenues to a perception of the truth. Improve the suggestion of each
object, however humble, however slight and transient the provocation ; what else is there to be
improved? Who knows what opportunities he
may neglect? It is not in vain that the mind
turns aside this way or that: follow its leading,
apply it whither it inclines to go. Probe the
universe in a myriad points. Be avaricious of
these impulses. Nature makes a thousand acorns
to get one oak. He is a wise man and experienced
who has taken many views, to whom stones and
plants and animals, and a myriad objects have
each suggested something, contributed something.
We cannot write well or truly but what we write
with gusto. The body and senses must conspire
with the mind. Experience is the act of the
whole man, — that our speech may be vascular.
The intellect is powerless to express thought without the aid of the heart and liver and of every
member. Often I feel that my head stands out too
dry when it should be immersed. A writer, a man

writing, is **the scribe of all** nature; **he is the corn** and **the grass** and **the** atmosphere writing. **It is** always essential that **we** *live* **to** do what **we are** doing, do it with **a** heart. There **are flowers of** thought and there are leaves of thought, and **most of** our thoughts are merely leaves to which the thread of thought is the stem. Whatever things **I perceive with my entire** man, those let me record and **it** will **be** poetry. The sounds which **I** hear with **the** consent and coincidence **of** all my senses, those are significant and musical; **at** least, they only are heard. I omit the unusual, **the** hurricanes and earthquakes, and describe **the** common. This has the greatest charm, **and is the true theme of** poetry. **You may have the extraordinary for your** province if you will; **let** me have the ordinary. Give me **the** obscure **life, the cottage** of the **poor** and humble, the work-days of **the** world, **the bar-** ren fields; the smallest share **of** all things but poetical perception. Give me but **the** eyes to see the things which **you** possess."

As he writes of **the strawberry, "** It is natural that the first fruit which the earth **bears** shall **emit** and be as it were **an** embodiment of that **vernal** fragrance **with** which **the air has** teemed," **so** he represented the purity and sweetness of **youth,** which **in him** *never* **grew old.**

" How watchful we must be to keep the crystal well clear, that it be not made turbid by our contact with the world, so that it will not reflect objects. If I would preserve my relation to Nature, I must make my life more moral, more pure and innocent. The problem is as precise and simple as a mathematical one. I must not live loosely, but more and more continently. How can we expect a harvest of thought who have not had a seed-time of character? Already some of my small thoughts, fruit of my spring life, are ripe, like the berries which feed the first broods of birds ; and some others are prematurely ripe and bright like the lower leaves of the herbs which have felt the summer's drought. Human life may be transitory and full of trouble, but the perennial mind whose survey extends from that spring to this, from Columella to Hosmer, is superior to change. I will identify myself with that which will not die with Columella and will not die with Hosmer."

As the song of the spring birds makes the richest music of the year, it seems a fit overture to have given a few of Thoreau's spring sayings upon his life and work. Few men knew better, or so well, what these were. In some senses he was a scientific man, in others not. I do not think he relished science in long words, or the thing Wordsworth calls —

> " Philosopher ! **a fingering slave,**
> One that would peep **and botanize**
> **Upon his mother's grave.**"

He loved Nature as a child, reverenced her veils that we should not conceitedly endeavor to raise. He did not believe the study of anatomy helped the student to a practical knowledge of the human body, and replied to a suggested prescription, " How do you know that his pills will go down ? " Nor that the eggs of turtles to be, seen through a glass darkly, were turtles, and said to the ornithologist who wished to hold his bird in his hand that " he would rather hold it in his affections." So he saw the colors of his with a kind heart, and let the spiders slide. Yet no man spent more labor in making out his bird by Wilson or Nuttall.

His was a broad catholic creed. As he thought of the Hindoo Mythology, " It rises on me like the full moon after the stars have come out, wading through some far summer stratum of sky." From Homer, who made a corner with Grecian mythology, to his beloved Indian, whose life of scalping and clam-bakes was a religion, he could appreciate the good of creeds and forms and omit the scruples. He says : —

" If I could, I would worship the paring of my nails. He who discovers two gods where there

was only known to be one, and such a one! I
would fain improve every opportunity to wonder
and worship as a sunflower welcomes the light."
" God could not be unkind to me if he should try.
I love best to have each thing in its season, doing
without it at all other times. It is the greatest of
all advantages to enjoy no advantage at all.   I
have never got over my surprise that I should have
been born into the most estimable place in all the
world, and in the very nick of time too. I heard
one speak to-day of his sense of awe at the thought
of God, and suggested to him that *awe* was the
cause of the potato-rot."

He again expressed himself in a lively way
about these matters: " Who are the religious?
They who do not differ much from mankind generally, except that they are more conservative and
timid and useless, but who in their conversation
and correspondence talk about kindness and Heavenly Father, instead of going bravely about their
business, trusting God even." He once knew a
minister, and photographs him: " Here's a man
who can't butter his own bread, and he has just
combined with one thousand like him to make a
dipt toast for all eternity."

Of a book published by Miss Harriet Martineau,
that Minerva mediocre, he observes: " Miss Martineau's last book is not so bad as the timidity which

fears its influence. As if the popularity of this or that book could be so fatal, and man would not still be man in the world. Nothing is so much to be feared as fear. Atheism may, comparatively, be popular with God." Religion, worship, and prayer were words he studied in their history; but *out-of-doors*, which can serve for the title of much of his writing, is his creed. He used this expression: " May I love and revere myself above all the gods that man has ever invented; **may I** never let the vestal fire go out in my recesses."

He thought the past and the **men of** the past, **as** they crop out in institutions, were not as valuable as the present and the individual alive. " They who will remember only this kind of right **do as if** they stood under a shed and affirmed that **they** were under the unobserved heavens. **The shed** has its use, but what is it to the heavens above." The institution of American slavery was a filthy and rotten shed which Thoreau used his utmost strength to cut away and **burn** up. From first to last he loved and honored abolitionism. Not one slave alone was expedited **to** Canada by Thoreau's personal **assistance.**

CHAPTER VI.

SPRING AND AUTUMN.

"Methinks I hear the sound of time long past,
  Still murmuring o'er us in the lofty void
Of these dark arches, like the ling'ring voice
Of those who long within their graves have slept."

ORBA, A TRAGEDY.

AS he is dropping beans in the spring, he hears the baywing : —

"I saw the world through a glass as it lies eternally. It reminded me of many a summer sunset, of many miles of gray rails, of many a rambling pasture, of the farmhouse far in the fields, its milk-pans and well-sweep, and the cows coming home at twilight; I correct my Human views by listening to their Volucral. I ordinarily plod along a sort of whitewashed prison entry, subject to some indifferent or even grovelling mood; I do not distinctly seize my destiny; I have turned down my light to the merest glimmer, and am doing some task which I have set myself. I take incredibly narrow views, live on the limits, and have no recollection of absolute truth. But suddenly, in some fortunate moment, the voice of eternal wisdom reaches *me* even in the strain of the sparrow, and liberates me; whets and clarifies my own senses, makes me a competent witness."

He says elswhere **of** the same sparrow: "**The** end of its strain **is like** the ring of **a** small piece **of** steel wire dropped on an anvil." How **he loved** Aurora! how he loved the morning! "You must **taste the** first glass of the day's nectar if you would get all the spirit of it. Its fixed air begins to stir and escape. The sweetness of the day crystallizes in the morning coolness." The morning was the spring of the day, and spring the morning of the year. Then he said, musing: "All Nature *revives* at this season. With her it **is** really **a** new life, but with these church-goers it **is** only a revival of religion or hypocrisy; they go down stream to still muddier waters. **It** cheers **me** more to behold the mass of gnats which **have** revived in the spring sun. If a man do not revive with Nature in the spring, how shall he revive when a white-collared priest prays for him?" This dash at theological linen is immediately followed by "small water-bugs in Clematis Brook."

Of the willow fish-creel in Farrar's Brook he says: —

"It was equal to a successful stanza whose subject was spring. I see those familiar features, that large type with which all my life is associated, unchanged. We too are obeying the laws of all nature. Not less important are the observers of the birds than the birds themselves. This rain is good **for thought, it** is especially **agreeable to me as I** enter the **wood** and hear the rustling dripping on the **leaves.** It domiciliates me in nature. The woods are more like a house for the **rain;** the few slight noises resound **more hollow** in them, the **birds hop** nearer, the very trees seem still and pensive. **We** love to sit **on** and **walk** over sandy *tracts* in the spring, like cicindelas. These tongues of **russet land, tapering** and sloping **into the flood, do almost** speak to me. One piece of ice, in breaking on the river, **rings when** struck **on** another, like **a trowel** on a brick. The loud *peop* of a pigeon woodpecker is heard in our **rear, and** anon the prolonged **and** shrill cackle calling the thin wooded hillsides and pastures to life. **You** doubt if the season **will be long** enough for such oriental and luxurious slowness. **I think that** my senses made **the truest** report the first time. There is a time to watch the ripples on Ripple Lake, to look for arrow-heads, to study the rocks and lichens, a time **to** walk on sandy deserts, and the observer of nature must improve **these seasons as much as** the farmer his.

" Those ripple **lakes** lie now in the midst of mostly bare, brown, or tawny dry woodlands, themselves the most living objects. They may say to the first woodland **flowers, — ' We** played with **the North** winds here before ye were born ! ' When the playful **breeze drops** on **the pool, it** springs **to** right and left, quick as a kitten playing with **dead** leaves. This pine warbler impresses me as if it were calling the trees to life ; I **think of** springing twigs. Its jingle rings through the wood **at short** intervals, as if, like an electric spark, it imparted a fresh spring life to them. The fresh land emerging from the water reminds me of the isle which was called up **from the bottom of** the sea, which was given **to Apollo. Or, like the skin** of a pard, the great mother leopard that **Nature is,** where she lies at length exposing **her** flanks to **the sun.** I feel as **if** I could land to kiss **and stroke** the very sward, it is **so fair.** It is homely and domestic to my eyes like the rug that lies before **my** hearth-side. As the walls of cities are fabled **to** have been built by music, so my **pines were** established by the song **of the** field-sparrow. **I heard** the jingle of the blackbird, — some of the most liquid **notes,** as if **produced** by some of the water of the Pierian spring flowing through some kind of musical water-pipe and at the same moment setting in motion **a** multitude of **fine** vibrating metallic springs, like a shepherd merely meditating most enrapturing tunes on such **a** water-pipe. **The** robin's song gurgles out of all conduits **now,** — they are choked **with it.**

"I **hear at** a distance **in** the meadow, still at

long intervals, the hurried commencement of **the** bobolink's strain: the bird is just touching the strings of his theorbo, his glavichord, his **water-organ,** and one or two notes globe themselves and **fall in** liquid bubbles from his teeming throat. . . . Beginning slowly and deliberately, the partridge's **beat** sounds **faster** and faster far away under **the boughs** and through the **aisle** of the wood, until it **becomes a regular roll.** How many things shall **we not see** and be and **do,** when we walk there where the partridge drums. **The rush-sparrow** jingles her small change, — pure sil**ver on the counter** of the pasture. How sweet it **sounds in a clear,** warm morning, in **a** wood-side **pasture, amid the** old corn-hills, **or in sprout-lands, clear and distinct** like ' a spoon in a cup,' the last part very clear and ringing. **I** hear the king-bird twittering or chat**tering like a** stout-chested swallow, and the sound **of** snipes winnowing the evening air. The cuckoo reminds me of some silence among the birds I had not noticed. I hear the squirrel chirp in the wall, like a spoon. **Times and** seasons may perhaps be best marked by the notes of reptiles; they express, as it were, the very feelings of the earth or nature. About May-day the ring of the first toad leaks into the general **stream of** sound, — **a** bubbling ring; **I am thrilled to my very spine, it is** so terrene a **sound, as crowded** with **protuberant** bubbles as the rind of an orange, sufficiently considered **by its** maker, in the night and the solitude. **I hear the** dumping sound of frogs, that know no winter. **It** is like the tap of a drum when human legions are mustering. It reminds me that Summer is now **in** earnest gathering her forces, **and** that ere long I shall see their waving plumes and hear the full bands and steady tread. What lungs! what health! what **terrenity (if not serenity)** it suggests! How **many walks I take along the brooks in the spring!** What shall I call **them? Lesser** riparial excursions? prairial rivular? If **you make the least** correct observation of **nature this** year, **you will** have occasion to repeat **it with illustrations the** next, and the season **and life itself is prolonged.** Days long enough and fair enough **for the worthiest** deeds. **The** day is an epitome of **the year. I** think that a perfect parallel may be drawn between the seasons of the day and of the **year.** If the writer would interest readers, **he** must report so much life, using a certain satisfaction **always as a** *point d'ap-**pui. **However mean** and limited, it must **be a** genuine **and** contented life **that** he speaks out **of.** **They** must have the essence and oil **of himself,** **tried** out **of the fat** of his experience and joy."

> " The Titan heeds his sky affairs,
> Rich rents and wide alliance shares ;
> Mysteries of color daily laid
> By the sun in light and shade ;
> **And sweet varieties of chance.**"

Color was a treat to Thoreau. He saw the seasons and the landscapes through their colors; and all hours and fields and woods spoke in varied hues which impressed him with sentiment. Nature does not forget beauty and outline even in a mud-turtle's shell. Is it winter? — he "loves the few homely colors of Nature at this season, her strong, wholesome browns, her sober and primeval grays, her celestial blue, her vivacious green, her pure, cold, snowy white. The mountains look like waves in a blue ocean tossed up by a stiff gale." In early spring he thinks, —

"The white saxifrage is a response from earth to the increased light of the year, the yellow crowfoot to the increased light of the sun. Why is the pollen of flowers commonly yellow? The pyramidal pine-tops are now seen rising out of a reddish, permanent mistiness of the deciduous trees just bursting into leaf. The sorrel begins to redden the fields with ruddy health. The sun goes down red again like a high-colored flower of summer. As the white and yellow flowers of the spring are giving place to the rose and will soon to the red lily, so the yellow sun of spring has become a red sun of June drought, round and red like a midsummer flower, productive of torrid heats. Again, I am attracted by the deep scarlet of the wild rose, half open in the grass, all glowing with rosy light."

" The **soft,** mellow, fawn-colored light **of the** July sunset seemed to **come** from the **earth itself.** My thoughts are drawn inward, even as clouds **and** trees are reflected in the smooth, still water. There is an inwardness even in the musquito's hum while I am picking blueberries in the dark wood. The landscape is fine as behind glass, the horizon edge distinct. The distant vales towards the north-west mountains lie up **open and** clear and elysian like so many Tempes. The shadows of trees are dark and distinct; the din of trivialness **is silenced. The** woodside after sunset is cool as a pot of green paint, and the moon reflects from the rippled surface like a stream **of** dollars. **The** shooting stars **are** but fireflies of the firmament. Late in September, **I** see the whole **of** the red-maple, — bright scarlet against the cold, green pines. The clear, bright scarlet leaves of the smooth sumac in many **places are** curled and drooping, hanging straight down, **so** as to make a funereal impression, reminding me **of a** red sash and a soldier's funeral. They impress me quite as black crape similarly arranged, — the bloody plants. In mid December the day is short; **it seems to be composed of** two twilights merely, **and there is sometimes a peculiar, clear,** vitreous, greenish sky in the west, as **it were a** molten gem."

" **In this January thaw I** hear the pleasant sound

of running water; **here is my Italy, my** heaven, my New England. I can understand **why** the Indians hereabouts placed heaven in the south-west, the soft south. The delicious, soft, spring-suggesting air! **The sky, seen** here and there through **the** wrack, bluish and greenish, and perchance with a vein **of red in** the west, seems like the **inside of** a shell deserted by its tenant, into which **I** have **crawled.** What beauty in the running brooks! What life! What society! The cold is **merely** superficial; it is summer still at the core, far, far **within. It** is in the cawing of the crow, the crowing of the cock, the warmth of the sun on our backs. I hear faintly the cawing **of a crow far,** far away, echoing from some unseen woodside, as if deadened by the spring-like vapor which the sun is drawing from the ground. **It** mingles with the slight murmur from the village, the sound of children at play, as one stream gently empties into another, and the wild and tame are one. What a delicious sound! It is not merely crow calling to crow. **If he has voice, I** have ears. . . . I think I never saw a more elysian blue than my shadow. I am turned into a tall, blue Persian from my cap to my boots, such as no mortal dye can produce, **with** an amethystine **hatchet in** my hand.

" **The** holes **in the** pasture where rocks **were taken out are now** converted **into perfect jewels.**

They are filled with water of crystalline transparency, through which I see to their emerald bottoms, paved with emerald. Even these furnish goblets and vases of perfect purity to hold the dews and rains; and what more agreeable bottom **can we** look to than this, which the earliest sun **and moisture** had tinged green? I see an early grasshopper drowning in one; it looks like a fate to be envied: April wells call them, vases clean, as if enamelled. What wells can be more charming? **You almost envy the** wood-frogs and toads that hop **amid** such gems as fungi, some pure and bright **enough for a** breastpin. Out of every crevice **between the dead** leaves oozes some vehicle of color, **the unspent** wealth of the year which Nature **is now casting** forth, as if it were only to empty herself. **And,** now **to your** surprise, these ditches are crowded **with** millions of little stars (*Aster Tradescanti*). Call them travellers' thoughts. What green, herbaceous, graminivorous thoughts the wood-frog must **have!** I wish that my thoughts were as reasonable as his."

" I notice many little, pale-brown, dome-shaped puff-balls, **puckered to a** centre beneath, which emit their **dust:** when **you pinch** them, a **smoke-like,** brown dust (snuff-colored) issues from **the** orifice at their top, like smoke from a chimney. **It is so fine and** light that it **rises into the** air and is wafted away like smoke. **They are** low, oriental domes or mosques, sometimes crowded together in nests like a collection of humble cottages on the **moor, in** the coal-pit or Numidian style. For there is suggested some humble hearth beneath, from **which** this smoke comes up, as it were, the homes of slugs and crickets. Amid the low and withering grass, their resemblance to rude, dome-shaped cottages where some humble but everlasting life is lived, pleases me not a little, and their smoke ascends between the legs of the herds and the traveller. I imagine **a hearth** and pot, and some snug but humble family passing its Sunday evening beneath each one. I locate there at **once** all that is simple and admirable in human life ; **there is no** virtue which their roofs exclude. I imagine with what faith and contentment I could come home to them at evening."

Thus social is Nature, if her lover bring a friendly **heart.** The love of beauty **and** truth which can light and cheer its possessor, not only in youth and health, but **to** the verge of the abyss, walked abroad with our Walden naturalist; for Nature never did betray the heart that loved her. To be faithful in few things, to possess your soul in peace and make the best use of the one talent, is deemed an acceptable offering, — *omne devotum pro significo.*

"I am a stranger in your towns; I can winter more to my mind amid the shrub-oaks; I have made arrangements to stay with them. The shrub-oak, lowly, loving the earth and spreading **over it,** tough, thick-leaved; leaves firm and sound in winter, and rustling like leather shields; leaves firm and wholesome, clear and smooth to the touch. Tough to support the snow, not broken down by it, well-nigh useless to man, a sturdy phalanx hard to break through, product of New England's **surface,** bearing many striped acorns. Well-tanned leather-color on the one side, sun-tanned, color of colors, color of the cow and the deer, silver-downy beneath, turned toward the late bleached **and russet** fields. What are acanthus leaves **and** the rest to this, emblem of my winter condition? I love and could embrace the shrub-oak with its scaly garment of leaves rising above the snow, lowly whispering to me, akin to winter thoughts and sunsets and to all virtue. Rigid as iron, clear as the atmosphere, hardy as virtue, innocent and sweet as a maiden, is the shrub-oak. I felt a positive yearning to one bush this afternoon. There was a match found for me at last, — I fell in love with **a** shrub-oak. Low, robust, hardy, indigenous, well-known to the striped squirrel and the partridge and rabbit, what is Peruvian bark to your bark! How many rents **I owe to you,** how **many eyes put** out, how

many bleeding fingers. How many shrub-oak
patches I have been through, winding my way,
bending the twigs aside, guiding myself **by** the
sun over hills and valleys and plains, resting in
clear grassy spaces. I love to go through a patch
of scrub-oaks in a bee line, — where you tear your
clothes and put your eyes out."

"Sometimes I would rather get a transient
glimpse, a side view of a thing, than stand front-
ing to it, as these polypodys. The object I caught
a glimpse **of as** I went by, haunts my thought a
long time, is infinitely suggestive, **and I do** not
care to front it and scrutinize **it; for I know** that
the thing that really concerns me **is not** there, but
in my relation to *that*. That is **a mere** reflecting
surface. Its influence **is** sporadic, wafted through
the air to me. Do you imagine its fruit to stick to
the back of its leaf **all** winter? At this season,
polypody is in the air. My thoughts are with them
a long time after my body has passed. It is the
cheerful community of the polypodys: are not wood-
frogs the philosophers who walk in these groves?"

As in winter: "How completely a load of hay
revives the memory of past summers. Summer in
us is only a little dried like it." The foul flanks
of the cattle remind him how early it still is in the
spring. He knows the date by his garment, and
says on the twenty-eighth of April, "The twenty-

seventh and to-day are **weather for a half-thick single coat. This first** off-coat warmth." The first week **of May,** " The shadow of the cliff is like a dark pupil on the side of the hill. That cliff and its shade suggests **dark eyes** and eyelashes and overhanging brows. **It is a** leafy mist throughout **the forest." And with** a rare comparison, " The green of the new grass the last week in April has **the** regularity of a parapet or rampart to a fortress. It winds along the irregular **lines** of tussucks like **the** wall of China **over hill and** dale. **As I am** measuring along the Marlboro' road, **a fine** little blue-slate butterfly fluttered over the chain. **Even** its feeble strength was required **to fetch** the year about. How daring, even rash, Nature appears, who sends out butterflies so early. Sardanapalus-like, she loves extremes and contrasts." **(It was** this day, April 28, 1856, that Thoreau first definitely theorized the succession of forest trees.) The sight and sound of the first humming-bird made him think he was in the tropics, in Demerara **or** Maracaibo. Or shall we take an autumn walk, the first September week?

" Nature improves this, her last opportunity, **to** empty her lap of flowers.

" I turn Anthony's corner. It **is** an early September afternoon, melting, warm, and sunny ; the thousand of grasshoppers leaping before you reflect gleams of light.   **A** little distance off, the field **is** yellowed with a Xerxean army of *Solidago nemoralis* (gray golden-rod) between me and the sun. It spreads its legions over the **dry** plains **now, as** soldiers muster in the fall, fruit of August and September sprung from **the** sun-dust.   The fields and hills appear in their yellow uniform (its recurved standard, a little more than a foot high), marching to the holy land, a countless host of crusaders.   The earth-song of the cricket comes up through all, and ever and anon the hot z-ing of the locust is heard.   The dry, deserted fields are one mass of yellow like a color shoved **to one** side on Nature's palette.   You literally **wade** in flowers knee-deep, and now the moist banks and low bottoms are beginning to be abundantly sugared with the *Aster Tradescanti*.   How ineffectual is the note of a bird now!   We hear it as if we heard it not and forget it immediately.   **The** blackbirds were pruning themselves and splitting their throats in vain, trying to sing as the other day ; all the melody flew off in splinters.   By the first week of **October, the hue** of maturity has come even **to** that fine, *silver-topped*, feathery grass, two or three feet high in clumps, on dry places ; I am riper for thought too.   Every thing, all fruits and leaves, even the surfaces of stone and stubble, are all ripe **in this** air.   **The** chickadees of late have winter

ways, flocking after you." "Birds generally **wear**
the russet **dress of** nature at this **season** (November 7), they have their fall no less than the plants;
the bright tints depart from their foliage of feathers, and they flit past like withered leaves in rustling flocks. The sparrow is a withered leaf. When
the flower season is over, when the great company
of flower-seekers have ceased their search, the
fringed gentian raises its blue face above the withering grass beside the brooks for **a** moment, having
at the eleventh hour **made up** its mind to join the
planet's floral exhibition. Pieces of water **are**
now reservoirs of dark indigo; as for the **dry oak-**
leaves, all winter is their fall."

"The tinkling notes of **goldfinches and bobo-**
links which we hear in August are of one character, and peculiar **to** the season. They are **not**
voluminous flowers, **but** rather nuts of sound,
ripened **seeds** of sound. It is the tinkling **of**
ripened grains in Nature's basket; like the sparkle
on water, **a** sound produced by friction on the
crisped **air.** The cardinals (*Lobelia cardinalis*)
are fluviatile, and stand along some river or brook
like myself. **It** is the three o'clock of the year
when the *Bidens Beckii* (water marigold) begins
to prevail. By mid-October, the year is acquiring
a grizzly look from the climbing mikania, golden-
rods, and ***Andropogon* scoparius** (purple wood-

grass). **And** painted ducks, **too,** often come to sail **and float amid the painted leaves.** Surely, **while geese fly overhead, we** can live here as **contentedly as they do at** York factory or Hudson's **Bay.** We shall perchance **be as well** provisioned and have as good society as they. **Let us** be of good cheer then, and expect the annual vessel which brings the spring to us, without fail. Goodwin, the one-eyed **Ajax, and** other fishermen, who sit thus alone from morning to **night at** this season, **must** be greater philosophers **than the** shoemakers. **The** streets are thickly strewn **with elm and button-wood** and other leaves, *feuille-morte* color. And what **is acorn color?** **Is it** not as good as chestnut? Now (the second November week) for twinkling light reflected from unseen windows in the horizon **in early twilight.** **The** frost seems **as if the** earth was letting off steam after the summer's **work is over.** If you do feel any fire at this season out of doors, you **may** depend upon **it,** it **is your** own. November, eat-heart, — is that the name of it? A man will eat **his** heart **in** this, if in any **month.** The old she-wolf is nibbling at your very extremities. The frozen ground eating away the soles of your shoes **is** only typical of the Nature that gnaws your heart. Going through a partly frozen meadow near the river, scraping the sweet-gale, I am pleasantly scented with its odoriferous fruit. The smallest (*Asplenium*) ferns under a shelving rock, pinned on rosette-wise, looked like the head of a breast-pin. The rays from the bare twigs across the pond are bread and cheese to me. . . . I see to the bone. See those bare birches prepared to stand the winter through on the bare hill-side. They never sing, ' What is this dull town to me ? ' The maples skirting the meadow (in dense phalanxes) look like light infantry advanced for a swamp fight. Ah! dear November, ye must be sacred to the Nine, surely."

" If you would know what are my winter thoughts, look for them in the partridge's crop. The winter, cold and bound out as it is, is thrown to us like a bone to a famishing dog. I go budding like a partridge. Some lichenous thoughts still adhere to us, our cold immortal evergreens. Even our experience is something like wintering in the pack, and we assume the spherical form of the marmot. We have peculiarly long and clear silvery twilights, morn and eve, with a stately withdrawn after redness, — it is indigoy along the horizon. . . . Wachusett looks like a right whale over our bow, ploughing the continent with his flukes well down. He has a vicious look, as if he had a harpoon in him. All waters now seen through the leafless trees are blue as indigo, reservoirs of dark indigo among the general russet, reddish-brown, and gray. I rode home on a hay rigging with a boy who had been collecting a load of dry leaves for the hog-pen, — this, the third or fourth ; two other boys asked leave to ride, with four large, empty box-traps, which they were bringing home from the woods. They had caught five rabbits this fall, baiting with an apple. Some fine straw-colored grasses, as delicate as the down on a young man's cheek, still rise above this crusted snow. I look over my shoulder upon an arctic scene. . . . The winters come now as fast as snow-flakes ; there is really but one season in our hearts. The snow is like a uniform white napkin in many fields. I see the old, pale-faced farmer walking beside his team (in the sled), with contented thoughts, for the five thousandth time. This drama every day in the streets. This is the theatre I go to."

CHAPTER VII.

PHILOSOPHY.

"La génie c'est la patience." — Buffon.
" As he had kyked on the newe mone." — Chaucer.

"IT was summer, and now again it is winter.
Nature loves this rhyme so well that she never
tires of repeating it. So sweet and wholesome is
the winter, so simple and moderate, so satisfactory
and perfect, that her children will never weary of
it. What a poem! an epic, in blank verse, inscribed
with uncounted tinkling rhymes. It is solid beauty.
It has been subjected to the vicissitudes of a million
years of the gods, and not a single superfluous
ornament remains. The severest and coldest of
the immortal critics shot their arrows at and pruned
it, till it cannot be amended. We might expect
to find in the snows the footprint of a life superior to our own; of which no zoölogy takes cogni-
zance; a life which pursued does not earth itself.
The hollows look like a glittering shield set round
with brilliants, as we go south-westward through
the Cassandra swamps toward the declining sun,
in the midst of which we walked. That beautiful

5   G

frost-work, which so frequently in winter mornings is seen bristling about the throat of every breathing-hole in the earth's surface, is the frozen breath of the earth upon its beard. I knew what it was by my own experience. Some grass culms eighteen inches or two feet high, which nobody noticed, are an inexhaustible supply of slender ice wands set in the snow. The waving lines within the marsh-ice look sometimes just like some white, shaggy wolf-skin. The fresh, bright chestnut fruit of some lichens, glistening in moist winter days, brings life and immortality to light. The sight of the masses of yellow hastate leaves and flower-buds of the yellow lily, already four or six inches long at the bottom of the river, reminds me that Nature is prepared for an infinity of springs yet. How interesting a few clean, dry weeds on the shore a dozen rods off, seen distinctly against the smooth reflecting water between ice!

"The surface of the snow everywhere in the fields, where it is hard blown, has a fine grain with low shelves, like a slate stone that does not split well; also, there are some shell-like drifts, more than once round. Over the frozen river only the bridges are seen peeping out from time to time like a dry eyelid. The damp, driving snow-flakes, when we turned partly round and faced them, hurt our eyeballs as if they had been dry scales: there are plenty of those shell-like drifts along the south sides of the walls now, and countless perforations, sometimes like the prows of vessels, or the folds of a white napkin or counterpane dropped over a bonneted head. Snow-flakes are the wheels of the storm chariots, the wreck of chariot wheels after a battle in the skies ; these glorious spangles, the sweeping of heaven's floor. And they all sing, melting as they sing, of the mysteries of the number six, six, six. He takes up the water of the sea in his hand, leaving the salt ; he disperses it in mist through the skies ; he recollects and sprinkles it like grain in six-rayed snowy stars over the earth, there to lie till it dissolves its bonds again.

" I see great thimbleberry bushes, rising above the snow with still a rich, rank bloom on them as in July, — hypæthral mildew, elysian fungus ! To see the bloom on a thimbleberry thus lasting into mid-winter ! What a salve that would make collected and boxed ! I should not be ashamed to have a shrub-oak for my coat-of-arms ; I would fain have been wading through the woods and fields and conversing with the sane snow. Might I aspire to praise the moderate nymph, Nature ! I must be like her, — moderate. Who shall criticise that companion ? It is like the hone to the knife. There I get my underpinnings laid and repaired, cemented and levelled. There is my country club; we dine at the sign of the shrub-oak, the new Albion House.

" A little flock of red-polls (*Linaria minor*) is busy picking the seeds of the pig-weed in the garden, this driving snow-storm. Well may the tender buds attract us at this season, no less than partridges, for they are the hope of the year, the spring rolled up; the summer is all packed in them. Again and again I congratulate myself on my so-called poverty. How can we spare to be abroad in the morning red; to see the forms of the leafless eastern trees against the clear sky, and hear the cocks crow, when a thin low mist hangs over the ice and frost in meadows? When I could sit in a cold chamber, muffled in a cloak, each evening till Thanksgiving time, warmed by my own thoughts, the world was not so much with me. When I have only a rustling oak-leaf, or the faint metallic cheep of a tree-sparrow, for variety in my winter walk, my life becomes continent and sweet as the kernel of a nut. Show me a man who consults his genius, and you have shown me a man who cannot be advised. . . . Going along the Nut Meadow, or Jimmy Miles road, when I see the sulphur lichens on the rails brightening with the moisture, I feel like studying them again as a relisher or tonic, to make life go down and digest well, as we use pepper and vinegar and salads. They are a sort of winter-greens, which we gather and assimilate with our eyes. The flattened boughs of the white-pine rest stratum above stratum like a cloud, a green mackerel-sky, hardly reminding me of the concealed earth so far beneath. They are like a flaky crust to the earth; my eyes nibble the piney sierra which makes the horizon's edge, as a hungry man nibbles a cracker. . . . That bird (the hawk) settles with confidence on the white-pine top, and not upon your weather-cock; that bird will not be poultry of yours, lays no eggs for you, for ever hides its nest. Though willed or *wild*, it is not wilful in its wildness. The unsympathizing man regards the wildness of some animals, their strangeness to him, as a sin. No hawk that soars and steals our poultry is wilder than genius; and none is more persecuted, or above persecution. It can never be poet-laureate, to say " pretty Poll," and " Poll want a cracker."

In these sayings may his life best be sought. It is an autobiography with the genuine brand, — it is unconscious. How he was affected by the seasons, who walked with them as a familiar friend, thinking thus aloud the thoughts which they brought; associations in linked sweetness long drawn out; dear and delightful as memories or hopes! He had few higher sources of inspiration than night, and having given a prayer of his to the moon, see **what one evening furnishes: it** is the first week **in** September.

" **The air** is very still, a fine sound of crickets, but **not** loud. **The** woods and single trees are **heavier** masses than in **the** spring, — night has more allies. I hear only **a** tree-toad **or** sparrow singing **at** long intervals, **as** in spring. **Now in the fields** I see **the white** streak of the neottia in **the** white twilight. **The** whippoorwill sings far off. I hear the **sound** from time to time **of a** leaping **fish** or **a frog, or** a muskrat or a turtle. I know not how it **is that** this universal cricket's creak **should** sound thus regularly intermittent, **as if** for the most part they fell in with one another and **creaked** in time, making **a certain** pulsing **sound,** a sort of breathing or panting of all nature. **You sit** twenty **feet** above the still river, see the sheeny pads and the **moon** and some bare tree-tops **in** the distant **horizon.** Those bare tree-tops add greatly to the wildness.

" Lower down **I** see **the moon in the water as** bright as in the **heavens,** only the water-bugs disturb its disk, and now **I** catch a faint glassy glare from the whole river surface, which before was simply dark. This is set in a frame of double darkness in the east ; *i.e.,* **the** reflected shore of woods and hills and the reality, **the shadow and the** substance bi-partite, answering **to each. I see** the northern

lights over my shoulder to remind me **of the Esqui**
maux, and that they are still my contemporaries
on this globe; that they, too, are taking their walks
on another part of the planet, in pursuit of seals
perchance. It was so soft and velvety **a** light as
contained a thousand placid days recently put **to**
rest in the bosom of the water. **So** looked the
North-twin Lake in the Maine woods. It reminds
me of placid lakes in the mid-noon of Indian
summer days, but yet more placid and civilized,
suggesting a higher cultivation, **as** wildness **ever**
does, which æons **of** summer days **have gone to**
make, like a summer day seen far **away. All the**
effects of sunlight, **with a** softer tone, and **all the**
stillness of the water and air superadded, **and**
the witchery of the hour. What gods are **they**
that require so fair a vase of gleaming water **to**
their prospect in the midst of the wild **woods**
by night?

"Else why this beauty allotted to night, a gem
to sparkle in the zone of *Nox?* They are strange
gods now out; methinks their names are not in
any mythology. The light that is in night, a smile
as in a dream on the face of the sleeping lake,
enough light to show what we see, any more would
obscure these objects. **I am** not advertised of any
deficiency of light. The faint sounds of birds
dreaming aloud in the **night,** the fresh cool air and

sound of the wind rushing over the rocks remind me of the tops of mountains. In this faint, hoary light all fields are like a mossy rock and remote from the cultivated plains of day. It is all one with Caucasus, the slightest hill-pasture.

"Now the fire in the north increases wonderfully, not shooting up so much as creeping along, like a fire on the mountains of the north, seen afar in the night. The Hyperborean gods are burning brush, and it spread, and all the hoes in heaven couldn't stop it. It spread from west to east, over the crescent hill. Like a vast fiery worm it lay across the northern sky, broken into many pieces; and each piece, with rainbow colors skirting it, strove to advance itself towards the east, worm-like on its own annular muscles. It has spread into the choicest wood-lots of Valhalla; now it shoots up like a single, solitary watch-fire, or burning brush, or where it ran up a pine-tree like powder, and still it continues to gleam here and there like a fat stump in the burning, and is reflected in the water. And now I see the gods by great exertions have got it under, and the stars have come out without fear in peace. Though no birds sing, the crickets vibrate their shrill and stridulous cymbals in the alders of the causeway, those minstrels especially engaged for night's quire."

He saw the great in the little: the translucent
leaves of the **Andromeda** *calyculata* seemed **in
January,** with **their soft red, more or less brown,
as he** walked towards the sun, **like cathedral win-**
dows; and he spoke **of the cheeks and temples of**
the soft crags of the sphagnum. **The hubs on**
birches are regular cones, as if they might be vol-
canoes in outline ; and the small **cranberries** occupy
some little valley a foot **or two over,** between two
mountains of **sphagnum** (that **dense,** cushion-like
moss that grows in swamps). **He says** distant
lightning is like veins **in** the **eye. Of that excel-**
lent nut, the chestnut, " the whole upper slopes **of**
the nuts are covered with the **same hoary wool as**
the points." **A** large, fresh stone-heap, eight **or**
ten inches above water, is **quite sharp,** like Tene-
riffe. These comparisons to him **were** realities, **not**
sports of the pen: to elevate the so-called little
into the great, with **him, was genius. In** that
sense **he** was no humorist. **He sees** a gull's wings,
that seem almost regular semicircles, like the new
moon. Some of the bevelled **roofs of the** houses
on Cape Ann are so nearly flat that they reminded
him of the low brows of monkeys. The enlarged
sail of the boat suggests a new power, like **a Gre-**
cian god. . . . Ajacean. The boat is like **a plough**
drawn by a winged bull. **He** asks, " Are there no
purple reflections **from the** culms of **thought** in my

5*

mind?" thinking of the colors of the poke-stem. In a shower he feels the first drop strike the right slope of his nose, and run down the ravine there, and says, "Such is the origin of rivers," and sees a wave whose whole height, "from the valley between to the top," was fifteen inches. He thus practically illustrates his faith, — how needless to travel for wonders; they lie at your feet; the seeing eye must search intently. The Wayland bird-stuffer shoots a meadow-hen, a Virginia rail, a *stormy petrel* and the *little auk*, in Sudbury meadows.

He wished so to live as to derive his satisfactions and inspirations from the commonest events, every-day phenomena; so that what his senses hourly perceived, his daily walk, the conversation of his neighbors, might inspire him; and he wished to dream of no heaven but that which lay about him. Seeing how impatient, how rampant, how precocious were the osiers in early spring, he utters the prayer, "May I ever be in as good spirits as a willow. They never say die." The charm of the journal must consist in a certain greenness, thorough freshness, and not in maturity. "Here, I cannot afford to be remembering what I said, did, my scurf cast off, — but what I am and aspire to become." Those annoyed by his hardness should remember that "the flowing of the sap under the dull rinds of the trees is a tide which few suspect." The same object is ugly or beautiful according to the angle from which you view it. He went to the rocks by the pond in April to smell the catnep, and always brought some home for the cat, at that season. To truly see his character, you must " see with the unworn sides of your eye." Once he enlarges a little on an offer he did not accept of a passenger. He had many: genial gentlemen of all sizes felt ready to walk or sail with him, and he usually accepted them, sometimes two in one. On this occasion he declines:

" This company is obliged to make a distinction between *dead* freight and passengers : I will take almost any amount of freight for you cheerfully, — any thing, my dear sir, but *yourself*. You are a heavy fellow, but I am well disposed. If you could go without going, then you might go. There 's the captain's state-room, empty to be sure, and you say you could go in the steerage : I know very well that only your baggage would be dropped in the steerage, while you would settle down into that vacant recess. Why, I am *going*, not staying ; I have come on purpose to sail, to paddle away from such as you, and you have waylaid me on the shore. . . . If I remember aright it was only on condition *that you were asked*, that you were to go with a man one mile or twain.

I could better carry a heaped load of meadow mud and sit on the thole-pins."

He believed, " We must not confound man with man. We cannot conceive of a greater difference than that between the life of one man and that of another."

" It is possible for a man wholly to disappear and be merged in his manners." *He thought a man of manners was an insect in a tumbler.* But genius had evanescent boundaries like an altar from which incense rises.

" Our stock in life, our real estate, is that amount of thought which we have had, and which we have thought out. The ground we have thus created is for ever pasturage for our thoughts. I am often reminded that, if I had bestowed on me the wealth of Crœsus, my aims must still be the same and my means essentially the same. The art of life, of a poet's life, is, not having any thing to do, to do something. Improve the suggestion of each object however humble, however slight and transient the provocation ; what else is there to be improved ? You must try a thousand themes before you find the right one, as nature makes a thousand acorns to get one oak. Both for bodily and mental health court the present. Embrace health wherever you find her. None but the kind gods can make me sane. If only they will let their south wind blow on me : I ask to be melted. You can only ask of the metals to be tender to the fire that melts them. To nought else can they be tender. Only he can be trusted with gifts, who can present a face of bronze to expectations."

At times, he asked : " Why does not man sleep all day as well as all night, it seems so very easy. For what is he awake?" " Do lichens or fungi grow on you?" The luxury of wisdom! the luxury of virtue! are there any intemperate in these things ? " Oh such thin skins, such crockery as I have to deal with ! Do they not know that I can laugh?" " Why do the mountains never look so fair as from my native fields?" " Who taught the oven-bird to conceal her nest ? " He states a familiar fact, showing that the notion of a thing can be taken for the thing, literally : " I have convinced myself that I saw smoke issuing from the chimney of a house, which had not been occupied for twenty years, — a small bluish, whitish cloud, instantly dissipated." Like other scribes, he wishes he " *could buy at the shops some kind of India-rubber that would rub out at once all that in my writing which it now costs me so many perusals, so many months, if not years, and so much reluctance to erase.*" His temperament is so moral, his least observation will breed a sermon, or a water-worn fish rear him to Indian heights of philosophy :

"How many springs shall I continue to see the common sucker (*Catostomus Bostoniensis*) floating dead on our river? Will not Nature select her types from a new font? The vignette of the year. This earth which is spread out like a map around me is but the lining of my inmost soul exposed. In me is the sucker that I see. No wholly extraneous object can compel me to recognize it. I am guilty of suckers. . . . The red-bird which I saw on my companion's string on election-days, I thought but the outmost sentinel of the wild immortal camp, of the wild and dazzling infantry of the wilderness. The red-bird which is the last of nature is but the first of God. We condescend to climb the crags of earth."

He believes he is soothed by the sound of the rain, because he is allied to the elements. The sound sinks into his spirit as the water into the earth, reminding him of the season when snow and ice will be no more. He advises you to be not in haste amid your private affairs. Consider the turtle: a whole summer, June, July, and August are not too good, not too much to hatch a turtle in. Another of his questions is: "What kind of understanding was there between the mind that determined that these leaves of the black willow should hang on during the winter, and that of the worm that fastened a few of these leaves to its cocoon in order to disguise it?" As an answer may be found the following: "It was long ago in a full senate of all intellects determined how cocoons had best be suspended, kindred mind with mind that admires and approves decided it so. *The mind of the universe which* **we** *share has been intended on* **each particular** *point.*" Thus persevering,—and, as he says of a dwelling on the Cape, he knocked all round the house at five doors in succession,— so at the great out-doors of nature, where he was accommodated.

> " Chide me **not, laborious band,**
> For the idle **flowers I brought;**
> Every aster in my hand
> **Goes** home loaded with a thought."

His fineness of perceiving, his delicacy **of** touch, has rarely been surpassed with **pen or pencil, a** fineness **as** unpremeditated as successful. **For** him the trout glances like a film from side to side and under the bank. The pitch oozing from pine logs is one of the beautiful accidents that attend **on** man's works, instead of **a** defilement. Darby's oak stands like an athlete, it **is an** agony of strength. Its branches look like stereotyped **gray** lightning on the sky. The lichens on the pine **remind** him of the forest warrior and his shield adhering **to** him.

In spring he notices **pewee days** and April show-

ers. The mountains are the pastures to which he
drives his thoughts, on their 20th of May. So the
storm has its flashing van followed by the long
dropping main body, with at very long intervals an
occasional firing or skirmishing in the rear, or on
the flank. " The lightning like a yellow spring
flower illumines the dark banks of the clouds.
Some æstrum stings the cloud that she darts head-
long against the steeples, and bellows hollowly,
making the earth tremble. It is the familiar note
of another warbler echoing amid the roofs." He
compares the low universal twittering of the chip-
birds, at daybreak in June, to the bursting bead on
the surface of the uncorked day. If he wishes for
a hair for his compass-sight, he must go to the sta-
ble ; but the hair-bird, with her sharp eyes, goes to
the road. He muses over an ancient muskrat
skull (found behind the wall of Adams's shop), and
is amused with the notion of what grists have come
to this mill. Now the upper and nether stones fall
loosely apart, and the brain chamber where the
miller lodged is now empty (passing under the
portcullis of the incisors), and the windows are
gone. The opening of the first asters, he thinks,
makes you fruitfully meditative ; helps condense
your thoughts like the mildews in the afternoon.
He is pretty sure to find a plant which he is shown
from abroad or hears of, or in any way becomes

interested in. The cry of hounds he lists to, as it were a distant natural horn in the clear resonant air. He says that fire is the most tolerable third party. When he puts the hemlock boughs on the blaze, the rich salt crackling of its leaves is like mustard to the ear, — dead trees love the fire. The distant white-pines over the Sanguinetto seem to flake into tiers; the whole tree looks like an open cone. The pond reminds him, looking from the mill-dam, of a weight wound up; and when the miller raised the gate, what a smell of gun-wash or sulphur! "I who never partake of the sacrament made the more of it." The solitude of Truro is as sweet as a flower. He drank at every cooler spring in his walk in a blazing July, and loved to eye the bottom there, with its pebbly Caddis-worm cases, or its white worms, or perchance a luxurious frog cooling himself next his nose. The squirrel withdraws to his eye by his aerial turnpikes. "The roof of a house at a distance, in March, is a mere gray scale, diamond shape against the side of a hill." "If I were to be a frog-hawk for a month, I should soon have known something about the frogs." He thinks most men can keep a horse, or keep up a certain fashionable style of living, but few indeed can keep up great expectations. He improves every opportunity to go into a grist-mill, any excuse to

H

see its cobweb-tapestry, such as putting questions to the miller, while his eye rests delighted in the cobwebs above his head and perchance on his hat.

So he walked and sang his melodies in the pure country, in the seclusion of the field. All forms and aspects of night and day were glad and memorable to him, whose thoughts were as pure and innocent as those of a guileless maiden. Shall they not be studied?

> "I will give my son to eat
> Best of **Pan's immortal** meat,
> Bread to eat, and juice to drink;
> So **the** thoughts that he shall **think**
> Shall not be forms of **stars, but stars,**
> Not pictures pale, but Jove and **Mars.**
> . . . .
> The Indian cheer, the frosty skies,
> Rear purer wits, inventive eyes.
>
> In the **wide thaw** and ooze of **wrong**
> Adhere like **this** foundation strong,
> The insanity of towns to stem
> With simpleness for stratagem."

If it is difficult (to some) to credit, it is no less certain that Thoreau would indulge himself in a rhapsody, — given the right topic, something the writer *cordially* appreciated. In speech or with the pen, the eloquent vein being touched, the spring of discourse flowed rapidly, as on this subject of the Corner-road : —

" Now I yearn for one of those old, meandering,

dry, uninhabited roads which lead away **from towns,** which **lead us** away from temptation, which **con-**duct to the outside of the earth over its uppermost crust; where you may forget in what country you are travelling; where no farmer can complain that you **are** treading down his grass; **no** gentleman who has recently constructed **a seat** in the country that you are trespassing, on which you can go off at half-cock and wave adieu to the village; along **which** you may travel like a pilgrim going **no-**whither; where travellers are not often **to be met,** where my spirit is free, where **the** walls and **flow-**ers are not cared for, where your head is more in heaven than **your** feet **are on** earth; which **have** long reaches, where you can see the approaching traveller half **a** mile off, and **be** prepared for him; not so luxuriant a soil **as** to attract men**; some** stump and root fences, which do not need atten-tion; **where** travellers have no occasion to stop, but pass along and leave you to your thoughts; where **it** makes no odds which way you face, whether you are going or coming, whether it is morning or evening, mid-noon or midnight; where earth is cheap enough by being public; **w**here you can walk and think with least obstruction, there being nothing to measure progress by; where **you can** pace when your breast **is** full, and cherish your moodiness; **where** you are not **in** false relations with men, are not dining or conversing with them ; by which you may go to the uttermost parts of the earth.

" Sometimes it is some particular half-dozen rods which I wish to find myself pacing over, as where certain airs blow, there my life will come to me ; methinks, like a hunter, I lie in wait for it. When I am against this bare promonotory of a huckleberry hill, then forsooth my thoughts will expand. Is it some influence as a vapor which exhales from the ground, or something in the gales which blow there, or in all things there brought together agreeably to my spirit? The walls must not be too high, imprisoning me, but low, with numerous gaps. The trees must not be too numerous nor the hills too near, bounding the view ; nor the soil too rich, attracting the attention to the earth. It must simply be the way and the life,—a way that was never known to be repaired, nor to need repair, within the memory of the oldest inhabitant. I cannot walk habitually in those ways that are likely to be repaired, for sure it was the devil only that wore them ; never by the heel of thinkers (of thought) were they worn. The saunterer wears out no road, even though he travel on it, and therefore should pay no highway (or rather *low-way*) tax ; he *may* be taxed to construct a higher way than that men travel. A way which no geese defile **or hiss along it, but only** sometimes **their** wild brethren fly far **overhead ; which** the kingbird and **the swallow** twitter over, and **the** song-sparrow sings on its rails ; where the **small** red butterfly is at home **on** the yarrow, and no **boy** threatens it with imprisoning hat, — there **I can** walk and stalk and **plod.** Which nobody **but Jonas** Potter travels beside **me ; where** no cow but his is tempted **to** linger for **the herbage by** its side ; where **the** guideboard is **fallen, and now** the **hand points to heaven** significantly, **to a** Sudbury ánd Marlboro' in the skies. That **'s a road I can travel, that** the particular Sudbury **I am bound for, six miles** an hour, **or** two, as you please ; and **few there be** that enter therein. Here I can walk **and recover** the lost child that I am, without any ringing **of a bell.** Where there was nothing ever discovered to detain a traveller, but all went through about their business ; where I never passed " the time of day " with any, — indifferent to me were the arbitrary divisions of time ; **where** Tullus Hostilius might have disappeared, **at** any rate has **never** been seen, — the road **to the** Corner!

" The ninety and nine acres **you go** through to get there, — I would rather see **it** again, though **I** saw it this morning, than Gray's Churchyard. **The** road whence you may hear a stake-driver, or whippoorwill, **a quail, in a** midsummer **day.** Oh, yes!

a quail comes nearest to the Gum-c bird heard
there. Where it would not be sport for a sportsman to go (and the Mayweed looks up in my face
not there). The pale lobelia and the Canada
snap-dragon, a little hardhack and meadow-sweet,
peep over the fence, nothing more serious to ob-
struct the view, and thimbleberries are the food
of thought (before the drought), along by the
walls. A road that passes over the Height-of-
land, between earth and heaven, separating those
streams which flow earthward from those which
flow heavenward.

"It is those who go to Brighton and to market
that wear out all the roads, and they should pay
all the tax. The deliberate pace of a walker never
made a road the worse for travelling on, — on the
promenade deck of the world, an outside passenger ;
where I have freedom in my thought, and in my
soul am free. Excepting the omnipresent butcher
with his calf-cart, followed by a distracted and
anxious cow, — the inattentive stranger baker,
whom no weather detains, that does not bake his
bread in this hemisphere, and therefore it is dry
before it gets here ! Ah ! there is a road where
you might adventure to fly, and make no preparations till the time comes ; where your wings will
sprout if anywhere, where your feet are not confined to earth. An airy head makes light walking,

when I am not confined and baulked by the sight of distant farm-houses, which I have not gone past. I must be fancy **free; I must** feel that, **wet or dry,** high **or low, it is the genuine surface of the** planet, and not a little chip-dirt **or a** compost heap, **or** made land, or redeemed. **A thinker's** weight is in his thought, not in his tread ; when **he** thinks freely, his body weighs nothing. **He cannot** tread down your grass, farmers !"

"Thus far to day your **favors** reach,
O fair appeasing presences !
Ye taught my lips a single speech
And a thousand silences."

CHAPTER VIII.

WALKS AND TALKS.

"Absents within the line conspire." — VAUGHAN.

" What I have reaped in my journey is, as it were, a small contentment in a never-contenting subject; a bitter-pleasant taste of a sweet-seasoned sour. All in all, what I found was more than ordinary rejoicing, in an extraordinary sorrow **of** delights." — LITHGOW.

" **What is it** to me that **I** can write these Table-Talks ? Others have **more** property in them than I have: *they* may reap the benefit, *I* have had only the pain. Nor should I know that I had ever thought at all, **but** that I am reminded of it by the strangeness of my appearance and my unfitness for any thing else." — HAZLITT.

> " Not mine the boast of countless herds,
>   Nor purple tapestries, nor treasures gold,
>   But mine the peaceful spirit,
>   And the dear muse, and pleasant wine
>   Stored in Bœotian urns." — BACCHYLIDES.

TO furnish a more familiar idea of Thoreau's walks and talks with his friends and their locality, some reports of them are furnished for convenience in the interlocutory form.

SECOND DIVISION BROOK.

And so you are ready for a walk ?

" Hence sand and dust are shak'd for witnesses."

When was I ever not ? Where shall we go ? To Conantum or White Pond, or is the Second Division our business for this afternoon ?

As you **will.** Under your piloting I feel **par-**
tially safe ; but not too far, not **too much.** Brevity
is the sole **of** walking.

And yet all true walking, all virtuous walking,
is a *travail.* The season is proper to the Brook. **I
am in the** mood to greet the Painted Tortoise ; nor
must **I** fail to examine the buds of the marsh marigold, now, **I** think, somewhat swollen. But few
birds have come in, though Minot says he has heard
a bluebird.

Did he ask his **old** question, — Seen **a robin?**
Minot is native and to the **manor born ;** was never
away from home but once, when he was drafted
as a soldier **in** the last war, and when he went **to**
Dorchester Heights, **and** has never ridden **on a**
rail. What do you make **of** him?

He makes enough of himself. The railroad has
proved too great a temptation for most of our farmers : the young men have a foreign air their fathers
never had. We shall not boast of *Mors Ipse,*
Grass and Oats, or Oats and Grass, and old Verjuice,
in the next generation. These rudimental Saxons
have the air of pine-trees and apple-trees, and might
be their sons got between them, — conscientious
laborers, with a science born within them, from out
the sap-vessels of their savage sires. This savagery
is native with man, and polished **New England
cannot** do without **it.** That makes **the** charm of

6

grouse-shooting **and deer-stalking to** those **Lord** Breadalbanes, walking **out of their doors** one hundred **miles to the sea, on** their own **property ; or** Dukes of Sutherland getting off at last their town-coat, donning **their hunters' gear,** exasperated by saloons and dress-coats.

Let me rest a fraction **on the bridge.**

I am **your well-wisher** in that. **The** manners of water are beautiful. **" As for** beauty, I need not look beyond **my oar's** length **for my** fill of it." As I heard my companion **say** this, my eye rested on the charming play **of** light on the water which he was slowly striking with his paddle. I fancied that I had never seen such color, **such** transparency, such eddies. It was the hue **of** Rhine wines, it **was** gold and green, and chestnut and hazel, in bewildering succession and relief, without cloud or **confusion.** A little canoe, with three men or boys **in it,** put out from a creek and paddled down stream, and afar and near we paid homage to the " Blessed Water," inviolable, magical, whose na-**ture is** beauty, which instantly began to play its sweet games, all circles and dimples, and lively gleaming motions, always Ganges, **the** *Sacred River,* and which cannot be desecrated or made to forget itself ; " For marble sweats and rocks have **tears."**

Hark ! Was that the **bluebird's** warble ?

I could not hear it, as now cometh the seventh abomination, the train.

And yet it looks like a new phenomenon, though it has appeared at the same hour each day for these ten years.

Already the South Acton passengers squeeze their bundles, and the member of the legislature hastens to drain the last drop of vulgar gossip from the Ginger-beer paper before he leaves the cars to fodder and milk his **kine.** I trust that **in heaven** will be no cows. **They** are created, apparently, **to give** the farmer a **sport** between planting **and harvest,** the joy of haying, dust, grime, and **tan, diluted** by sun strokes.

The cause of cows is, that they make good **walking** where they feed. **In the paths of the thicket** the best engineer is the cow.

We cross where the high bank will give us a view over the river at Clam-shell, and where I may possibly get an arrow-head from this Concord Kitchen-mödding.

A singular proclivity, thou worshipper of Indians! for arrow-heads; and I presume, like certain other worships, uncurable!

Apply thy Procrustes-bed to my action, and **permit** me **to** continue my search. They **speak of** Connecticuts and Hudsons : our slow little stream, **in** its spring overflow, draws **on the** surtout of greater rivers; a river, — fair, solitary path, — the one piece of real estate belonging to the walker, unfenced, undeeded, sacred to musquash and pickerel, and George Melvin, gunner, more by the token he was drowned in it.

Are not those gulls, gleaming like spots of intense white light, far away on the dark bosom of the meadows?

Yes, indeed! they come from the sea each spring overflow, and go a-fishing like Goodwin. See! I have got a quartz arrow-head, — and perfect. This bank is made of the clams baked by the Indians.   Let us look a moment at the minnows as we cross the brook; I can see their shadows on the yellow sand much clearer than themselves, and can thus count the number of their fins.   I wonder if the Doctor ever saw a minnow.   In his report on reptiles, he says he has never seen but one *Hylodes Pickeringii,* in a dried state.   It is well also to report upon what you have not seen.   He never troubled *himself* with looking about in the country.   The poet more than the *savant* marries man to nature.   I wish we had some fuller word to express this fine picture we see from Clam-shell bank: *kinde* was the old English word, but we do not designate the power that works for beauty alone, whilst man works only for use.

See, O man of nature! yon groups of weather-

stained houses we now o'ertop. There live some
Christians, put away on life's plate like **so many
rinds** of cheese; there descend, **like dew on flowers,** the tranquillizing years, into their prickly life-
petals. **Save** the **rats** scrabbling along **the old**
plastering, the sawing of pluvial pea-hens, **or the**
low of the recuperating cow, what repose! **And**
in the midst, such felons of **destiny,—** .

" O mother Ida, hearken ere I die."

What avails **against hot-bread,** cream-of-tartar,
and Oriental-company tea, with an afternoon nap?
I have met **Œnones whom I could have spared**
better than **these horn-pouts of gossip.**

Is there **a fixed sum of hyson allotted to each**
sibyl?

> **"Only** a learned and a manly soul
> **I** purposed her, that should with even powers
> The rock, the spindle, and the shears control
> **Of** Destiny, and spin her own full hours."

The bluebird, **sir!** the **first** bluebird! there he
sits and warbles. **Dear** bird **of** spring, first speech
of the original beauty, first note in the annual concert of love, why soundest thy soft and plaintive
warble on my ear, like the warning **of a** mournful
past?

As the poet sings, if not of the new birds:—

> **" We** saw thee in thy balmy nest,
> Bright dawn of our eternal day;

> We saw thine eyes **break** from their east,
> **And** chase the trembling shades away :
> **We** saw thee, and we blest the sight,
> **We** saw thee by thine own sweet light.
>
> She sings thy tears asleep, and dips
> Her kisses in thy weeping **eye** ;
> She spreads the red leaves of thy lips,
> That in their buds yet blushing lie :
> She 'gainst those mother diamonds tries
> **The points of her** young eagle's eyes."

Excuse soliloquy.

Go on, go on : I can **hear** the bluebird just the same.

I am glad **we are at the sand-bank. Radiantly** here the brook parts **across the shallows its ever-** rippling tresses of **golden light. It steals away** my battered senses **as I gaze therein ; and, if I re-** member me, 'tis in some murmuring line : —

> " Thus swam away my thoughts **on thee,**
> And in thy joyful ecstasy
> **Flowed** with thy **waters** to thy **sea.**"

And the quantity of thy rhyme, **I** judge. **Let** us to the ancient woods : I say let us value the woods. They are full of solicitations. My wood-lot has no price, full of mysterious values. What forms, **what colors,** what powers, **null to** our igno-rance, but opening fast enough to our wit. **I** love **this** smell that comes from the brush of the pitch-pine, **as** the spring sun bakes its first batch of violets here. **And here is the brook itself, the petted** darling of the meadows, wild minstrel **of an ancient** song, poured through **the** vales **for ever.** The sands of Pactolus were not **more golden than** these of thine, and black the eddying pools, where the old experienced trout sleeps on his **oars. As** hurries the water to the **sea, so** seeks **the soul its** universe. **And this is the** May-flower, sweet **as** Cytherea's breath ; **and in yonder lowlands grows** the climbing fern. Simple **flowers ! Yet was not** Solomon in **all his** glory arrayed like **one of these.**

> " To clothe the fiery thought
> In simple word succeeds,
> For still the craft of genius is
> **To mask a** king in weeds."

OLD SUDBURY **INN.**

There, you have it ! Howe's tavern, on **the old** Worcester turnpike. I was never **before here,** *au revoir !*

A new place **is** good property, **if we** have the prospect of owning **it, hey,** Betty Martin ! 'Tis one of the ancient taverns of **the** noble old Commonwealth: observe the date, 1719, painted **on the** sign. From that **to** this the same **family have had** it in their keeping, and **many a** glass has **been** drunk and paid for **at the** bar, whose defence you observe moves curiously up and down like a portcullis, and the room is ceiled all round, instead of plastered. There is a seigniorial property attached to it, some hundred acres; and see the old buttresses of time-channelled oak along the road, in front, that must have been set at the same time with the inn. A spacious brook canters behind the house; yonder is a noble forest; and there above us, Nobscot, our nearest mountain. Indeed, the tract across to Boone's Pond and Sudbury is all a piece of wild wood. Come, away for Nobscot! taking the sandy path behind the barn. Do you see that strange, embowered roof, peeping out of its great vase of apple-blossoms? for this, O man of many cares! is the 23d of May, and just as much Blossom-day as ever was.

I see the peeping chimney, — romance itself. May I hope never to know the name of the remarkable genius who dwells therein.

Very proper, no doubt, — Tubs or Scrubs.

Believe it not, enemy to Blossom-day romance. My soul whispers of a fair, peculiar region behind those embracing bouquets.

Where one should surely find an anxious cook and a critical family.

Hush! hush! traduce not the venerable groves. Here, or in some such devoted solitude, should dwell the Muse and compose a treatise on the worship of Dryads.

Dry as powder-post. Have you seen the scarlet tanager?

No.

The Puseyite unmistakable among our birds, — true, high-church scarlet. Hear! the pewee's soft, lisping, pee-a-wee! **Now,** as we rise and leave the splendid chestnut forest, the **view** opens. Nobscot **is a** true, low mountain, and these small creatures look off the best. I love the broad, healthy, new-springing pastures, ornamented with apple-tree pyramids, **the** pastoral architecture **of the cow;** the waving saxifrage and delicate **houstonia, that** . spring-beauty; **and the free,** untrammelled **air of** the mountains, — it never **swept the dusty plain.** There's our **Cliff** and meeting-house **in Concord,** and Barrett's hill, and Anursnac; **next comes** high Lincoln with his gleaming spires, **and** modest **W**ayland low in the grass, the Great Sudbury Meadows (sap-green), and Framingham and **Na-**tick. How many dark belts of pines stalk across the bosky landscape, like the traditions of the old Sagamores, **who** fished in yonder Long Pond that now colors its town with reddish water **a** country boy *might* bathe in if hard pushed!

I faintly hear the sound of the church-going bell, I suppose, of Framingham.

(As the country wife beats her brass pan **to** collect her bees.) In the landscape is found the magic of color. The world is all opal, and these ethereal tints the mountains wear have the finest effects of music on us. Mountains are great poets, and one glance at this fine New Hampshire range of Watatic, Monadnock, Peterboro', and Uncannunnuk, undoes a deal of prose and reinstates poor, wronged men in their rights, life and society begin to be illuminated and transparent, and we generalize boldly and well. Space is felt as a privilege. There is some pinch and narrowness to the best. Here we laugh and leap to see the world, and what amplitudes it has of meadow, stream, upland, forest, and sea, which yet are but lanes and crevices to the great space in which the world swims like a cockboat on the ocean. There below are those farms, but the life of farmers is unpoetic. The life of labor does not make men, but drudges. 'Tis pleasant, as the habits of all poets may testify, to think of great proprietors, to reckon this grove we walk in a park of the noble; but a continent cut up into ten-acre lots is not attractive. The farmer is an enchanted laborer, who, after toiling his brains out, sacrificing thought, religion, love, hope, courage, to toil, turns out a bankrupt, as well as the shopman.

I must meditate an ode to be called, " Adieu, my Johnny-cake."

Ay, ay: hasty-pudding for the masculine eye,

chicken and jellies for girls. Yonder on that hill
is Marlboro', a town (in autumn at least, when **I**
visited it) that wears **a** rich appearance **of** rustic
plenty and comfort, — ample farms, **good** houses,
profuse yellow apple-heaps, pumpkin mountains in
every enclosure, orchards left ungathered ; and in
the Grecian piazzas of the houses, squashes ripening between the columns. At Cutting's were oats
for **the** horse, but no dinner for men, so **we went
to a** chestnut **grove and** an old **orchard for our
fare.**

Now for an inscription upon

OLD SUDBURY INN.

Who set the oaks
Along the road ?
Was it not Nature's hand,
Old Sudbury Inn ? for I have stood
And wondered at the sight,
The oaks my delight.

And the elms,
So boldly branching to the sky,
And the interminable forests,
Old Sudbury Inn ! that wash thee, nigh
On every side,
With a green and rustling tide.

Such oaks ! such elms !
And the contenting woods,

And Nobscot good.
Old Sudbury Inn! creature of moods,
That could I find
Well suited to the custom of my mind.

Most homely seat,
Where Nature eats her frugal meals
And studies to outwit,
Old Sudbury Inn! what thy inside reveals,
Long mayst thou be
More than a match for her and me.

And so it comes every year, this lovely Blossom-day: —

"The cup of life is not so shallow
   That we have drained the best,
That all the wines at once we swallow,
   And lees make all the rest.

Maids of as soft a bloom shall marry,
   As Hymen yet hath blessed,
And fairer forms are in the quarry
   Than Angelo released."

And to-day the air is spotted with the encouraging rigmarole of the bobolink, — that buttery, vivacious, fun-may-take-me cornucopia of song. Once to hear his larripee, larripee, buttery, scattery, wittery, pittery; some yellow, some black feathers, a squeeze of air, and this *summer* warming song! The bobolink never knew cold, and never could, — the musician of blossoms. Hark! the veery's liquid strain, with trilling cadence; his holy brother, the wood-thrush, pitches his flute-notes in the pine alleys, where at twilight is heard the strange prophecy of the whippoorwill. The oven-bird beats his brass *witcher-twitcher* in the heated shades of noon, mixed with the feathery roll-call of the partridge. As we take our nooning, I will recall some lines on this famous bird.

Song, — THE ·PARTRIDGE.

Shot of the wood, from thy ambush low,
  Bolt off the dry leaves flying,
With a whirring spring like an Indian's bow,
  Thou speed'st when the year is dying;
And thy neat gray form darts whirling past,
So silent all, as thou fliest fast,
Snapping a leaf from the copses red,
Our native bird on the woodlands bred.

I have trembled a thousand times,
  As thy bolt through the thicket was rending,
Wondering at thee in the autumn chimes,
  When thy brother's soft wings were bending
Swift to the groves of the spicy south,
Where the orange melts in the zephyr's mouth,
And the azure sunshine humors the air,
And Winter ne'er sleeps in his pallid chair.

And thy whirring wings I hear,
  When the colored ice is warming

> The twigs of the forest sere,
>   While the northern wind a-storming
> Draws cold as death round the Irish hut
> That lifts its blue smoke in the railroad cut,
> And the hardy chopper sits dreaming at home,
> And thou and I are alone in the storm.
>
> Brave bird of my woodland haunt,
>   Good child of the autumn dreary,
> Drum of my city and bass of my chaunt,
>   With thy rushing music so cheery,
> Desert not my bowers for the southern flowers,
> Nor my pale northern woods for her ruby hours;
> Let us bide the rude blast and the ringing hail,
> Till the violets peep on the Indian's trail.

Above our heads the night-hawk rips; and, soaring over the tallest pine, the fierce hen-harrier screams and hisses; cow, cow, cow, sounds the timorous cuckoo: thus our cheerful and pleasant birds do sing along else silent paths, strewn with the bright and bluest violets, with houstonias, anemones, and cinque-foils. Academies of Music and Schools of Design, truly! and to-day on all the young oaks shall be seen their bright crimson leaves, each in itself as good as a rich and delicate flower; and the sky bends o'er us with its friendly face like Jerusalem delivered.

And Mrs. Jones and Miss Brown —

No, indeed: I declare it boldly let us leave out

man in such days; his history may be written at nearly any future period, **in dull weather.**

Yet hath the same toiling **knave in yonder field** a kind **of** grim advantage.

The grime I perceive, and hear the **toads sing.**

Yet the poet says, —

> "Not in their houses stand **the stars,**
> But o'er the pinnacles **of thine."**

And also listen to *my* poet : —

> "Go thou to thy learned task,
> I stay with the flowers of Spring;
> Do thou **of** the Ages ask,
> What to me the Hours will bring."

Oh, the soft, **mellow green of the swamp-sides!** Oh, the sweet, **tender green of the** pastures! **Do** you observe how like the colors of currant-jelly are **the** maple-keys where the sun shines through them? **I** suppose to please you **I** *ought* **to be** *unhappy*, but the contrast is too strong.

See the *Rana palustris* bellying the world in the warm pool, and making up his froggy mind to accept the season **for** lack of **a** brighter ; and will not a gossipping dialogue between two comfortable brown thrashers cure the heartache **of** half the world ? Hear the charming song-sparrow, the Prima-donna of the wall side ; and the meadow-lark's **sweet,** timid, yet gushing lay hymns the praise **of the** Divine Beauty.

And were you ever in love?

Was that the squeak of a night-hawk?

Yes, flung beyond the thin wall of nature, whereon thy fowls and beasts are spasmodically plastered, and swamped so perfectly in one of thy own race as to forget this illusory showman's wax figures.

A stake-driver! pump-a-gaw, pump-a-gaw, like an old wooden pump. They call the bittern *butter-bump* in some countries. Every thing is found in nature, even the stuff of which thou discoursest thus learnedly.

I would it were not, O Epaminondas Holly!

What, sir! and have you had a touch of the chicken-pox?

I shall not let the cat out of the bag.

Go in peace! I must do my best and catch that green-throated gentleman. To take frogs handsome requires a quick eye and a fine touch, like high art. They dive under the sludge; their colors are of the water and the grass, chameleon-like. How ridiculous is yonder colt, the color of sugar gingerbread, set upon four long legs and swishing a bald tail! and how he laughs at us men folks nibbling our crackers and herring! May our wit be as dry as our *matinée*. Now the water mouse-ear, typha, or reed-mace; *Drosera rotundi-folia*, Solomon's seal, violets of all sorts, bulbous *arethrum*, yellow lily, **dwarf** cornel, lousewort, yellow Star of Bethlehem, *Polygala paucifolia*, *Arum triphyllum*, **cohosh** —

Hush! hush! **what names!** Hadst thou spoken **to me of Violet,** that child of beauty !

> " Where its long rings unwinds the **fern,**
> The violet, nestling low,
> **Casts back** the white lid of its urn,
> **Its purple streaks to show.**
>
> Beautiful **blossom!** first to rise
> And smile beneath Spring's wakening **skies** ;
> The courier **of** the band
> Of coming flowers, — what feelings sweet
> Flow, as the silvery germ we meet
> Upon its needle-wand ! "

CONANTUM.

As good as the domains of royalty, and **is the** possession of an ancient New England farmer.

From this bridge I see only a simple field, with its few **old** apple-trees. It rises neatly to the west.

When we traverse the whole of the long seigniorage, I think you will agree that this is a good place for a **better** than Montaigne-chateau (the stake-driver pump-a-gawing again). From **this** corner to Fairhaven bay the domain extends, **with** not **an** ounce of cultivated soil. First, a tract of woodland, with its pleasant wood-paths, its **deep**

and mossy swamp, where owls and **foxes have holes,**
and **the long** lichens **sway their** soft, **green tresses**
from the rotting spruce. Behind **yon old barn**
stands the original **farmhouse ;** the mouldering
shell has ripened birth and death, marriage feasts
and funeral tables, **where now the** careless flies
only buzz and **the century-old** crow alights on **the**
broad roof that almost touches the ground. **The**
windows are gone, the door half ruined, the chimney down, the **roof falling in, —sans** eyes, sans
ears, sans life, sans **every thing. Not even a con-**
templative cat shakes his irresponsive sides on **this**
solitude, and the solid grass grows **up to the** edges
of the enormous door-stone. Our ancestors took a
pride **in** acquiring **the** largest **and flattest** rock
possible **to lay before the** hospitable sill. **We do**
get unscrupulously rid of the ancestral mansion,
and the pot of beans of the careful grandson bakes
upon the architectural desolation of " my grand-
papa." Ascend this height, and you will see (part
second) the lovely valley of **the** Concord **at** your
feet, —

> " See where the winding vale its lavish stores
>   Irriguous spreads."

There is the Musketaquid, the grass-ground river.

A goodly view ! and noble walking !

Let us continue **on a few steps more** till we
reach the little meadow, a natural arboretum, where

grows **the black ash, the bass, and the cohosh,** cornels, viburnums, sassafras, and **arethusas :** —

> " **Each spot** where tulips prank their **state**
> **Has** drunk the life-blood of the great;
> The violets yon field which stain
> Are moles of cheeks which time hath **slain.**"

How the earliest kiss of June heaps **the** trees with leaves, and makes land and orchard, hillside **and** garden, verdantly attractive ! Man feels the blood of thousands in his **body, and** his heart pumps the sap of **all** this forest of vegetation through his proper arteries. Here is **his** work, and here he is **a** most willing workman. He **displaces** birch and chestnut, larch and alder, and will set out oak and beech to cover **the land** with leafy colonnades. Then it seems what **a** fugitive summer-flower, papilionaceous, is he, whisking about **amid these** longevities. Gladly he could spread himself abroad among them, love the tall trees as if he were their father, borrow by his love the manner of his trees, **and** with nature's patience watch the giants, from the youth to the age of the golden fruit or gnarled timber, nor think it long. This great domain, all but this one meadow, is under the holding of one old prudent husbandman ; and here is an old cellar-hole, where in front yet grows the vivacious lilac in profuse flower, — a plant to set. **It** has out-lived man and dog, hen and pig, house and wife, —

" all, all are gone," except the " old familiar face "
of the delightsome lilac. And now we stand on
the verge of broad Fairhaven, and below us falls
the scaly frost-abraded precipice to the pitch-pines
and walnuts that stand resigned to their lower
avocations. There is about us here that breath of
wildness, in whose patronage the good Indians
dwelt; there is around us in these herbaceous odors,
in these lustral skies, all that earthly life hath ever
known of beauty or of joy. Thus sings the lark
as he springs from his nest in the grassy meadow;
thus in the barberry hedge, along the gray and pre-
carious wall, the melodious song-sparrow chants in
his brownish summer-suit and that *brevet* of honor
on his breast, the black rosette, constituting him
" Conantum's Malibran." It is Time's holiday, the
festival of June, the leafy June, the flower-sped
June, the bird-singing June,

> " And sweeter than the lids of Juno's eyes."

Let us get a good look from these cliffs at Baker
Farm that lies on that opposite shore. There is
Clematis Brook, Blue Heron Pond, and Mount
Misery.

WHITE POND.

Yesterday was Spring: to-day beginneth the
second lesson, what doth Summer typify?

Hot ovens, a baking-pan, **the taking our turn at** the spit. Grasshoppers creak over dry fields, and devil's-needles whizz across your hat as if they were scorched. Black snakes conclude it is pretty **com-**fortable, considering January. **Oh!** the heat **is** like solid beds **of feathers.**

I think **you** said we were going to White Pond?

A favorable **July** afternoon's plunge; the river flashes in **the** sun like a candle. This little forget-me-not of ours **is as** pure **a blue as** the German's. Ants, bees, millers, **June flies,** horse flies, open shop; woodchucks set **up at** the mouths of their holes and our learned advocate, the *Mephitis chinga,* probes the wood-roads for **beetles;** robins, bull-frogs, bobolinks, Maryland yellow-throats, and oven-birds perform operas all **day** long; the **brave** *senecio* spots the sides of ditches with its dusky gold. How sweet its root smells!

This is **a** right pleasant stroll along **the** Assa-bet?

First-class! The caterpillars make minced-meat of the wild cherries. Nature does **so** love to pet worms, — an odd taste. The great iris is now perfect, and the maple-leaved viburnum, — two flower-belles; the turtles dream at their ease, with but their noses above water among the floating-heart and *potamogetons,* — a good investment in a blaze; verdure, verdure, — meadows, copses, foregrounds and distances.   Showers raise up their heads in the west to catch the leafy prospect.

Is it not against the dignity of man that a little light and heat can so despoil him ?

See that nest of breams, the parents swimming over it, — some fun now in being tickled by a cool stream.   And there lives a lordly baron, a great manorial seignior, with a private road to his castle of Belvoir, as good a king as can be found in Christendom.   We had best stop at Duganne's spring and get a drink: it is as cold as charity. The swallows dart away over the river and Nut-meadow Brook, but a few feet above the surface, taking insects ; the turtles have writ their slow history on this Duganne sand-bank.   There stretches the old Marlboro' road, and now, gleaming beneath the trees, you may see the water of White Pond.

'Tis not as large as Walden: the water looks of the like purity.   •

Yes, 'tis a pretty little Indian basin, lovely as Walden once was, and no pen could ever at all describe its beauties.   We can almost see the sachem in his canoe in the shadowy cove.   How wonderful, as we make the circuit of the shore, are the reflections ; but once we saw them in au-tumn, and then the marvellous effect of the col-ored woods held us almost to the going down of the sun.   The water, slightly rippled, took their proper character from the pines, birches, and few oaks which composed the grove, and the submarine wood seemed made of Lombardy poplar, with such delicious green, stained by gleams of mahogany from the oaks, and streaks of white from the birches, every moment more excellent : it was the world through a prism. Is all the beauty to perish? Shall no one remake this sun and wind, the sky-blue river, the river-blue sky, the waving meadow, the iron-gray house, just the color of the granite rock below, the paths of the thicket, the wide, straggling, wild orchard, in which Nature has deposited every possible flavor in the apples of different trees, — *whole zones and climates she has concentrated into apples?* We think of the old benefactors who have conquered these fields; of the old man, who is just dying in these days, who has absorbed such volumes of sunshine, like a huge melon or pumpkin in the sun, who has owned in every part of Concord a wood-lot, until he could not find the boundaries of them, and never saw their interiors. But, we say, where is he who is to save the present moment, and cause that this beauty be not lost? Shakespeare saw no better heaven or earth, but had the power and need to sing, and seized the dull, ugly England (ugly to this), and made it amiable and enviable to all reading men ; and now we are forced into likening

this to that, whilst if one of us had the chanting
constitution that land would no more be heard of.
But let us have space enough, let us have wild
grapes and rock-maple with tubs of sugar; let us
have huge, straggling orchards; let us have the
Ebba Hubbard pear, hemlock, savin, spruce, walnut
and oak, cider-mills with tons of pummace, peat,
cows, horses, Paddies, carts and sleds. But, with
all this, not the usurpation of the past, the great
hoaxes of the Homers and Shakespeares hindering
the books and the men of to-day. What say you
of Festus? You people who have been peda-
gogues scarcely tolerate the good things in the
moderns. I can repeat you a few classic lines of
that poem as good as those of your old dramatists:

> " How can the beauty of material things
>   So win the heart and work upon the mind,
>   Unless like natured with them?
>
>   .   .   .   .
>
>   When the soul sweeps the future like a glass,
>   And coming things, full freighted with our fates,
>   Jut out, dark, on the offing of the mind.
>   .   .   .   .
>
>   The shadow hourly lengthens o'er my brain,
>   And peoples all its pictures with thyself.
>   .   .   .   .
>
>   To the high air sunshine and cloud are one.
>   .   .   .   .
>
>   And lasses with sly eyes,
>   And the smile settling in their sun-flecked cheeks,
>   Like noon upon the mellow apricot.
>   .   .   .   .

> **The wave is never weary of the wind.**
>
> . . . .
>
> For marble **is** a shadow weighed with **mind.**
>
> . . . .
>
> The last high, upward slant of sun upon the trees,
> **Like a** dead soldier's sword upon **his pall.**
>
> . . . .
>
> **Be** every man a people in his mind."

And that is a pretty little poem of Swedenborg's, written in prose : " The ship is in the harbor; the sails **are** swelling; the east wind blows; let us weigh anchor, and put forth to sea."

Oh, certainly! Oaks and horse-chestnuts are quite obsolete, and the Horticultural Society are about to recommend **the** introduction of the cabbage as a shade-tree ; **so much** more comprehensible **and** convenient, all grown **from the seed** upward to **its** extreme generous **crumple, within** thirty days, — past contradiction the **ornament of** the modern world, **and** then good **to eat,** — choice good, as acorns and horse-chestnuts **are not.** We will have **shade** trees for **breakfast. Then** the effrontery of one man's exhibiting **more wit or** merit than another! **Man** of **genius,** said **you?** man of virtue! I tell **you both are malformations, dropsies** of the brain or the **liver,** and must **be strictly punished** in my new commonwealth. **Nothing that is** not extempore shall **now be tolerated ; pyramids** and cities shall give place **to tents ; the man, soul,** sack, and skeleton, which many years or ages have built up, shall go for nothing ; his dinner, the rice and mutton he ate two hours ago, now fast flowing into chyle, is all we consider. And the problem how to detach new dinner from old man, what we respect from what we repudiate, is the problem for the academies.

"Oh, knit me, that am crumbled dust!"

And what saith Adsched of the melon, for that criticism needs a sop to Cerberus ?

> " Color, taste, and smell, — smaragdus, honey, and musk ;
> Amber for the tongue, for the eye a picture rare ;
> If you cut the fruit in slices, every slice a crescent fair ;
> If you have it whole, the full harvest moon is there."

And which of us would not choose to be one of these insects, — rose-bugs of splendid fate, living on grape-flowers, apple-trees, and roses, and dying of an apoplexy of sweet sensations in the golden middle days of July ! Hail, vegetable gods ! I could not find it in my heart to chide the man who should ruin himself to buy a patch of well-timbered oak-land; I admire the taste which makes the avenue to a house (were the house never so small) through a wood, as this disposes the mind of the host and guest to the deference due. We want deference ; and when we come to realize that thing mechanically, we want acres. Scatter this hot and crowded population at respectful distances each from each, over the vacant world. The doctor and his friends fancied it was the cattle made all this wide space necessary; and that if there were no cows to pasture, less land would suffice. But a cow does not require so much land as my eyes require betwixt me and my neighbor. The poet asks : — .

> " Where is Skymir, giant Skymir?
>   Come, transplant the woods for me !
>   Scoop up yonder aged ash,
>   Centennial fir, old boundary pine,
>   Beech by Indian warriors blazed,
>   Maples tapped by Indian girls,
>   Oaks that grew in the Dark Ages ;
>   Heedful bring them, set them straight
>   In sifted soil before my porch,
>   Now turn the river on their roots,
>   That no leaf wilt, or leading shoot
>   Drop his tall-erected plume."

Now just hop over with your eyes to yonder garden, which realizes Goldsmith's description, " The rusty beds, unconscious of a poke," — or is it Cowper ; the rusty nail over the latch of the gate ; the peach-trees are rusty, the arbors rusty, and I think the proprietor, if there be one, is buried under that heap of old iron. But look across the fence into Captain Hardy's land : there's a musician for you, who knows how to make men dance for him in all weathers, — all sorts of men, Paddies, felons, farmers, carpenters, painters, — yes ! and trees and grapes, and ice and stone, hot days, cold

days. Beat that true Orpheus lyre, if you can.
He knows how to make men sow, dig, mow, and lay
stone-wall, and make trees bear fruit God never
gave them ; and foreign grapes yield the juices of
France and Spain, on his south side. He saves
every drop of sap, as if it were his blood. His
trees are full of brandy. See his cows, his horses,
his swine. And he, the piper that plays the jig
which they all must dance, biped and quadruped
and centipede, is the plainest, stupidest harlequin
in a coat of no colors. His are the woods, the
waters, hills, and meadows. With one blast of his
pipe, he danced a thousand tons of gravel from yonder blowing sand-heap to the bog-meadow, where
the English grass is waving over thirty acres ; with
another, he winded away sixty head of cattle in
the spring, to the pastures of Peterboro', in the
hills.

And the other's ruins ask : —

> " Why lies this hair despised now,
>   Which once thy care and art did show ?
>   Who then did dress the much-loved toy,
>   In spires, globes, angry curls and coy,
>   Which with skill'd negligence seemed shed
>   About thy curious, wild young head ?
>   Why is this rich, this pistic nard
>   Spilt, and the box quite broke and marred ? "

CHAPTER IX.

WALKS AND TALKS CONTINUED.

"Felix ille animi, divisque simillimus ipsis,
  Quem non mordaci resplendens gloria fuco
  Solicitat, non fastosi mala gaudia luxus,
  Sed tacitos sinit ire dies, et paupere cultu
  Exigit innocuæ silentia vitæ " — POLITIAN.

  "If over this world of ours
    His wings my phœnix spread,
    How gracious o'er land and sea
    The soul-refreshing shade!

  "Either world inhabits he,
    Sees oft below him planets roll;
    His body is all of air compact,
    Of Allah's love his soul.

  "Courage, Hafiz, though not thine
    Gold wedges and silver ore,
    More worth to thee thy gift of song,
    And thy clear insight more." — HAFIZ.

"The wretched pedlear more noise he maketh to cry his soap than a rich merchant all his dear worth wares." — ANCREN RIWLE.

FLINT'S POND.

SUPPOSE we go to Flint's.

Agreed.

That country with **its** high **summits in Lincoln** is good for breezy days. I love the mountain view from the Three Friends' Hill beyond the pond, looking **over** Concord. **It** is worth the while to see the mountains in our horizon once a day. They are the natural temples, the elevated brows of the earth, looking at which the thoughts of the beholder are naturally elevated and sublime, — etherealized. I go to Flint's Pond, also, to see a rippling lake and a reedy island in its midst, Reed Island. A man should feed his senses with the best the land affords. These changes in the weather, — how much they surprise us who keep no journal! but look back for a year, and you will most commonly find a similar change at the same time, like the dry capsules of the violets along the wood-road. Temperatures, climates, and even clouds, may be counted, like flowers, insects, animals, and reptiles, among the Constants, — inevitable reappearances ; and things yet further typify each other, like the breeze rushing over the waterfall.

Nay, do not pierce me with your regularity, though you might say, like Peter to the sentimental lady, " Madam, my pigs never squeal."

Not so : learn to see its philosophy in each thing. It is a significant fact, that though no man is quite well or healthy, yet every one believes, practically, that health is the rule, and disease the exception ; and each invalid is wont to think himself in a minority, and to postpone somewhat of endeavor to another state of existence. But it may be some encouragement **to men to** know that in **this re-**spect they stand on **the** same platform, that **disease** is in fact the rule of **our** terrestrial life, **and the** prophecy of a *celestial* life. **Where is** the coward **who** despairs because **he is sick?** Seen in this light, our life with all its diseases will look healthy; and, in one sense, **the more healthy as** it **is the** more diseased.

Upon your principle **" I am thus** wet because I am thus **dry."**

Disease is not **an** accident of **the individual, nor** even of the generation, but of life itself. **In some** form, and to some **degree or** other, **it is one of the** permanent conditions of life. **It** is a **cheering fact,** nevertheless, that men affirm health unanimously, and esteem themselves miserable failures. Here was no blunder. They gave us life on exactly **these** conditions, and methinks we shall live it with more heart when we clearly perceive that these are the terms on which we **have it.** Life is a warfare, **a** struggle, **and the** diseases of the body answer **to** the troubles **and** defects **of the** spirit. Man begins by quarrelling with the animal in him, and the result is immediate disease. In proportion as the spirit is more ambitious and persevering, the more obstacles it will meet with. It is as a seer that man asserts his disease to be exceptional.

Your philosophers and their tax of explanations remind me of the familiar Snail :—

> " Wise emblem of our politic world,
>   Sage snail, within thine own self curled ;
>   Instruct me swiftly to make haste,
>   Whilst thou my feet go slowly past.
>   Compendious snail ! thou seem'st to me
>   Large **Euclid's** strict epitome,
>   That big still with thyself dost go,
>   And livest an aged embryo."

And I might make that other criticism upon
society and its institutions : —

> " While man doth ransack man
>   And builds on blood, and rises by distress ;
>   And th' Inheritance of desolation leaves
>   To great-expecting hopes."

Then mark how man and his affairs fall in rounds :
the railroad keeps time like one of Simon Willard's
clocks, saturated with insurance. How much the
life of certain men *goes* to sustain, to make respected, the institutions of society ! They are the
ones who pay the heaviest tax. They are, in effect,
supported by a fund which society possesses for
that end, or they receive a pension ; and their life
seems to be a sinecure, but it is not. Unwritten
laws are the most stringent. He who is twice
erratic has become the object of custom : —

> " There are whom Heaven has blessed with store of **wit.**
>   You want as much again to manage it."

Then am I a customer, and a paying one. Montaigne took much pains to be made a citizen of

Rome: I should much prefer to have the freedom of a peach-orchard, — once a great part of this town of Lincoln was such, — or of some plantations of apples and pears I have seen, to that of any city. You do not understand values, said Sylvan. I economize every drop of sap in my trees, as if it were wine. A few years ago these trees were whipsticks: now every one of them is worth a hundred dollars. Look at their form: not a branch nor a twig is to spare. They look as if they were arms and hands and fingers, holding out to you the fruit of the Hesperides. Come, see, said he, what weeds grow behind this fence. And he brought me to a pear-tree. Look, he said: this tree has every property that should belong to a plant. It is hardy and almost immortal. It accepts every species of nourishment, and can live almost on none, like a date. It is free from every form of blight. Grubs, worms, flies, bugs, all attack it. It yields them all a share of its generous juices; but, when they left their eggs on its broad leaves, it thickened its cuticle a little, and suffered them to dry up and shook off the vermin. It grows like the ash Ygdrasil.

A bushel of wood-ashes were better than a cart-load of mythology. If I did not love Carlyle for his worship of heroes, I should not forgive him for setting out that ash. There is the edge of the

7*

Forest Lake, like an Indian tradition, gleaming across the pale-face's moonshine. From this Three Friends' Hill (when shall we three meet again ?) the distant forests have a curiously rounded or bowery look, clothing the hills quite down to the water's edge and leaving no shore ; the ponds are like drops of dew, amid and partly covering the leaves. So the great globe is luxuriously crowded without margin. The groundsel, or " fire-weed," which has been touched by frost, already is as if it had died long months ago, or a fire had run through it. The black birches, now yellow on the hill-sides, look like flames ; the chestnut-trees are burnished yellow as well as green. It is a beautifully clear and bracing air, with just enough coolness, full of the memory of frosty mornings, through which all things are distinctly seen, and the fields look as smooth as velvet. The fragrance of grapes is on the breeze, and the red drooping barberries sparkle amid their leaves. The horned (*cornuta*) utricularia on the sandy pond shores is not affected by the frost. The sumacs are among the reddest leaves ; the witch-hazel is in bloom, and the crows fill the landscape with a savage sound. The mullein, so conspicuous with its architectural spire, the prototype of candelabrums, must be remembered. We might relish in autumn a Berkshire brook, which falls, and now beside the road, and now under it, cheers the traveller for miles with its loud voice. If Herrick be the best of English poets, as sometimes, when in the vein, you say (a true Greek), this landscape could give him all he needed, — he who sang a cherry, Julia's hair (we have plenty of that), Netterby's pimple (yes), his own hen Partlet, and Ben **Jonson** (we have all of these, excepting a large assortment of Ben Jonsons). We possess a wider variety here among the maples; but the poetry and the prose of that age was more solid and cordial.

There is a versifier of *ours* who has made some accurate notices of our native things, — Street. I fear you must let me give you a proof of this, nothing of a Herrick. Mate me if you will these passages. He is a good colorist.

> " Yon piny knoll, thick-covered with the brown,
> Dead fringes, in the sunshine's bathing flood
> Looks like dark **gold**.
>
> .   .   .   .
>
> **The thicket** by the road-side casts its cool
> **Black** breadth of shade across the heated dust.
>
> .   .   .   .
>
> The thistle-downs, through the rich,
> Bright blue, quick float, like gliding stars, and **then**
> Touching the sunshine flash and seem to melt
> Within the dazzling brilliance.
>
> .   .   .   .
>
> Another sunset, crouching low
> Upon a rising pile of cloud,
> Bathes deep the island with its glow,
> Then shrinks behind its gloomy shroud.
>
> .   .   .   .

> ... the little violet
> Pencilled with purple on one snowy leaf.
>
> .   .   .   .   .   .
>
> And golden-rod and aster stain the scene
> With hues of sun and sky.
>
> .   .   .   .   .   .
>
> The last butterfly
> Like a winged violet, floating in the meek
> Pink-colored sunshine, sinks his velvet feet
> Within the pillared mullein's delicate down.
>
> .   .   .   .   .   .
>
> Here showers the light in golden dots,
> There sleeps the shade in ebon spots.
>
> .   .   .   .   .   .
>
> Floated the yellow butterfly,
> A wandering spot of sunshine by.
>
> .   .   .   .   .   .
>
> ... the buckwheat's scented snow."

Not less acute and retentive his ear : —

> ... "that flying harp, the honey-bee.
>
> .   .   .   .
>
> ... the spider's clock
> Ticked in some crevice of the rock.
>
> .   .   .   .
>
> The light click of the milkweed's bursting pods.
>
> .   .   .   .
>
> ... the spider lurks
> A close-crouched ball ; out-darting as a hum
> Dooms its trapped prey, and looping quick its threads
> Chains into helplessness those buzzing wings.
> The wood-tick taps its tiny muffled drum
> To the shrill cricket-fife."

He saw peculiarities no one else describes, — exquisite touches of creation for his insight.

" The whizzing of **yon** humming-bird's **swift wings**,
Spanning gray, glimmering circles **round its shape.**

                Yon aster, that displayed
A brief while since its lustrous bloom, has now
Around the shells that multiply its life
Woven soft downy plumes.

The gossamer, motionless, hung from the spray,
Where the weight of the dew-drops had torn it away,
And the seed of the thistle, **that** whisper could swing
Aloft on its wheel, as though borne on a wing,
When the yellow-bird severed it, dipping across,
Its **soft** plumes unruffled **fell** down on the moss.

Lives in the ripple edging **flowery shapes**
With melting lacework.

             . . . from the earth the fern
Thrusts its green, close-curled wheel, the downy sprout
Its twin-leaves.

Beside yon mullein's braided stalk.

            . . . the snail
Creeps in its twisted fortress.

           . . . the twisting cattle-path."

He has his prettinesses : —

           . . . " the holy moon,
A sentinel upon the steeps of heaven.

A cluster of low roofs is prest
Against the mountain's leaning breast.

> One mighty pine, **amid** the straggling **trees,**
> **Lifts** its unchanging **pyramid to heaven.**
>
> He marked **the** rapid **whirlwind shoot,**
> Trampling the pine-tree **with its foot.**
>
> The bee's low **hum, the whirr of wings,**
> And the **sweet songs of grass-hid things."**

So Vaughan has **a hint of this insight : —**

> " As this **loud** brook's incessant fall
> **In streaming** rings re-stagnates all,
> Which reach **by** course the bank, and then
> **Are no more seen.**
>
> **Shall my short hour, my inch,**
>   **My one poor sand.**
>
> Her art, **whose** pensive weeping eyes
> **Were once sin's loose and tempting spies.**
>
>   Heaven
> Is a plain watch, and without figures winds
> All ages **up.**
>
> **How shrill are silent tears !"**

But Vaughan is like the interiors of Fra Angelico.

Has this pond an outlet, as methinks it should, when you hold the reflections caught from its waters thus precious?

It has: a brook runs from the southerly end,

that joins another from Beaver **Pond,** and chasing
swiftly down **fine** meadows, amid rocky knolls **in**
Weston, goes to turn water-wheels at Stony **Brook.**
Man fits into Nature like a seal in its ring. **But**
enfoncer, or how is it in French? Clap down in
the middle of to-day's pudding, and eat thereof, —
they whip **lads at** school for **looking off** their
books; despatch your Sunday plate of broth.
The parson carries **the sins of** the village **by virtue**
of his cloth, upon his back.

ROUND **HILL IN SUDBURY MEADOWS.**

You judge it is three miles and **one-half to the**
point where you propose to take the boat?

Yes: in the rear of the blacksmith's house, — **he**
who calls the bittern " Baked Plum-pudding and
Cow-poke," and the woodchuck " Squash-belly."
A composed, moderate, self-understanding man;
— here's the pinnace (as our neighbor names his
candle-stick) for a voyage among the lilies. Why
look ye so intently at the bottom?

I commonly sit, not *in*, but above, the water.

Be assured, sir, your feet are not wholly in the
Concord. 'Tis dry enough in July, outside, — push
off; she will not sink more than four feet, — the
depth here. Full many **a** glorious morning have
I seen, but not a more superb one than this. How
in its glassy folds the dark, wine-colored river lays

its unswept carpet across the fragrant meadows. The button-bushes and willows resound with the gleeful chorus of redwings and bobolinks, while the courageous king-bird hovers quivering over his nest. If there is any one thing birds do like, it is to sing in sunshiny mornings. Why, this is the mouth of the Pantry Brook: it comes out of the mysterious interstices of Sudbury, where the mud is up to your middle, and where some of Sam Haynes's folks died. I wish I had a photograph of Sam, the fisherman, as the man did when he was told that Crœsus was the richest man who ever lived : if he beat Sam's stories, he must have been rich. And there is Round Hill, the river bending, yet not before we anchor in the Port of Lilies, perfumed love-tokens floating in a lapsing dream of turquoise and gold, like Cleopatra's barge ; some experiments in rose-tints, too, were tried with that dear creature, the water-lily, and did well.

When you thus eulogize Nature, it reminds me how great an advantage he possesses who can turn a verse over all the human race. I read in Wood's Athenæ Oxonienses a score of pages of learned nobodies, of whose once odoriferous reputations not a trace remains in the air ; and then I come to the name of some Carew or Herrick, Suckling or Chapman, as fresh and lustrous as these floating sunlight creams. As a poet says : —

"There are beggars in Iran and Araby,
Said was hungrier than all ;
Men said he was a fly
That came to every festival,
Also he came to the mosque
In trail of camel and caravan,
Out from Mecca to Isphahan ; —
Northward he went to the snowy hills, —
At court he sat in the grave divan.
His music was the south wind's sigh,
His lamp the maiden's downcast eye,
And ever the spell of beauty came
And turned the drowsy world to flame.
By lake and stream and gleaming hall,
And modest copse, and the forest tall,
Where'er he went the magic guide
Kept its place by the poet's side.
Tell me the world is a talisman,
To read it must be the art of man ;
Said melted the days in cups like pearl,
Served high and low, the lord and the churl ;
Loved harebells nodding on a rock,
A cabin hung with curling smoke,
And huts and tents, nor loved he less
Stately lords in palaces,
Fenced by form and ceremony."

There, on Round Hill, is a true woodman's hut. The hill is low, but from its position enjoys a beautiful outlook upon Sudbury meadows. Yes: this is a good place to fish. Can you keep worms in your mouth, like Indians? Maybe they won't bite.

Which, — fish, worms, or Indians? Things that are done it is needless to speak about, or remon-

strate against : things that are past are needless to
blame.

PETER OR BOSE.

I fancied the saying, that man was created a little lower than the angels, should have been, a little
lower than the *animals !*

Does it not flavor of puerile conceit, that fancy ?

The conceit of man is dark; but, as we go to
Goose-shore swimming-place, on the Assabet, with
Peter running before, I feel sorry that Goethe
introduced a black dog in Faust, as the kernel of
the elephant.   And the wild animals are superior to the tame, as the Indian treads before the
civilized man.   Observe Peter capering through
bush and briar, plunging into pool or stream, with
his smiling tail, and he sweats through his nose,
au revoir !   What dull pedants the mirth-provok-
ing creatures consider us ! and how more than
tame poor Cowper's three tame hares may have
deemed him, in his nightcap, made by Mrs. Un-
win !   Peter catches no cold, though he wets his
feet, and never has the doctor.   As the Indians
amused the Jesuits in Canada, by sitting all day in
a nude manner, frozen to the ice, and fishing com-
placently through holes in it, as if lolling on feather
beds, so I have known Peter take a nap all night
on a snow-bank in January.

There, he's at the base of that mud-hole; Lyell was never deeper in geology than he is.

I saw a man, a few days since, working by the river with a horse carting dirt, and the horse and his relations to him struck me as very remarkable. There was the horse, a mere animated machine, though his tail was brushing off the flies, his whole condition subordinated to man's, with no tradition (perhaps no instinct) in him of a time when he was wild and free, — completely humanized. No contract had been made with him that he should have the Saturday afternoons, or the Sundays, or any holidays, his independence never being recognized; it being now quite forgotten, both by man and horse, that the horse was ever free. For I am not aware that there are any wild horses, known surely not to be descended from tame ones. He was assisting that man to pull down that bank and spread it over the meadow, only keeping off the flies with his tail, and stamping and catching a mouthful of grass or leaves from time to time, on his own account; all the rest for man. It seemed hardly worth while that he should be *animated* for this. It was plain that the man was not educating the horse, not trying to develop his nature, but merely getting work out of him, —

"Extremes are counted worst of all."

That mass of animated matter seemed more completely the servant of man than any inanimate. For slaves have *their* holidays; a heaven is conceded to them (such as it is); but to the horse, none. Now and forever he is man's slave. The more I considered, the more the man seemed akin to the horse, only his was the stronger will of the two; for a little further on I saw an Irishman shovelling, who evidently was as much tamed as the horse. He had stipulated that to a certain extent his independence should be recognized; and yet he was really but a little more independent. What is a horse but an animal that has lost its liberty; and has man got any more liberty for having robbed the horse, or has he lost just as much of his own, and become more like the horse he has robbed? Is not the other end of the bridle, too, coiled around his own neck? hence stable-boys, jockeys, and all that class that are daily transported by fast horses. There he stood, with his oblong, square figure (his tail mostly sawed off), seen against the water, brushing off the flies with the stump, braced back, while the man was filling the cart.

> "The ill that's wisely feared is half withstood, —
> He will redeem our deadly, drooping state."

I regard the horse as a human being in a humble state of existence. Virtue is not left to stand alone. He who practises it will have neighbors.

Man conceitedly names the intelligence and industry of animals instinct, and overlooks their wisdom and fitness of behavior. I saw where the squirrels had carried off the ears of corn more than twenty rods from the corn-field, to the woods. A little further on, beyond Hubbard's Brook, I saw a gray squirrel with an ear of yellow corn, a foot long, sitting on the fence, fifteen rods from the field. He dropped the corn, but continued to sit on the rail where I could hardly see him, it being of the same color with himself, which I have no doubt he was well aware of. He next went to a red maple, where his policy was to conceal himself behind the stem, hanging perfectly still there till I passed, his fur being exactly the color of the bark. When I struck the tree, and tried to frighten him, he knew better than to run to the next tree, there being no continuous row by which he might escape ; but he merely fled higher up, and put so many leaves between us that it was difficult to discover him. When I threw up a stick to frighten him, he disappeared entirely, though I kept the best watch I could, and stood close to the foot of the tree.

They *are* wonderfully cunning !

That is all you can say for *them*. There is something pathetic to think of in such a life as an average Norfolk *man* may be supposed to live, drawn out to eighty years; and he has died, perchance, and there is nothing but the mark of his cider-mill left. Here was the cider-mill, and there the orchard, and there the hog-pasture, and so men lived and ate, and drank, and passed away like vermin. Their long life was mere duration. As respectable is the life of the wood-chuck, which perpetuates its race in the orchard still. That is the life of these *select men* spun out. They will be forgotten in a few years, even by such as themselves, as vermin. They will be known like Tucker, who is said to have been a large man, who weighed 250, who had five or six heavy daughters who rode to Suffolk meeting-house on horseback, taking turns; they were so heavy that one could only ride at once. What, then, would redeem such a life? We only know that they ate and drank, and built barns and died, and were buried, and still, perchance, their tombstones cumber the ground, — "time's dead low water." There never has been a girl who learned to bring up a child, that she might afterwards marry.

Perhaps you depreciate humanity, and overestimate somewhat else. A whimsical person said once, he should make a prayer to the chance that brought him into the world. He fancied that when the child had escaped out of the womb, he cried, " I thank the bridge that brought me safe over: I would not for ten worlds take the next one's chance!" Will they, one of these days, at Fourierville, make boys and girls to order and pattern? I want, Mr. Christmas-office, a boy between No. 17 and No. 134, half-and-half of both, or you might add a trace of 113. I want a pair of little girls like 91, only a tinge more of the Swede, and a tinge of the Moorish. And then men are so careless about their really good side. James Baker does not imagine that he is a rich man, yet he keeps from year to year that lordly park of his, by Fairhaven Pond, lying idly open to all comers, without crop or rent, like another Lord Breadalbane, with its hedges of Arcady, its sumptuous lawns and slopes, its orchard and grape-vines, the mirror at its foot, and the terraces of Holloway on the opposite bank. Yet I know he would reprove me, as the poet has written : —

> " Said Saadi, — When I stood before
> Hassan the camel-driver's door,
> I scorned the fame of Timour brave, —
> Timour to Hassan was a slave.
> In every glance of Hassan's eye
> I read rich years of victory.
> And I, who cower mean and small
> In the frequent interval,
> When wisdom not with me resides,
> Worship toil's wisdom that abides !
> I shunned his eyes, — the faithful man's,
> I shunned the toiling Hassan's glance."

Work, yes ; and good conduct additional. You

have been, so I have read, a schoolmaster. I trust
you advised your neophytes to keep company with
none but men of learning and reputation ; to behave themselves upon the place with candor, cau-
tion, and temperance ; to avoid compotations ; to
go to bed in good time, and rise in good time ; to
let them see you are men that observe hours and
discipline ; to make much of yourself, and want
nothing that is fit for you. The life of Cæsar himself has no greater example for us than our own.
We must thrust against a door to know whether
it is bolted against us or not. Where there is no
difficulty, there is no praise ; and every human excellence must be the product of good fortune, improved by hard work and genius.

CHAPTER X.

THE LATTER YEAR.

> "Come, sleep! Oh, sleep! the certain knot of **peace,**
> **The baiting-place of wit, the** balm of woe,
> **The poor man's wealth,** the prisoner's release,
> The indifferent judge between the high and low."
>
> SIDNEY.

> "You meaner beauties of the night
> That poorly satisfy our eyes,
> More by your number than your light;
> You common people of the skies,
> **What are you** when the moon **shall rise?"**
>
> H. WOTTON.

> . . . "In the dust be equal made
> With the poor crooked scythe and spade."
>
> SHIRLEY.

> "Astrochiton Heracles, King of fire, Chorus-leader **of the** world, Sun, **Shepherd of** mortal life, who castest long shadows, riding spirally the **whole heaven** with burning disk, rolling the twelve-monthed year, the **son of Time, thou** performest orbit after orbit." — NONNUS.

> "It is not but the tempest that doth **show**
> **The seaman's** cunning, but the field that tries
> **The captain's courage."** — BEN JONSON.

DO you observe how long the cultivated trees hold their leaves, such as apples, cherries, and peaches? As if they said, "We can longer maintain our privileges than yonder uncultured generation." The black willows stand bare along the edges of the river; the balm-of-Gileads and a

few triumphant elms yet hang out their dusky
banners on the outward walls of the latter year.
That Indian summer, too, made its tranquil appearance, — put in leg-bail for the greasy old redskins.
After the verdure goes, after the harvest of the
year is gathered in, there is a stationary period, —
the year travels on a paved road.   It is with leaves
as with fruits and woods and animals : when they
are mature, their different characters appear.   That
migration of the birds is a cunning get-off.   The
most peaceful, the sunniest autumn day in New
England has a blue background, like some cultivated person at the bottom of whose palaver is
ice.   I hear the barking of a red squirrel whose
clock is set a-going by a little cause in cool
weather, when the spring is tense, and a great
scolding and ado among the jays.   The house-
wives of Nature wish to see the rooms properly
cleaned and swept, before the upholsterer comes and
nails down his carpet of snow.   The swamp burns
along its margin with the scarlet berries of the
black alder, or prinos; the leaves of the pitcher-
plant (which old Josselyn called *Hollow-leaved Lavender*) abound, and are of many colors, from plain
green to a rich striped yellow, or deep red.

> "The hickory-shell, cracked open by its fall,
> Shows its ripe fruit, an ivory ball, within ;
> And the white chestnut-burr displays its sheath
> White glistening with its glossy nuts below.

> Scattered around, the wild rose-bushes hang,
> Their ruby buds tipping their thorny sprays;
> The everlasting's blossoms seem as cut
> In delicate silver, whitening o'er the slopes;
> The seedy clematis, branched high, is robed
> With woolly tufts; the snowy Indian-pipe
> Is streaked with black decay; the wintergreen
> Offers its berries; and the prince's-pine,
> Scarce seen above the fallen leaves, peers out,
> A firm, green, glossy wreath."

Now you allude to it, does not a deception like that of the climate pervade the men? The downright cheer of old England struggling through its brogue, the dazzling stiletto affliction of Italy and France, with us are lacking. Like our climate, and our scale of classes, the sentiment of New England is changeable. It is one of the year's expiring days, one of his death-bed days. The children, playing at the school-house a mile off, the rattle of distant carts, farmers' voices calling to their cattle, cocks crowing in unknown barn-yards, every sound speeds through the attenuated air, as the beat of the death-tick echoes in the funeral-chamber! The trees are as bare as my purse. How significant is the effect of these blue smokes, as if they came from some olfactory altar of the Parsees, imploring the protection of yon threadbare luminary! Methinks is something divine in the culinary art, — the silent columns of light-blue vapor rising slowly. Beneath them many a rusty kettle sings: —

"To intersoar unseen delights the more."

I cannot doubt but the range of the thermometer invades the morals of the people. The puritan element survives in our cultivated conservatism, if there is gilding on the chain. Certain families resolve to divide themselves from the mass by ingenious marriages. And talent tries to keep its head above low-water, yet the agreeable orators, who go to Plymouth and delectate the mass, if you come at them in parlors, are simple creatures, and our great historian took the weight of his waistcoat before he went forth.

'Tis well he was not forced to conceal the ravelled sleeve of care by buttoning up his outer garment. A few years past, yonder breezy representative may have been an usher in a school.

Where, doubtless, filligree was taught.

FROSTY WEATHER.

Winter is fairly broached. When the year becomes cold, then we know how the pine and cypress are the last to lose their leaves.

I should say he is in such a condition that tapping is impossible : —

> " The moon has set, the Pleiades are gone ;
> 'Tis the mid-noon of night ; the hour is by,
> And yet I watch alone."

How hollow echoes the frozen road, under the

wheels of the teamster's wagon! The muzzles of the patient steers are fringed in ice, and their backs whitened with hoar-frost. For all the singing-birds, the chickadees remain; the sawing and scraping of the jay and the crows do remotely pertain to music. A single night snaps the year in two. In the declaration of Tang, it is said, O sun, when wilt thou expire? We will die with thee.

> "Sweet mother! I can weave the web no more,
> So much I love the youth, so much I lingering love."

Shadows hang like flocks of ink from the pitch-pines; the winter sunset, the winter twilight, falls slowly down and congeals the helpless valleys; the sky has a base of lustrous apple-green, and then flows softly up to the zenith that tender roseate flush, like a virgin's cheek when she is refusing the youth. Is winter a cheat? "Neighbor," as Margaret says when she finds Faust is, "lend me your smelling-bottle."

The weather forms its constitution in our people, and they are equal to it. As we catch a morsel of warmth behind the sunny rock, I'll sing you a song about old King Cole:—

TEAMSTERS' SONG.

> How the wind whistled! the snow, how it flew!
> The teamsters knew not if it were still or no,

And the **trains stood** puffing, all kept away back,
And the **drifts lay deep o'er the railroad track** ;
While the snow it flew, and the wind it blew,
And the teamsters bawled, — what a jolly crew !

Their caps are all dressed with the muskrat fur,
But the colder the weather (the truth I aver),
Still less do they turn to the soft, silky lining ;
Their ears are of stone, — 'tis easy divining, —
And their hearts full of joy, while the snow whirls fast,
And the lash of the North swings abroad on the blast.

And the sky is steel on the white cloud flecked,
And the pines are ghosts in their snow-wreaths decked,
And the stormy surge of the gale is rising
While the teamster enjoys the tempest surprising,
With his lugging-sled and his oxen four ;
When the wind roars the hardest, he bawls all
    the more.

Did you never admire the steady, silent, windless fall of the snow in some lead-colored day, silent save the little ticking of the flakes as they touch the twigs? It is chased silver, moulded over the pines and oak-leaves. Soft shades hang like curtains along the closely draped wood-paths. Frozen apples become little cider-vats. The old, crooked apple-trees, frozen stiff in the pale shivering sunlight that appears to be dying of consumption, gleam forth like the heroes of one of Dante's cold hells ; we would not mind a change in the mercury of the dream. The snow crunches under the foot, the chopper's axe rings funereally through the tragic air. At early morn the frost on button-bushes and willows was silvery, and every stem and minutest twig and filamentary weed became a silver thing, while the cottage-smokes came up salmon-colored into that oblique day. At the base of ditches were shooting crystals, like the blades of an ivory-handled pen-knife, and rosettes and favors fretted of silver on the flat ice. The little cascades on the brook were ornamented with trans-parent shields, and long candelabrums, and sperma-ceti-colored fools' caps, and plaited jellies, and white globes, with the black water whirling along trans-parently underneath. The sun comes out, and all at a glance rubies, sapphires, diamonds, and emeralds start into intense life on the angles of the snow-crystals.

You remember that Dryden says, common-sense is a rule in every thing but matters of faith and revelation.

Because he lived in Will's coffee-house. He would have had an *ideal* sense, had he experienced a New England winter. Frost is your safest shoe-leather in the marshes. How red the androm-eda-leaves have turned! Snow and ice remind us of architecture. No lathe ever made such hand-some scrolls and friezes.

And to the arctic man these cold matters make paradise. As Kudlago, the Eskimo, who was going home aboard ship from warmer climes, cried, in his dying moment, "*Teiko-se Ko, teiko-se Ko?*" — Do you see ice, do you see ice?

By fall and fount, by gleaming hill,
And sheltered farm-house still and gray,
By broad, wild marsh and wood-set rill,
Dies cold and sere the winter's day.
Oh, icy sunlight, fade away!

Thou pale magnificence of fate!
Thy arch is but the loitering cloud,
A tall pine-wood thy palace-gate,
The alder-buds thy painted crowd,
Some far-off road thy future proud,
Much cold security allowed.

Art and architecture, I suppose, you consider the same thing. If I visited galleries where pictures are preserved, I would go now, though Hawthorne says he would as soon see a basilisk as one of the old pictures at the Boston Athenæum. I think the fine art of Goethe and company very dubious; and it is doubtful whether all this talk about prints of the old Italian school means any thing (Giotto and the rest). It may do very well for idle gentlemen.

I reply, there is a fire to every smoke. There were a few Anakim who gave the thing vogue by their realism. If Odin wrought in iron or in ships, these worked as rancorously in paint. Michel Angelo, Ribiera (the man that made the skull and the monk, who is another skull looking at it), and the man who made in marble the old Torso Hercules; the Phidias, man or men, who made the Parthenon friezes, had a drastic style, which a blacksmith or a stone-mason would say was starker than their own. And I adhere to Van Waagen's belief, that there is a pleasure from works of art which nothing else can yield. Yes, we should have a water-color exhibition in Boston; but I should like better to have water-color tried in the art of writing. Let our troubadours have one of these Spanish slopes of the dry ponds or basins which run from Walden to the river at Fairhaven, in their September dress of color, under a glowering sky, — the Walden sierras given as a theme, — and they required to daguerreotype that in good words : —

> " I long to talk with some old lover's ghost
> Who died before the god of love was born."   ·

I will do my best ; but, as we were speaking of architecture, remember that this art consists in the imitation of natural Principles, and not like the other arts in the imitation of natural Forms. I

never know the reason why our people have not
reached some appropriate style of architecture. In
Italy and Switzerland and England, the picturesque
seems to spring forth from the soil, in the shapes
of buildings, as well seasoned as its trees and flowers themselves. But look at the clapboard farm-
house we are passing! Is there not a needless
degree of stiffness and too little ornamentation?

Moderate your criticism, my dear Gilpin : utility
lies at the bottom of our village architecture ; the
structure springs out of that. This simple edifice,
created out of white pine-boards and painted white ;
this case of shingles and clapboards appears to its
owner — who built it and lives in it — any thing
but ugly or unpicturesque : so far from it, it fits
him like a shell. Our climate has something to
answer for with respect to this scarcity of ornament
and beauty. The subtle influence of the weather
crops out in the very clapboards, as it does also in
the garments of the farmer, who gets their benefits :
the untamable burning summer, the fatally pene-
trative winter, with warm places sometimes inter-
calated, when the honey-bees come forth and the
black ploughed fields shine like a horse after he
has been rubbed down. Brick and stone are too
damp, and the wall-paper will mould and the cellar
run with water, even in the dryest wooden house,
unless it be warmed throughout, so pungent is the

condensing essence of winter. Then, if you put on outside adorning, it will be warred upon to such a degree by the elements as to be scarcely appropriate to the plain fancies of our farmers: the face of the house is only a mirror of the climate. The roof should have sufficient steepness to carry off rain and snow readily, with as few breaks and angles as possible ; the windows not too large, — in fact, warmth and coolness must, in one of these New England houses, be consulted at the same time, situated as they are in an excessive climate. On the sea-coast the old houses are usually one story high, thus offering the least surface to the wind. The low cottage, all on one floor, will not keep us cool in summer ; and the high Italian style is a comb of ice in February. Then I know that Mr. Gilpin censures the location of the farm-buildings so close upon the road, and that he wishes to set them at the end of an avenue a long distance from the entrance-gate ; that he equally detests the position of the barn within a few rods of the house, — privacy, good taste, refinement, as he says, are thus all sacrificed at one blow. Our farmers cut the timber for their mansions in their own woods, shape it themselves, and bring it upon the ground. Utility, economy, comfort, and use, — a dry, warm cellar, a sweet, airy milk-room, a large wood-shed, a barn with its cellars and accommodations, and all in the most solid style, — these matters make the study of the farmer. He desires a house to live in, not to look at. He must have a pump in the kitchen and one in the cow-yard ; and the kitchen, indeed, needs to be much considered. It should be warm, airy, well-lighted, connected with cellar, shed, yard, road, — and in fact it is a room in use most of the time. The barn and house must be placed with reference to the farm itself : near a village, school, church, store, post-office, station, and the like. All this, it is true, has little to do with the fine art of architecture. Our native democrat, whose brains, boots, and bones are spent in composing a free republic and earning money, is growing up to the fine arts, even if at present utility sways the balance.

This creature, whose portrait you have thus fancifully drawn, looks like a mere machine for gravitating to pork and potatoes, an economical syllogism. I say beauty must have an equal place with utility, if not a precedent. Your farmer shirks architecture and landscape-gardening, with one leg in the barn and the other in the kitchen, and the compost-heap in the midst ; and whose highest ambition is to have a patent-leather top to his carriage. Go to! you libel my jolly countryman. He is no such thieving rat as this, with a singed tail and his ears snipped off. The duke king of T'se had a thousand teams, each of four horses; but on the day of his death the people did not praise him for a single virtue.

O brother Gilpin! hearken ere you die. Those inveterate prejudices of yours for Vitruvius and Inigo Jones have left you too little sympathy with the industrious, able yeoman of New England. I have but drawn a few lines of his portrait. The climate is close, the soil difficult, the clapboard edifice not alluring in its aspect. Let this be so: the creator of it, the citizen, stands up like a king in the midst of the local penury. How well he can write and cipher! how intelligent! He receives the news from all lands each day in his paper, and has his monthly journals and lyceum lectures. There is a sweetness, a native pride, in the man, that overtops the rugged necessities of his condition, and shoots its fine branches heavenward. His healthful economic industry, and that practical education derived from a constant use of natural elements, and a life-long struggle against difficulties, renders him incredibly expert and capable of seizing all expedients whereby he can better his conditions. The New England farmer has proved that an independent man, a democratic citizen, on a poor soil and in unfavorable positions, can overcome the outward obstacles. He has solved the problem of democracy, and must give place to some new forms of society, when all the arts shall be employed in the construction of the estate.

> " Born nature yields each day a brag which we now first behold,
> And trains us on to slight the new as if it were the old;
> And blest is he who playing deep, yet haply asks not why,
> Too busy with the crowded day to fear to live or die."

WALDEN.

I believe you take some note of the seasons. Pray, what is this ? On our old path to Walden Pond I cannot really decide whether I or the world have had the opiate. Assuredly it must be autumn, if it is not summer. How tacitly the pond sleeps ! These pine-stumps, after the pitch is dry, make excellent seats. The semi-clouded sky images itself so truthfully in the slumbering water that sky and water form one piece, and the glancing swallows flying above that invisible surface seem to be play-ing with their own images reversed. Not with the very utmost scrutiny can I distinguish between the twain. And so you think the superiorities of the Englishman grow out of his insular climate. Shake-speare's beauties were never cradled on the rack of a New English summer. If our landscape stew with heat, the brain becomes another stew-pan. As most of our days are unutterably brilliant, I enjoy the few scattered gray and lowering ones, half-shade and half-shine, the negative days : —

> " In the turbulent beauty
>   Of a gusty autumn day,
>   Poet on a sunny headland
>   Sighed his soul away.
>   Farms the sunny landscape dappled,
>   Swan-down clouds dappled the **farms,**
>   Cattle lowed in hollow distance
>   Where far oaks outstretched their arms.
>   Sudden gusts came full of meaning,
>   All too much to him they said,
>   South winds have long memories,
>   Of that be none afraid.
>   I cannot tell rude listeners
>   Half the tell-tale south wind **said,**
>   'Twould bring the blushes of yon maples
>   To a man and to a maid."

The golden loveliness of autumn, — was that your phrase?

Rather **fine,** methinks, **for the like of me !**

A pretty rustic wreath **could be braided of wild berries now,** including such as the **dark blue** magical **berries of** the red-osier cornel, the maple-leaved **viburnum with its** small bluish-black berries, and, though **so fragile, we might add, for** the passing hour, **the purple might of the** great elderberry clusters. **Why not wreathe wild** grapes, prinos, **and smilax berries together,** and **the** berries of the **andromeda ? Then the** purple-stemmed **golden-rod and the blue** gentian's flowers should **not be omitted from this votive offering to Ceres ;** and it **should be suspended from a white-maple** whence **we could steal a** glimpse **through the** charming

Septembrian sunflood with its sense of fulness and everlasting life, over the quivering river that is blue and sunny, silvery, golden, and azure at once, transparent olives and olive-greens glazed to a complete polish, and bounded by the softest shimmer, not transparent. I have been reading a report on herbaceous plants. The mere names of reeds and grasses, of the milkweeds and the mints, the gentians, the mallows and trefoils, are poems. Erigeron, because it grows old early, is the old man of the spring ; *Pyrola umbellata* is called *chimaphila*, lover of winter, since its green leaves look so cheerful in the snow ; also called prince's-pine. The plantain (*Plantago major*), which follows man wherever he builds a house, is called by the Indians white-man's foot ; and I like well to see a mother or one of her girls stepping outside of the door with a lamp, for its leaf, at night, to dress some slight wound or inflamed hand or foot. My old pet, the *Liatris*, acquires some new interest from being an approved remedy for the bite of serpents, and hence called rattlesnake's-master. Fire-weed, or *Hieracium*, springs up abundantly on burnt land. The aromatic fields of dry *Gnaphalium* with its pearly incorruptible flowers, and the sweet-flags with their bayonet-like flash, wave again, thanks to this dull professor, in my memory, on even a cold winter's morning. Even the naming of the localities — ponds, shady woods, wet pastures, and the like — comfort us. But this heavy country professor insults some of my favorites, — the well-beloved *Lespedeza*, for instance ; the beautiful *Epigœa*, or Mayflower, — pride of Plymouth hermits. The hills still bear the remembrance of sweet berries ; and I suppose the apple or the huckleberry to have this comfortable fitness to the human palate, because they are only the palate inverted : one is man eating, and the other man eatable. The *Mikania scandens*, with its purplish-white flowers, now covers the button-bushes and willows, by the side of streams ; and the large-flowered bidens (*chrysanthemoides*), and various-colored polygonums, white and reddish and red, stand high among the bushes and weeds by the river-side ; and, in modest seclusion, our scarlet imperialists, the lordly Cardinals.

You have a rare season in your shanty by the pond.

I have gained considerable time for study and writing, and proved to my satisfaction that life may be maintained at less cost and labor than by the old social plan. Yet I would not insist upon any one's trying it who has not a pretty good supply of internal sunshine ; otherwise he would have, I judge, to spend too much of his time in fighting with his dark humors. To live alone comfortably, we must have that self-comfort which rays out of Nature, — a portion of it at least.

I sometimes feel the coldest days
  A beam upon the snow-drift thrown,
As if the sun's declining rays
  Were with his summer comforts sown.

The icy marsh, so cold and gray,
  Hemmed with its alder copses brown,
The ruined walls, the dying day,
  Make in my dream a landscape crown.

And sweet the walnuts in the fall,
  And bright the apples' lavished store;
Thus sweet my winter's pensive call,
  O'er cold, gray marsh, o'er upland hoar.

And happier still that we can roam
  Free and untrammelled o'er the land,
And think the fields and clouds are home,
  Nor forced to press some stranger's hand.

CHAPTER XI.

MULTUM IN PARVO.

> "There's nothing left
> Unto Andrugio but Andrugio: and that
> Not mischief, force, distress, nor hell can take;
> **Fortune my** fortunes not my mind shall shake."
>
> MARSTON.

"**There, your** Majesty, what a glimpse, as into infinite extinct Continents, filled with ponderous, thorny inanities, invincible nasal drawling of didactic Titans, and the awful attempt to spin, on all **manner** of wheels, road-harness out of split cobwebs: Hoom! Hoom-m-m! **Harness not** to be had on those terms." — CARLYLE.

"My dears, you are like the heroines of romance, — **jewels in abundance**, but scarce a rag to your backs." — MADAME DE SÉVIGNÉ.

AS already noticed, Thoreau believed **that one** of the arts of life was **to** make **the** most out of it. He loved **the** *multum in parvo*, **or** potluck; **to boil up the little into** the **big.** Thus, he was **in the habit of saying,** — Give me healthy senses, **let me be thoroughly alive, and** breathe **freely in the very flood-tide of the living world.** But **this should have availed him little, if he had not been at the same time** copiously **endowed with the power of recording** what he **imbibed.** His **senses truly lived twice.**

Many thousands of travellers pass **under** the telegraph-poles, and descry in them **only** a line of barked chestnuts: to our poet-naturalist they came forth a Dodona's sacred grove, and like the old Grecian landscapes followed the phantasy of our Concord Orpheus, twanging on their road.

" As I went under the new telegraph wire, I heard it vibrating like a harp high over head: it was as the sound of a far-off glorious life, a supernal life which came down to us and vibrated the lattice-work of this life of ours, — an Æolian harp. It reminded me, I say, with a certain pathetic moderation, of what finer and deeper stirrings I was susceptible. It said: Bear in mind, child, and never for an instant forget, that there are higher planes of life than this thou art now travelling on. Know that the goal is distant, and is upward. There is every degree of inspiration, from mere fulness of life to the most rapt mood. A human soul is played on even as this wire: I make my own use of the telegraph, without consulting the directors, like the sparrows, which, I observe, use it extensively for a perch. Shall I not, too, go to this office? The sound proceeds from near the posts, where the vibration is apparently more rapid. It seemed to me as if every pore of the wood was filled with music. As I put my ear to one of the posts, it labored with the strains, as if every fibre was affected, and being seasoned or timed, rearranged according to a new and more harmonious law : every swell and change and inflection of tone pervaded it, and seemed to proceed from the wood, the divine tree or wood, as if its very substance was transmuted.

" What a recipe for preserving wood, to fill its pores with music! How this wild tree from the forest, stripped of its bark and set up here, rejoices to transmit this music. When no melody proceeds from the wire, I hear the hum within the entrails of the wood, the oracular tree, acquiring, accumulating the prophetic fury. The resounding wood,— how much the ancients would have made of it! To have had a harp on so great a scale, girdling the very earth, and played on by the winds of every latitude and longitude, and that harp were (so to speak) the manifest blessing of Heaven on a work of man's. Shall we not now add a tenth Muse to those immortal Nine, and consider that this invention was most divinely honored and distinguished, upon which the Muse has thus condescended to smile, — this magic medium of communication with mankind? To read that the ancients stretched a wire round the earth, attaching it to the trees of the forest, on which they sent messages by one named Electricity, father of Lightning and Magnetism, swifter far than Mercury,— the stern commands of war and news of peace; and that the winds caused this wire to vibrate, so that it emitted a harp-like and Æolian music in all the lands through which it passed, as if to express the satisfaction of the gods in this invention! And this is fact, and yet we have attributed the instrument to no god. I hear the sound working terribly within. When I put my ear to it, anon it swells into a clear tone, which seems to concentrate in the core of the tree, for all the sound seems to proceed from the wood. It is as if you had entered some world-cathedral, resounding to some vast organ. The fibres of all things have their tension, and are strained like the strings of a lyre. I feel the very ground tremble underneath my feet, as I stand near the post. The wire vibrates with great power, as if it would strain and rend the wood. What an awful and fateful music it must be to the worms in the wood. No better vermifuge were needed. As the wood of an old Cremona, its every fibre, perchance, harmoniously transposed and educated to resound melody, has brought a great price, so methinks these telegraph-posts should bear a great price with musical instrument-makers. It is prepared to be the material of harps for ages to come; as it were, put a-soak in and seasoning in music."

> "How could the patient pine have known
> 　The morning breeze would come?
> Or humble flowers anticipate
> 　The insect's noonday hum?"

Much more was he, who drew this ravishing noise off a stale post, a golden wire of communication with the blessed divinities! With poetic insight he married practical perception, avoiding that flying off in space like the writings of some who pursued the leading of the Rev. Bismiller, where there is the theatrical breadth of a pasteboard sky, with not much life rolling in it,

> "But troops of smoothing people that collaud
> All that we do."

Or, as he observes, "Not till after several months does an infant find its hands, and it may be seen looking at them with astonishment, holding them up to the light; and so also it finds its toes. How many faculties there are which we have never found! We want the greatest variety within the smallest compass, and yet without glaring diversity, and we have it in the color of the withered oak-leaves." He speaks of fleets of yellow butterflies, and of the gray squirrels on their winding way, on their unweariable legs. Distant thunder is the battle of the air. "A cow looking up at the sky has an almost human or wood-god, fawn-like expression, and reminded me of some frontispiece to Virgil's Bucolics. When the red-eye (*Vireo*) ceases, then, I think, is a crisis. The pigeons, with their *quivet*, dashed over the Duganne desert." . . . When the snow-birds flew off, their wave actually broke over him, as if he were a rock. He sees two squirrels answering one to the other, as it were, like a vibrating watch-spring, — they withdrew to their airy houses. . . . "When turning my head I looked at the willowy edges of Cyanean meadow, and onward to the sober-colored but fine-grained Clam-shell hills, about which there was no glitter, I was inclined to think that the truest beauty was that which surrounded us, but which we failed to discern ; that the forms and colors which adorn our daily life, not seen afar in the horizon, are our fairest jewelry. The beauty of Clam-shell hill near at hand, with its sandy ravines, in which the cricket chirps, — this is an *occidental* city, not less glorious than we dream of in the sunset sky.

" At Clematis Brook I perceive that the pods or follicles of the common milkweed (*Asclepias syriaca*) now point upward. They are already bursting. I release some seeds with the long, fine silk attached : the fine threads fly apart at once (open with a spring), and then ray themselves out into a hemispherical form, each thread freeing itself from its neighbor, and all reflecting rainbow or prismatic tints. The seeds beside are furnished with wings, which plainly keep them steady, and prevent their whirling round. I let one go, and it rises slowly and uncertainly at first, now driven this way, then that, by currents which I cannot perceive, and I fear it will shipwreck against the neighboring **wood ; but no ! as it** approaches **it, it surely** rises above **it, and** then feeling the **strong north wind it is** borne off rapidly **in** the opposite **direction,** ever rising higher and higher, and tossing **and heaved** about with **every** fluctuation of the gale, **till at a h**undred feet above **the earth, and fifty rods** off, steering **south, I lose sight of it. I** watched this milkweed-seed, for **the time, with as** much interest as his friends **did Mr. Lauriat** disappearing in the skies. **How many** myriads go sailing away at this season, **—high** over **hill** and **meadow and** river, to plant their race in new localities, — on various tacks, **until** the wind lulls, **who** can tell how **many miles !** And for this end these silken streamers **have been** perfecting all summer, snugly packed **in this light** chest, **a** prophecy **not** only of the fall, but **of** future springs. Who could believe in the prophecies of a Daniel **or of** Miller, **that** the world would end this summer, **while one** milkweed with faith matured its seeds ? Densely **packed in a** little oblong chest, armed with soft, downy **prickles, and** lined with a smooth, silky **lining, lie some** hundreds of seeds, pear-shaped, **or like a steelyard's** poise, which have derived their nutriment through a band **of ex-tremely fine,** silken threads, attached by their **ex-tremities** to the core. **At** length, when **the seeds** are matured and cease to require nourishment from the parent plant, being weaned, and the pod with dryness and frost bursts, the extremities of the silken thread detach themselves from the core, and from being the conduits of nutriment to the seed become the buoyant balloon which, like some spiders' webs, bear the seeds to new and distant fields. They merely serve to buoy up the full-fed seeds, far finer than the finest thread. Think of the great variety of balloons which, at this season, are buoyed up by similar means. I am interested in the fate, or success, of every such venture which the autumn sends forth."

A well-known writer says he looked at the present moment as a man does upon a card upon which he has staked a considerable sum, and who seeks to enhance its value as much as he can without exaggeration. Thoreau had a like practice, — the great art is judiciously to limit and isolate one's self, and life is so short we must miss no opportunity of giving pleasure to one another. No doubt our author's daily writing, his careful observation in his own mind, lay as a mass of gold, out of which he should coin a good circulating medium for the benefit of other minds. Nothing which has not sequence is of any value in life. And he held to that oft-repeated dictum, "Whatever is very good sense must have been common-sense in all times. I fairly confess I have served myself all I could by writing: that I made use of the judg-

ment of authors, dead and living. If I have written well, let it be considered it is what no man
can do without good sense, — a quality that renders one not only capable of being a good writer,
but a good man. To take more pains and employ
more time cannot fail to produce more complete
pieces. The ancients constantly applied to art,
and to that single branch of an art to which their
talent was most powerfully bent; and it was the
business of their lives to correct and finish their
works for posterity : —

> "Nor Fame I slight, nor for her favors call ;
> She comes unlook'd for, if she comes at all. —
> Who pants for glory finds but short repose."

Then thinkers are so varied. The Mahometans
taught fate in religion, and that nothing exists that
does not suppose its contrary. Some believe that
cork-trees grow merely that we may have stoppers
to our bottles. St. Augustine, in his City of
God, mentions a man who could perspire when he
pleased. Napoleon classed the Old and New Tes-
taments, and the Koran, under the head of politics.
One says, a fact of our lives is valuable, not according as it is true, but as it is significant. Thoreau
would scarcely have upheld this. But he could
assert " that no greater evil can happen to any one
than to hate reasoning. Man is evidently made
for thinking : this is the whole of his dignity, and

the whole of **his merit.**   To think as he ought is the
whole **of** his duty."

After our dear lover of Nature had retired from
Walden, a rustic rhymer hung up on **the** walls of
his deserted sanctuary some irregular verses, as an
interpretation :—

WALDEN HERMITAGE.

Who bricked this chimney small
I well do know;
Know **who** spread the mortar on the wall,
And the shingles nailéd through ;
Yes, have **seen** thee,
Thou small, rain-tinted hermitage!
And spread aside the pitch-pine tree
That shaded the brief edge
Of thy snug **roof,** —
'Twas water-proof!

Have seen thee, Walden lake !
Like burnished glass to take
With thy daguerreotype
Each cloud, each tree,
More firm yet free.
Have seen and known, —
Yes, as I hear and **know**
Some echo's faintest tone.
All, all have fled,
Man, and cloud, and shed.

    " What man was this,
      Who thus could build,

Of what complexion,
At what learning skilled?
That the lake I see down there,
Like a glass of simmering air?"
So might that stranger say.
To him I might reply, —
"You ask me for the man.   Hand me yesterday,
Or to-morrow, or a star from the sky:
More mine are they than he;
But that he lived, I tell to thee.

" Might I say
He was brave,
As a cold winter's day,
Or the waves that toss their spray;
Brave,
So is the lion brave,
And the wind that braids a song
On the corded forest's gong.

" That man's heart was true,
As the sky in living blue,
And the old contented rocks
That the mountains heap in blocks.
Wilt thou dare to do as he did,
Dwell alone and bide thy time?
Not with lies be over-rid,
And turn thy griefs to rhyme?
True! do you call him true?
Look upon the eaglet's eye,
Wheeled amid the freezing blue,
In the unfathomable sky,
With cold and blasts and light his speed to try!

" And should I tell thee that this man was good ?
  Never thought his neighbor harm,
  Sweet was it where he stood,
  Sunny all, and warm.
  Good ?
  So the rolling star seems good,
  That miscalculates not,
  Nor sparkles a jot
  Out of its place,
  Period of unlettered space."

  Now might once more some stranger ask,
  I should reply:
" Why this man was high
  And lofty is not his task,
  Nor mine, to tell:
  Springs flow from the invisible.
  But on this shore he used to play,
  There his boat he hid away,
  And where has this man fled to-day ?
  Mark the small, gray hermitage
  Touch yon curved lake's sandy edge;
  The pines are his you firmly see,
  All before the cliff so high.

" He never goes, —
  But must thou come,
  As the wind blows,
  He sits surely at home.
  In his eye the thing must stand,
  In his thought the world command;
  As a clarion shrills the morn,
  On his arms the world be borne.

> Beat with thy paddle on the boat,
> Midway the lake, — the wood repeats
> The ordered blow, the echoing note
> Has ended in the ear, yet its retreats
> Contain more possibilities;
> And in this Man the nature lies
> Of woods so green,
> And lakes so sheen,
> And hermitages edged between."

A literary disciple, whose shanty stood on London streets, thus vents *his* history: "I am quite familiar at the Chapter Coffee-house, and know all the geniuses there. A character is now unnecessary: an author carries his character in his pen. Good God, how superior is London to that despicable Bristol! The poverty of authors is a common observation, but not always a true one. No author can be poor who understands the arts of booksellers. [But he don't.] No: it is my pride, my damned, native, unconquerable pride, that plunges me into distraction." And another asks, "What could Stephen Duck do? what could Chatterton do? Neither of them had opportunities of enlarging their stock of ideas. No man can coin guineas but in proportion as he has gold." Even that touch upon booksellers' arts did not prevent our brother from starving to death three months after in London.

Thoreau **would not** have said, **with** Voltaire, " *Ah, croyez-moi, l'erreur a son merite,*" — believe me, **sin has** something worthy in it, — which is the same as Goethe's " Even in God I discover defects ; " but he would recognize the specific value of events. The directions **of men are** singular. **He knew** one **in** Sudbury **who used to fat** mud-turtles, having **a** great appetite for them ; another used **to eat those imposthumes on wild rose-bushes, which** are made **by** worms and contain an **ounce of** maggots each. **But why** criticise poor human nature, when a black snake **that has just laid** her eggs **on a** tussock in the **meadow** (some were hatching, **and some** hatched), upon being alarmed, **swallows them all** down in a lump for safe keeping, and **no doubt** produces them afresh at a convenient time ? Nature, as Thoreau said, does have her dawn each day ; and her economical code of laws does not consult taste or high **art,** as in the **above** salvation of so inconvenient a morsel as a snake's offspring. He sometimes caught sight of the inside of things by artificial means ; and notices that the young mud-turtle is a hieroglyphic of snappishness a fortnight before it is hatched, like the virtue **of** bottled cider. " When **the** robin ceases, then **I think is an exit, . . .   the concert is** over." He could see a revolution in **the end of a** bird's song, and used working abroad **like the** artist who painted **out-of-doors, and** believed **that**

lights and a room were absurdities, and that *a picture* could be painted anywhere. So must a man
be moral everywhere, and he must not expect that
Nature will take a scrubbing-brush and clean her
entries for his steps, seeing how sentimental a
fellow is our brother.

The *Bombyx pini*, the pine spider, the most
destructive of all forest insects, is infested, so says
Ratzeburg, by thirty-five parasitical ichneumonidæ.
And infirmity that decays the wise doth ever make
the better fool.

> "Not to know at large of things remote
> From use, obscure and subtle, but to know
> That which before us lies in daily use."

The love of our poet-naturalist for the open air,
his hypæthral character, has been dwelt upon.
Such was his enjoyment in that outward world, it
seemed as if his very self became a cast of nature,
with the outlines of humanity fair and perfect; but
that intensity of apprehension did, with certain
minds, accuse him of egotism. Yet not self, but
rather that creation of which he was a part, asserted
itself there. As it is said : —

> "For chiefly here thy worth, —
> Greatly in this, that unabated trust,
> Amplest reliance on the unceasing truth
> That rules the darting sphere about us,
> That drives round the unthinking ball,
> And buds the ignorant germs on life and time,

9*

> Of men and beasts and birds, themselves the sport
> Of a clear, healthful prescience, still unspent."

He admired plants and trees: truly, he loved them. Doubt not that it was their infinite beauty which first impressed them on him, and then he greatly held that art of science which, taking up the miscellaneous crowd, impaled them on the picket-fences of order, and coined a labelled scientific plan from the phenomenal waste-basket of vulgar observation. And a hearty crack in Latin he rejoiced at; not merely because he had digested it early, but as a stencil-tool for the mind. He prized a substantial name for a thing beyond most sublunary joys. Name it! name it! he might have cried to the blessed fortune.

"He shall be as a god to me who can rightly define and divide. The subjects on which the master did not talk were, — extraordinary things, feats of strength, disorder, and spiritual beings. What the superior man seeks is in himself: what the mean man seeks is in others. By weighing we know what things are light and what heavy; by measuring we know what things are long and what short. It is of the greatest importance to measure the motions of the mind."

> "Mills of the gods do slowly wind,
> But they at length to powder grind."

He loved what the Prussian king says to his

brother, — "I write this letter with the rough common-sense of a German, who speaks what he thinks, without employing equivocal terms and loose assuagements which disfigure the truth." But it may be feared he would have stopped running, when Fichte thus lays his finger on the destination of man: "My consciousness of the object is only a yet unrecognized consciousness of my production of the representation of an object;" although he admired the poet's description, —

> "My mother bore me in the southern wild,
> And I am black, but, oh! my soul is white, —
> White as an angel is the English child, ₊
> But I am black as if bereaved of light."

For pure, nonsensical abstractions he had no taste. No work on metaphysics found room on his shelves unless by sufferance; there being some Spartan metaphysicians who send you their books, like the witty lecturer who sent out cards of invitation to his lectures, when you had to come. Neither did he keep moral treatises, though he would not say, what we call good is nothing else than egoism painted with verbiage, like the Frenchman. "Stick your nose into any gutter, entity, or object, this of Motion or another, with obstinacy, you will easily drown if that be your determination. Time, at its own pleasure, will untie the knot of destiny, if there be one, like a shot of electricity through an elderly, sick household cat." We do not bind ourselves to men by exaggerating those peculiarities in which we happen to differ from them.

" I perceive on the blue vervain (*Verbena hastata*) that only one circle of buds, about half-a-dozen, blossoms at a time; and there are about thirty circles in the space of three inches, while the next circle of buds above at the same time shows the blue. Thus the triumphant blossoming circle travels upward, driving the remaining buds off into space. It is very pleasant to measure the progress of the season by this and similar clocks. So you get not the absolute, but the true time of the season. These *genera* of plants suggest a history to nature, — a *natural* history, in a new sense. Any anomaly in vegetation makes Nature seem more real and present in her working, as the various red and yellow excrescences on young oaks. As if a poet were born who had designs in his head! Animals are often manifestly related to the plants, which they feed upon or live among, as caterpillars, butterflies, tree-toads, partridges, chewinks. I noticed a yellow spider on a golden-rod. The interregnum in the blossoming of flowers being well over (August 24th), many small flowers blossom now in the low grounds, having just reached their spring. What a miserable name to the *Gratiola aurea*, hedge-hyssop. Whose hedge does it grow by, pray, in this part of the world? *Rubus semper-virens*, the small, low blackberry, is now (August 27th) in fruit; the *Medeola Virginica*, cucumber-root, is now in green fruit; and the *Polygala cruci-ata*, cross-leaved polygala, with its handsome calyx and leaves."

On such Latin thorns do botanists hang the Lilies of the Vale, — things that can only be crucified into order upon the justification of a splitting-hair microscope. We are assured they have no nerves, sharing the comfort with naturalists.

" The ivy-leaves are turning red; fall dande-lions stand thick in the meadows. The leaves on the hardhack are somewhat *appressed*, clothing the stem and showing their downy under-sides, like white waving wands. I walk often in drizzly weather, for then the small weeds (especially if they stand on bare ground), covered with rain-drops like beads, look more beautiful than ever. They are equally beautiful when covered with dew, fresh and adorned, almost spirited away in a robe of dewdrops. At the Grape Cliffs the few bright red leaves of the tupelo contrast with the polished green ones, — the tupelos with drooping branches. The grape-vines, over-running and bending down the maples, form little arching bowers over the meadow five or six feet in diameter, like parasols held over the ladies of the harem in the East. The rhomboidal joints of the tick trefoil (*Desmodium paniculatum*) adhere to my clothes, and thus disperse themselves. The oak-ball is a dirty drab now. When I got into the Lincoln road, I perceived a singular sweet scent in the air, which I suspected arose from some plant now in a peculiar state owing to the season (September 11th) ; but though I smelled every thing around I could not detect it, but the more eagerly I smelled the further I seemed to be from finding it ; but when I gave up the search, again it would be wafted to me, the intermitting perfume ! It was one of the sweet scents which go to make the autumn air, — which fed my sense of smell rarely, and dilated my nostrils. I felt the better for it. Methinks that I possess the sense of smell in greater perfection than usual, and have the habit of smelling of every plant I pluck. How autumnal now is the scent of ripe grapes by the road-side ! The cross-leaved polygala emits its fragrance as if at will. You must not hold it too near, but on all sides and at all distances. How beautiful the sprout-land, a young wood thus springing up ! Shall man then despair ? Is he not a sprout-land too ?

" In Cohosh Swamp the leaves have turned a very deep red, but have not lost their fragrance.

I notice wild apples growing luxuriantly in the midst of the swamp, rising red over the colored, painted leaves of the sumac, reminding me that they were colored by the same influences, — some green, some yellow, some red. I fell in with a man whose breath smelled of spirit, which he had drunk. How could I but feel it was his own spirit that I smelt? A sparrow-hawk, hardly so big as a night-hawk, flew over high above my head, — a pretty little, graceful fellow, too small and delicate to be rapacious. I found a grove of young sugar-maples. How silently and yet start-lingly the existence of these was revealed to me, which I had not thought grew in my immediate neighborhood, when first I perceived the entire edges of its leaves and their obtuse sinuses! Such near hills as Nobscot and Nashoba have lost all their azure in this clear air, and plainly belong to earth. Give me clearness, nevertheless, though my heavens be moved further off to pay for it. It is so cold I am glad to sit behind the wall; still, the great bidens blooms by the causeway side, beyond the bridge. On Mount Misery were some very rich yellow leaves (clear yellow) of the *Populus grandidentata*, which still love to wag and tremble in my hands."

This qualification hides the plant celebrated by the entombed novelist, Walter Scott, when he speaks of —

> " the shade
> By-the light quivering aspen made."

It is a poplar whose leaves are soft and tremulous, and some botanist has smashed his Latinity on the little, trembling, desponding thing. We shall next be required to ask, " What's yours?" To Henry these names were a treat, and possessed a flavor beyond the title of emperor.

The river never failed to act as a Pacific for his afternoon, and few things gave him so great a delight as a three hours' voyage on this mitigated form of Amazon.

> " Seek then, again, the tranquil river's breast.
> July awakes new splendor in the stream,
> Yet more than all, the water-lily's pomp,
> A star of creamy perfume, born to be
> Consoler to thy solitary voyage.
> In vast profusion from the floor of pads,
> They floating swim, with their soft beauty decked ;
> Nor slight the pickerel-weed, whose violet shaft
> Controls the tall reed's emerald, and endows
> With a contrasted coloring the shore.
> No work of human art can faintly show
> The unnoticed lustre of these summer plants,
> These floating palaces, these anchored orbs,
> These spikes of untold richness crowning earth.
> The muskrat glides, and perch and pout display
> Their arrowy swiftness, while the minnows dart
> And fright the filmy silver of the pool ;
> And the high-colored bream, a ring of gems,
> Their circular nests scoop in the yellow sands,
> And never ask, Why was this beauty wasted
> On these banks ? nor soon believe that love in vain
> Is lavished on the solitude, nor deem

Absence **of** human life **absence of all !**
Why is **not** *here* **an answer to thy thought ?**
Or mark in August, when the twilight falls :
Like wreaths of timid **smoke her curling mist**
Poured from some smouldering fire across
The meadows cool, whose modest shadows thrown
So faintly seem to fall asleep with day.
Oh, softly pours the thin and curling mist !
Thou twilight hour ! abode of peace how deep,
May we not envy him **who in** thee dwells ?
And, **like thy** soft and gently falling beauty,
His **repose, —** dreams on the flood-tide of the soul."

Or let us hear this dear lover of wood and glen, **of early morn and deep** midnight, sing a strain of the autumnal wind as **it goes hurrying** about, regardless of **the plucked mannikins** freezing **amid its** polarities : —

" The wind roars amid the pines like **the surf. You** can hardly hear the crickets for the **din or the cars.** Such a blowing, stirring, bustling day **! what** does **it mean** ? All light things decamp, straws and loose leaves change their places. It shows the **white and silvery** under-sides of the leaves. **I** perceive **that some** farmers are busy cutting turf now. You dry **and** burn the very earth itself. I see the volumes **of** smoke, — not quite the blaze, —from burning brush, **as I** suppose, far in **the** western horizon : the farmers' simple enterprises ! They improve this season, — which is the dryest, **— their** haying being done and their harvest not **begun, to do** these jobs : burn brush, build walls, dig ditches, cut turf, also topping corn and digging potatoes. May not the succory, tree-primrose, and other plants, be distributed from Boston on the rays of the railroad? The shorn meadows looked of a living green at eve, even greener than in spring. This reminded me of the *fenum cordum*, the after-math; *sicilimenta de pratis*, the second mowing of the meadow, in Cato. His remedy for sprains would be as good in some cases as opedeldoc. You must repeat these words: '.Hauat, hauat, hauat ista pista sista damia bodanna ustra.' And his notion of an auction would have had a fitness in the South: 'If you wish to have an auction, sell off your oil, if it will fetch something, and any thing in the wine and corn line left over; sell your old oxen, worthless sheep and cattle, old wool, hides and carts; old tools, old slaves and sick slaves; and if you can scrape up any more trash, sell it along with them.' I now begin to pick wild apples.

" We scared a calf out of the meadows, which ran, like a ship tossed on the waves, over the hills: they run awkwardly, — red, oblong squares, tossing up and down like a vessel in a storm, with great commotion. I observe that the woodchuck has two or more holes, a rod or two apart: one, or the front door, where the excavated sand is heaped up; another, not so easily discovered, which is very

small, round, and without sand about it, being that
by which he emerged, and smaller directly at the
surface than beneath, on the principle by which a
well is dug. I saw a very fat woodchuck on a
wall, evidently prepared to go into the ground, —

> " Want and woe which torture us,
> Thy sleep makes ridiculous."

As the woodchuck dines chiefly on crickets, he
will not be at much expense in seats for his winter
quarters.   Since the anatomical discovery, that
the *thymoid* gland, whose use in man is *nihil*, is for
the purpose of getting digested during the hiber-
nating jollifications of the woodchuck, we sympa-
thize less at his retreat.   Darwin, who hibernates
in science, cannot yet have heard of this use of
the above gland, or he would have derived the
human race to that amount from the *Mus montana,*
our woodchuck, instead of landing him flat on the
simiadæ, or monkey. We never can remember
that our botanist took a walk that gave him a poor
turn or disagreed with him. It is native to him
to say, —

" It was pleasant walking where the road was
shaded by a high hill, as it can be only in the
morning ; also, looking back, to see a heavy shadow
made by some high birches reaching quite across
the road.   Light and shadow are sufficient contrast

and furnish **sufficient excitement when we are well.**
Now **we were** passing **a sunshiny mead,** pastured
with cattle and sparkling **with dew, — the sound of
crows and** swallows **was heard in the air,** and
leafy-columned elms stood **about,** shining **with**
moisture. The **morning freshness and unworldli-**
ness of that domain! **When you are starting**
away, leaving your more familiar fields for a little
adventure **like a** walk, you **look at every object**
with a traveller's, or at **least** historical, eyes; **you**
pause **on the** foot-bridge **where** an ordinary walk
hardly commences, and begin **to** observe and moral-
ize. It **is worth the while to see your** native
village **thus,** sometimes. **The dry** grass **yields a**
crisped **sound to my feet; the cornstalks, standing**
in stacks in **long rows** along the edges **of the corn-**
fields, remind me of stacks of muskets. As soon
as berries are gone, grapes come. The flowers of
the meadow-beauty are literally little reddish chal-
ices now, though many **still** have petals, — little
cream-pitchers. There was a **man** in a boat, in the
sun, just disappearing in the distance around a
bend, lifting high his **arms, and** dipping his paddles,
as if he were a vision bound to the land of the
blessed, **far off as in** a picture. When I see Concord to purpose, I see **it as if** it were not real, but
painted; and **what wonder if I** do not speak to
thee ? "

And there was nothing **our** poet loved **or sang**
better, albeit **in prose, than the** early morning :—

> "Alone, despondent **? then art** thou alone,
> On some near hill-top, ere of **day** the orb
> In early summer tints the floating heaven,
> While sunk around thy sleeping race o'ershade
> With more oblivion their dim village-roofs.
>
> Alone ?   **Oh,** listen hushed !
> What living hymn awakes such studious air **?**
> **A** myriad **sounds that in** one song converge,
> **As the added light lifts the** far hamlet
> **Or** the distant wood.   **These** are the carols
> Of the unnumbered birds that drench the sphere
> With their prodigious harmony, prolonged
> And ceaseless, **so** that at **no** time it dies,
> Vanquishing the expectation with delay.
> Still crowding notes from the wild robin's **larum**
> In the walnut's bough, to the **veery's** flute,
> Who, from the inmost shades of the wet wood,
> His liquid lay rallies in martial trills.
> And mark the molten flecks fast on those skies ;
> They move not, musing on their rosy heights
> **In pure,** celestial radiance.
>
> Nor these forms,
> That chiefly must engross and ask thy praise.
> It is a startling theme, this **lovely** birth
> Each morn of a new day, **so wholly new,**
> So absolutely penetrated by itself, —
> This fresh, this sweet, this ever-living grace,
> This tender joy that still unstinted clothes
> An orb of beauty, of all bliss the abode.
> Cast off the night, unhinge the dream-clasped **brow,**
> Step freely forth, exulting in thy joy ;
> Launch off, and sip the dewy twilight time ;
> **Come ere** the last great stars have fled, ere dawn

> "Like a spirit seen, unveil the charm
> Of bosky wood, deep dell, or odorous plain;
> Ere, blazed with more than gold, some slow-drawn mist
> Retreats its distant arm from the cool meads."

As in the song, such a "getting up we never saw," our author sallying forth like Don Quixote, ere the stingiest farmer commenced milking his cow-yard cistern. All that he did was done with order due: the late walk came *out* at two in the morning, and the early one came on at the same crisis.

> "His drink the running stream, his cup the bare
> Of his palm closed, his bed the hard, cold ground."

Cleanness, punctuality, the observation of the law he truly followed. "Treat with the reverence due to age the elders of your own family, so that the elders in the families of others shall be similarly treated; treat with the kindness due to youth the young in your own family, so that the young in the families of others shall be similarly treated: do this, and the empire may be made to go round in your palm." He might have said, with Victor Hugo, "The finest of all altars is the soul of an unhappy man who is consoled, and thanks God. Nisi Dominus custodierit domum, in vanum vigilant qui custodiant eam (Unless God watches over our abode, they watch in vain who are set to keep it). Let us never fear robbers or murderers.

They are external and small dangers: let us
fear ourselves; prejudices are the true thefts,
vices the fatal murders." And his notions about
the privileges of real property remind us of the
park of King Van, which contained seventy square
le; but the grass-cutters and the fuel-gatherers
had the privilege of entrance. He shared it with
the people; and was it not with reason they
looked on it as small? Of every ten things he
knew, he had learned nine in conversation; and he
remembered that between friends frequent reproofs
lead to distance, and that in serving the neighbor
frequent remonstrances lead to disgrace. Nor did
he follow that old rule of the nuns, — Believe
Secular men little, Religious still less. He was
one of those men of education who, without a
certain livelihood, are able to maintain a fixed
pursuit.

"Thou **art not gone,** being gone, where'er thou **art:**
Thou leav'st **in us thy** watchful eyes, in **us thy** loving heart."

CHAPTER XII.

HIS WRITINGS.

"The dark-colored ivy and the untrodden grove of God, with its myriad fruits, sunless and without wind in all **storms;** where always the frenzied Dionysus dwells."— SOPHOCLES.

"When, like the stars, the singing angels shot
  To earth." GILES FLETCHER.

"Patience! why, 'tis the soul of peace,
It makes men look like gods! The best of men
That e'er wore earth about him was a Sufferer,
A soft, meek, patient, humble, tranquil spirit;
The first true gentleman that ever breathed."
DECKER.

" 'I know not' **is one word;** 'I know' is **ten words."**— CHINESE PROVERB.

"Friendship has passed me like a ship at sea."— FESTUS.

O NE of the objects of our poet-naturalist was to acquire the art of writing a good English style. So Goethe, that slow and artful formalist, spent himself in acquiring a good German style. And what Thoreau thought of this matter of writing may be learned from many passages in this sketch, and from this among the rest: "It is the fault of some excellent writers, and De Quincey's first impressions on seeing London suggest it to me, that they express themselves with too great fulness and detail. **They give the** most faithful, natural, **and** lifelike account **of their** sensations, mental **and** physical, but they lack moderation and sententiousness. They do not affect us as an ineffectual earnest, and a reserve of meaning, like a stutterer: they say all they mean. Their sentences are not concentrated and nutty, — sentences which suggest far more than they **say, which** have an atmosphere about them, which do not report an old, but make **a new** impression; sentences which suggest **on many things, and are as durable as a Roman aqueduct: to frame these, — that is the *art* of** writing. **Sentences which are expressive, towards which so** many **volumes, so much life, went; which lie like** boulders on **the** page **up and down, or across;** which contain the seed **of** other sentences, **not mere** repetition, but creation ; and which **a man might sell his** ground **or** cattle to build. De Quincey's **style is nowhere** kinked **or** knotted up into something **hard and significant, which you** could swallow **like a diamond, without** digesting.''

As **in the story, '' And that 's** Peg Woffington's **notion of an actress !** Better it, Cibber and Bracegirdle, **if you** can !'' This moderation **does, *for the most part*,** characterize his works, **both of prose and** verse. They have their stoical merits, their uncomfortableness ! It is one result to be lean and sacrificial, yet **a** balance **of** comfort and a house of freestone on the sunny side of Beacon Street can be endured in a manner by weak nerves. But the fact that our author lived for a while alone in a shanty near a pond or *stagnum*, and named one of his books after the place where it stood, has led some to say he was a barbarian or a misanthrope, — it was a writing-case : —

> " This, as an amber drop enwraps a bee,
>   Covering discovers your quick soul, that we
>   May in your through-shine front your heart's thoughts see."

Here, in this wooden inkstand, he wrote a good part of his famous " Walden ; " and this solitary woodland pool was more to his muse than all oceans of the planet, by the force of that faculty on which he was never weary of descanting, — Imagination. Without this, he says, human life, dressed in its Jewish or other gaberdine, would be a kind of lunatic's hospital, insane with the prose of it, mad with the drouth of society's remainder-biscuits ; but add the phantasy, that glorious, that divine gift, and then —

> " The earth, the air, and seas I know, and all
>   The joys and horrors of their peace and wars ;
>   And now will view the gods' state and the stars."

Out of this faculty was his written experience chiefly constructed, — upon this he lived ; not upon the cracked wheats and bread-fruits of an outward platter. His essays, those masterful creations, taking up the commonest topics, a sour apple, an autumn leaf, are features of this wondrous imagination of his; and, as it was his very life-blood, he, least of all, sets it forth in labored description. He did not bring **forward his** means, unlock **the closet of** his Maelzel's automaton chess-player. **The reader cares not that** the writer of a **novel, with two** lovers **in hand,** should walk out **on the** fool's-cap, and **begin balancing some peacock's** feather **on his** nose.

> " Begin, murderer, — **leave thy damnable** faces, and begin ! "

He loved antithesis in verse. **It** could **pass for** paradox, — something subtractive **and unsatisfactory,** as the four herrings provided by Caleb **Balderstone** for Ravenswood's dinner: come, **he says, let us see** how miserably uncomfortable we **can** feel. Hawthorne, too, enjoyed **a grave** and a pocket full of miseries to **nibble upon.**

In **his** discourse of **Friendship,** Thoreau starts with **the idea of "** *underpropping* **his** love by such pure **hate, that it would** *end* in sympathy," like sweet butter from sour cream. And in this : —

> " **Two** solitary stars, —
> Unmeasured systems far
> Between us roll ; "

getting off into the agonies of space, where every **thing freezes, yet adds as** inducement, —

> "But by our conscious light we are
>   Determined to one pole."

In other words, there was a pole apiece. He continues the antithesis, and says there is "no more use in friendship than in the tints of flowers" (the chief use in them), "pathless the gulf of feeling yawns," and the reader yawns, too, at the idea of tumbling into it. And so he "packs up in his mind all the clothes which outward nature wears," like a young lady's trunk going to Mount Desert.

We must not expect literature, in each case, to run its hands round the dial-plate of style with cuckoo repetition: the snarls he criticises De Quincey for not getting into are the places where *his* bundles of sweetmeats untie. As in the Vendidad, "Hail to thee, O man! who art come from the transitory place to the imperishable:"—

> "In Nature's nothing, be not nature's toy."

This feature in his style is by no means so much bestowed upon his prose as his poetry. In his verse he more than once attained to beauty, more often to quaintness. He did not court admiration, though he admired fame; and he might have said:

> "Whoe'er thou beest who read'st this sullen writ,
>   Which just so much courts thee as thou dost it."

He had an excellent turn of illustration. Speaking of the *débris* of Carnac, he says:—

> " Erect ourselves, and let those columns lie ;
>   If Carnac's columns still **stand on the** plain,
>   **To enjoy our opportunities they** remain."

The little Yankee squatting on Walden Pond was not deceived by an Egyptian stone **post, or sand heap. In another verse :** —

> " **When life** contracts into a **vulgar span,**
>   And human nature tires to **be a man,** —
>   Greece ! who am I that should remember thee ? "

And he let Greece slide.   At times he hangs **up old authors, in** the **blaze of a New** England noon.

> " Plutarch **was good, and so was Homer too,**
>   Our Shakespeare's **life was rich to live again ;**
>   What Plutarch read, that was **not good nor true,**
>   Nor Shakespeare's books, unless his books were men."

> " **Tell** Shakespeare to attend some leisure hour,
>   For now I 've business with this drop of dew."

He could drop Shakespeare ; and it were well if both **he and Dante were prescribed,** rather than poured **out of bath-tubs. Every** one must, however, admire **the** essay **of Mr. Brown on** the Bard **of Avon, and the** translation **of** Dante by Mr. **Black : neatness is** the elegance of **poverty.**

The following verses **are pretty, the** last line from Milton's " Penseroso," with the **change of a** syllable.   He did not fear to *collect* **a** good line any more than **a** good flower : —

RUMORS FROM AN ÆOLIAN HARP.

"There is a vale which none hath seen,
  Where foot of man has never been,
  Such as here lives with toil and strife,
  An anxious and a sinful life.

There every virtue has its birth,
  Ere it descends upon the earth,
  And thither every deed returns,
  Which in the generous bosom burns.

There love is warm, and youth is young,
  And poetry is yet unsung;
  For Virtue still adventures there,
  And freely breathes her native air.

And ever, if you hearken well,
  You still may hear its vesper bell,
  And tread of high-souled men go by,
  Their thoughts conversing with the sky."

He has no killing single shots, — *his* thoughts flowed.

"Be not the fowler's net,
    Which stays my flight,
  And craftily is set
    T' allure my sight.

But be the favoring gale
    That bears me on,
  And still doth fill my sail
    When thou art gone.

Some **tender buds** were left upon my **stem**
  In mimicry of life.
    .   .   .   .   .

Some tumultuous little rill,
  Purling round its storied pebble.
    .   .   .   .   .

Conscience is instinct bred in the house.
    .   .   .   .   .

Experienced river!
  Hast thou flowed for ever?"
    .   .   .   .   .

As an instance of his humor in verse: —

"I make ye an **offer**,
  Ye gods, hear the scoffer!
The scheme will not hurt you,
If ye will find goodness, I will find **virtue.**
I have pride still unbended,
And blood undescended;
I cannot toil blindly,
Though ye behave kindly,
And I swear by the rood
I 'll be slave to no god."

"Nature doth have her dawn each day, .
  But mine are far between;
Content, I cry, for sooth to say,
  Mine brightest are I ween.

For when my sun doth deign to rise,
  Though it be her noontide,
Her fairest field in shadow lies,
  Nor can my light abide.

> Through his discourse I climb and see,
>   As from some eastern hill,
> A brighter morrow rise to me
>   Than lieth in her skill.
>
> As 'twere two summer days in one,
>   Two Sundays come together,
> Our rays united make one sun,
>   With fairest summer weather."
>
> July 25th, 1839.

This date is for those who, unlike Alfieri, are by nature *not* almost destitute of curiosity; and the subject, Friendship, is for the like : —

> " For things that pass are past, and in this field
> The indeficient spring no winter flaws."

What subtlety and what greatness in those quartrains ! then how truly original, how vague ! His Pandora's box of a head carried all manner of sweets. No one would *guess* the theme, Yankee though he be. He has that richness : —

> " Looks as it is with some true April day,
> Whose various weather strews the world with flowers."

As he well affirms, if it be applied antithetically, a man cannot wheedle nor overawe his genius. Nothing was ever so unfamiliar and startling to a man as his own thoughts. To the rarest genius it is the most expensive to succumb and conform to the ways of the world. It is the worst of lumber if the poet wants to float upon the breeze of popularity. The bird of paradise is obliged constantly to **fly** against the wind. The poet is no tender slip of fairy stock, but the toughest son of earth and of heaven. He will prevail to be popular in spite of his faults, **and** in spite of his beauties too. He makes us free of his hearth and heart, which is greater than to offer us the freedom of a city. Orpheus does not hear the strains which issue from his lyre, but only those which are breathed into it. The poet will write for his peers alone. He never whispers in a private ear. The true poem is not that which the public read. His true work will not stand in any prince's gallery.

> " My life has been the poem I would **have writ,**
> **But I could not** both live and utter it.
>
> .　　.　　.　　.　　.
>
> I hearing get, who had but ears,
> And sight, who had but eyes before.
> I moments live, who lived but years,
> **And·truth discern, who** knew **but** learning's lore."

He has this bit of modesty : —

THE POET'S DELAY.

> " **In vain I see** the morning **rise,**
> In vain **observe the** western blaze,
> Who idly look to other skies,
> Expecting life by other ways.
>
> Amidst such boundless wealth without,
> I only still am poor within,

> The birds have sung their summer out,
>   But still my spring does not begin.
>
> Shall I then wait the autumn wind,
>   Compelled to seek a milder day,
> And leave no curious nest behind,
>   No woods still echoing to my lay."

Again he asks, " Shall I not have words as fresh as my thought ? Shall I use any other man's word ? A genuine thought or feeling would find expression for itself, if it had to invent hieroglyphics. I perceive that Shakespeare and Milton did not foresee into what company they were to fall. To say that God has given a man many and great talents, frequently means that he has brought his heavens down within reach of his hands." He sometimes twanged a tune of true prose on the strings of his theorbo, as where, instead of Cowper's church-going bell, he flatly says : —

> "Dong sounds the brass in the east,"

which will pass for impudence with our United Brethren. It is difficult to comprehend his aloofness from these affectionate old symbols, drawling out from the sunshiny past, and without which our New England paradise is but a " howling wilderness," although he loves the *echo* of the meeting-house brass. It is his species of paradoxical quintessence. He draws a village : " it has a meeting-house and **horse-sheds, a** tavern and **a black-** smith's shop **for centre, and a** good deal of **wood to cut and cord yet."**

> "A man that looks on glass,
> **On it** may stay his eye ;
> **Or, if** he pleaseth, **through it pass,**
> And the heavens espy."

His notions of institutions **were like his views of sepulchres.** Another **has said, " It is** my business **to rot** dead **leaves,"** symbolizing **a** character working **like water. " A** man might **well** pray that he **may not taboo or curse** any portion **of nature by** being **buried in it. It is,** therefore, much **to the** credit **of** Little **John, the famous** follower of **Robin** Hood, that **his grave was ' long celebrous for the** yielding **of excellent whetstones.' Nothing but great** antiquity can make grave-yards **interesting to me. I** have no friends there. The **farmer who has** skimmed his farm might perchance leave his body **to nature** to be ploughed in. **' And** the king **seide, What is the** biriel which **I** se ? And the citeseynes **of that cite answeride to** him, It is the sepulchre of **the man of God** that cam fro Juda.' "

He makes us a photograph of style, which touches some of **his** chief strength. " There is a sort of homely truth and naturalness in some books which is very rare to find, and yet looks cheap enough. Homeliness is almost **as** great a merit in a book as **in a house, if the** reader would abide there. It is next to beauty, and a very high art. Some have this merit only. Very few men can speak of Nature, for instance, with any truth. They overstep her modesty, somehow or other, and confer no favor. They do not speak a good word for her. The surliness with which the wood-chopper speaks of his woods, handling them as indifferently as his axe, is better than the mealy-mouthed enthusiasm of the lover of nature." So Philina cried, " Oh! that I might never hear more of nature and scenes of nature! When the day is bright you go to walk, and to dance when you hear a tune played. But who would think a moment on the music or the weather? It is the dancer that interests us, and not the violin; and to look upon a pair of bright black eyes is the life of a pair of blue ones. But what on earth have we to do with wells and brooks and old rotten lindens?

> " I sing but as the linnet sings,
>   That on the green bough dwelleth;
> A rich reward his music brings,
>   As from his throat it swelleth:
> Yet might I ask, I 'd ask of thine
> One sparkling draught of purest wine,
>   To drink it here before you."

> He viewed the wine, he quaffed it up:
>   " Oh! draught of sweetest savor!
> Oh! happy house, where such a cup
>   Is thought a little favor!

> If well you fare, remember me,
> And thank kind Heaven, from envy free,
>   As now for this I thank you."

Goethe never signed the temperance-pledge: **no more** did Thoreau, but he drank **the kind** of wine " which never grew in **the** belly **of the grape,**" but in that **of the corn.** He was made more dry by drink-**ing.** These affections were **a** kind of *résumé*, or in-fant thanatopsis, sharp on both **edges.** Yet, in spite of this abundant moderation, he says, " I trust that you realize what an exaggerator I am, — that **I lay myself** out to exaggerate whenever I have an **oppor-**tunity, — pile Pelion upon Ossa, to reach heaven **so.** Expect no trivial truth from me, unless I am on **the** witness stand. I will come as near **to lying as you** will drive a coach-and-four. **If it isn**'t thus and so with me, it is with something.**"** As for writing **letters,** he mounts above prose. " Methinks I will write to you. Methinks you will be glad to hear. We will **stand on** solid foundations to one another, — I **am a column planted on** this shore, you on that. **We meet the same** sun in his rising. We were built slowly, and have come **to our** bearing. **We** will not mutually fall **over** that we may meet, **but** will grandly and eternally guard the straits."

> " My life is like a stroll upon the beach, —
> I have but few companions by the shore.
>
>   .   .   .   .   .

> Go where he will, the wise man is at home ;
> His hearth the earth, his hall the azure dome ;
> Where his clear spirit leads him, there 's his road."

The well-known speech to his large and respectable circle of acquaintance beyond the mountains is a pretty night-piece. " **Greeting : My** most serene and irresponsible **neighbors, let us see that we have the whole** advantage of **each** other. **We will be useful, at least, if not admirable to one another.** I know **that the mountains which** separate us are **high,** and covered with perpetual snow ; but despair **not. Improve the serene** weather **to scale** them. If need **be, soften the** rocks with vinegar. For here lies the verdant plain of **Italy ready to** receive you. Nor shall I be slow **on my** side **to penetrate** to your Provence. **Strike** then boldly **at** head or heart, or any **vital part.** Depend upon it the timber **is well seasoned and** tough, and will bear **rough usage ;** and if it should crack, there is plenty more **where it** came from. I am no piece of crockery, that cannot be jostled against my neighbor without **being in** danger **of being broken** by the collision, **and must** needs ring false **and** jarringly to the end of my **days when once I** am cracked, **but** rather one of **the** old-fashioned wooden trenchers, which **one while stands** at **the head of the** table, and at **another is a** milking-stool, and **at** another **a** seat **for children ; and, finally, goes down to its grave** not unadorned with honorable scars, and does not die till it is worn out. Nothing can shock a brave man but dulness. Think how many rebuffs every man has experienced in his day, — perhaps has fallen into a horse-pond, eaten fresh-water clams, or worn one shirt for a week without washing. Indeed, you cannot receive a shock, unless you have an electric affinity for that which shocks you. Use me, then ; for I am useful in my way, and stand as one of many petitioners, — from toadstool and henbane up to dahlia and violet, — supplicating to be put to any use, if by any means you may find me serviceable : whether for a medicated drink or bath, as balm and lavender ; or for fragrance, as verbena and geranium ; or for sight, as cactus; or for thoughts, as pansy. These humbler, at least, if not those higher uses." So good a writer should

> "live
> Upon the alms of his superfluous praise."

He was choice in his words. " All these sounds," says he, " the crowing of cocks, the baying of dogs, and the hum of insects at noon, are the evidence of nature's health or *sound* state." For so learned a man he spared his erudition ; neither did he, as one who was no mean poet, use lines like these to celebrate his clearness : —

> " Who dares upbraid these open rhymes of mine
> With blindfold Aquines, or darke Venusine ?

> Or rough-hewn Teretisius, writ in th' antique vain
> Like an old satire, and new Flaccian?
> Which who reads thrice, and rubs his ragged brow,
> And deep indenteth every doubtful row,
> Scoring the margent with his blazing stars,
> And hundredth crooked interlinears
> (Like to a merchant's debt-roll new defaced,
> When some crack'd Manour cross'd his book at last),
> Should all in rage the curse-beat page out-rive,
> And in each dust-heap bury me alive."

There are so few obscurities in Thoreau's writing, that the uneasy malevolence of ephemeral critics has not discovered enough to cite, and his style has that ease and moderateness he appears to taste.

He had the sense of humor, and in one place indulges himself in some Latin fun, where he names the wild apples, creatures of his fancy. "There is, first of all, the wood-apple, *Malus sylvatica;* the blue-jay apple; the apple which grows in dells in the woods, *sylvestrivallis;* also in hollows in pastures, *campestrivallis;* the apple that grows in an old cellar-hole, *Malus cellaris;* the meadow-apple; the partridge-apple; the truants' apple, *cessatoris;* the saunterer's apple, — you most lose yourself before you can find the way to that; the beauty of the air, *decus aeris;* December-eating; the frozen-thawed, *gelato-soluta;* the brindled apple; wine of New England; the chickaree apple; the green apple, — this has many synonymes; in its perfect state it is the *Cholera morbifera aut* **dysente-** **rifera,** *puerulis* **dilectissima ;** the hedge-apple, **Ma-** **lus sepium ;** the slug apple, *limacea ;* the apple whose fruit we tasted in our youth ; our particular **apple, not** to be found in any catalogue, *pedestrium solatium,*" and many others. His **love of this sour** vegetable **is** characteristic : **it is the wild flavor,** the acidity, the difficulty of eating it, which pleased. To no gastronomic societies Thoreau appertained, unless drawn there by the butt. The lover of gravy, the justice lined with capon, apoplectic professors in purple skulls who reckon water a nuisance, **never** loved his **pen** that praised poverty : " Quid est paupertas ? odibile bonum, sanitatis **mater,** curarum remotio, absque sollicitudine semita, **sa-** pientiæ reparatrix, negotium sine damno, intracta- bilis substantia, possessio absque calumnia, incerta fortuna, sine sollicitudine felicitas." *

Or in what he names complemental verses : —

> " Thou dost presume too much, **poor needy** wretch,
>   **To claim a station in the firmament,**
>   Because **thy** humble cottage, **or thy tub,**
>   Nurses **some lazy** or pedantic virtue,
>   With roots and pot-herbs.   **We, more high, advance**
>   **Such** virtues only as admit excess, —
>   **Brave,** bounteous acts, regal magnificence

* **A free** rendition : " What is poverty ? Kerosene lamps, tak- ing tea out, **Dalley's** pain-killer, horse-cars, scolding help, book- **seller's accounts, modern** rubber boots, what nobody discounts, the **next tax-bill,** sitting in your minister's pew."

> All-seeing prudence, magnanimity
> That knows no bound, and that heroic virtue
> For which antiquity hath left no name,
> But patterns only, such as Hercules,
> Achilles, Theseus ; — back to thy loath'd cell ! "

He had that pleasant art of convertibility, by which he could render the homely strains of Nature into homely verse and prose, holding yet the flavor of their immortal origins ; while meagre and barren writers upon science do perhaps intend to describe that quick being of which they prose, yet never loose a word of happiness or humor. The art of describing realities, and imparting to them a touch of human nature, is something comfortable. A few bits of such natural history as this follow : —

" A hornets'-nest I discovered in a rather tall huckleberry-bush, the stem projecting through it, the leaves spreading over it. How these fellows avail themselves of these vegetables ! They kept arriving, the great fellows (with white abdomens), but I never saw whence they came, but only heard the buzz just at the entrance. At length, after I had stood before the nest for five minutes, during which time they had taken no notice of me, two seemed to be consulting at the entrance, and then made a threatening dash at me, and returned to the nest. I took the hint and retired. They spoke as plainly as man could have done. I examined this nest again : I found no hornets buzzing about ; the

entrance seemed to have been enlarged, so I con-
cluded it had been deserted, but looking nearer I
discovered two or three dead hornets, men-of-war,
in the entry-way. Cutting off the bushes which
sustained it, I proceeded to open it with my knife.
It was an inverted cone, eight or nine inches by
seven or eight. First, there were half-a-dozen lay-
ers of waved, brownish paper resting loosely over
one another, occupying nearly an inch in thickness,
for a covering. Within were the six-sided cells, in
three stories, suspended from the roof and from one
another by one or two suspension-rods only; the
lower story much smaller than the rest. And in
what may be called the attic or garret of the structure were two live hornets partially benumbed
with cold. It was like a deserted castle of the
Mohawks, a few dead ones at the entrance to the
fortress. The prinos berries (*Prinos verticillatus*)
are quite red; the dogwood has lost every leaf, its
bunches of dry, greenish berries hanging straight
down from the bare stout twigs, as if their pedun-
cles were broken. It has assumed its winter aspect,— a Mithridatic look. The black birch (*Betula
lenta*) is straw-colored, the witch-hazel (*Hamamelis
Virginica*) is now in bloom. I perceive the fragrance of ripe grapes in the air. The little conical
burrs of the agrimony stick to my clothes; the pale
lobelia still blooms freshly, and the rough hawk-

weed holds up its globes of yellowish fuzzy seeds,
as well as the panicled. The declining sun falling
on the willows and on the water produces a rare,
soft light I do not often see, — a greenish-yellow.

> " Thus, perchance, **the Indian hunter,**
>   Many a lagging year agone,
>   Gliding o'er thy rippling waters,
>   Lowly **hummed** a natural **song.**

> **"Now the** sun 's behind the willows,
>   **Now he** gleams along the waves,
>   Faintly o'er the wearied billows
>   **Come the spirits of the braves.**

" The reach **of the river** between Bedford **and**
Carlisle, seen from a distance, has a **strangely ethe-**
real, celestial, **or elysian** look. It is of a light sky-
blue, alternating with smoother white **streaks, where**
the surface reflects the light differently, like **a milk-**
pan full of the milk of Valhalla partially **skimmed,**
more gloriously **and heavenly fair and pure** than
the sky itself. We have names **for the rivers** of
hell, but none for **the** rivers **of heaven, unless** the
Milky Way may be one. It **is such a smooth and**
shining **blue,** like a panoply of **sky-blue plates, —**

> ' **Sug'ring all** dangers with **success.'**

" Fairhaven **pond, seen from the** cliffs in the
moonlight, is a sheeny lake of apparently a boundless primitive forest, untrodden by man ; the windy

surf sounding freshly and wildly in the single pine behind you, the silence of hushed wolves in the wilderness, and, as you fancy, moose looking off from the shores of the lake ; the stars of poetry and history and unexplored nature looking down on the scene. This light and this hour takes the civilization all out of the landscape. Even at this time in the evening (8 P.M.) the crickets chirp and the small birds peep, the wind roars in the wood, as if it were just before dawn. The landscape is flattened into mere light and shade, from the least elevation. A field of ripening corn, now at night, that has been topped, with the stalks stacked up, has an inexpressibly dry, sweet, rich ripening scent: I feel as I were an ear of ripening corn myself. Is not the whole air a compound of such odors indistinguishable ? drying corn-stalks in a field, what an herb garden ! What if one moon has come and gone with its world of poetry, so divine a creature freighted with its hints for me, and I not use them."

He loved the πολυφλοίσβοιο θαλάσσης, the noisy sea, and has left a pleasant sketch of his walks along the beach ; but he never attempted the ocean passage. The shore at Truro, on Cape Cod, which he at one time frequented, has been thus in part described.

A little Hamlet hid away from men,

Spoil for no painter's eye, no poet's pen,

Modest as some brief flower, concealed, obscure,
It nestles on the high and echoing shore;
Yet here I found I was a welcome guest,
At generous Nature's hospitable feast.
The barren moors no fences girdled high,
The endless beaches planting could defy,
And the blue sea admitted all the air,
A cordial draught, so sparkling and so rare.

The aged widow in her cottage lone,
Of solitude and musing patient grown,
Could let me wander o'er her scanty fields,
And pick the flower that contemplation yields.
This vision past, and all the rest was mine, —
The gliding vessel on the ocean's line,
That left the world wherein my senses strayed,
Yet long enough her soft good-by delayed
To let my eye engross her beauty rare,
Kissed by the seas, an infant of the air.
Thou, too, wert mine, the green and curling wave,
Child of the sand, a playful child and brave;
Urged on the gale, the crashing surges fall;
The zephyr breathes, how softly dances all!

Dread ocean-wave! some eyes look out o'er thee
And fill with tears, and ask, Could such things be?
Why slept the All-seeing Heart when death was near?
Be hushed each doubt, assuage thy throbbing fear!
Think One who made the sea and made the wind
Might also feel for our lost human kind;
And they who sleep amid the surges tall
Summoned great Nature to their funeral,

> And she obeyed.   We fall not far from shore;
> The sea-bird's wail, the surf, our loss deplore;
> The melancholy main goes sounding on
> His world-old anthem o'er our horizon.

As Turner was in the habit of adding what *he* thought explanatory verses to his landscapes, so it may be said of some books, besides the special sub-ject treated they are *diversified* with quotations. Thoreau adhered closely to his topic, yet in his " Week" as many as a hundred authors are quoted, and there are more than three hundred passages either cited or touched upon.   In fact, there are some works that have rather a peculiar value for literary gentry, like Pliny, Montaigne, and Burton's Anat-omy of Melancholy, upon which last work it was the opinion of Lord Byron many authors had con-structed a reputation.

A list follows of the writings of Thoreau, as they appeared chronologically.   These have been since printed in separate volumes, if they did not so appear at first (with few exceptions), under the titles of " Excursions, 1863," " The Maine Woods, 1864," " A Yankee in Canada, 1866," " Cape Cod, 1865," and in addition a volume of letters, 1865. These works were printed in Boston : —

A WALK TO WACHUSETT. — In the " Boston Miscellany."
IN THE DIAL. — 1840–1844 : —

> Vol. I. — Sympathy.   Aulus Persius Flaccus.   **Nature doth have her dawn each day.**

Vol. II. — Sic Vita. Friendship.

Vol. III. — Natural History of Massachusetts. In "Prayers," the passage beginning "Great God." The Black Knight. The Inward Morning. Free Love. The Poet's Delay. Rumors from an Æolian Harp. The Moon. To the Maiden in the East. The Summer Rain. The Laws of Menu. Prometheus Bound. Anacreon. To a Stray Fowl. Orphics. Dark Ages.

Vol. IV. — A Winter Walk. Homer, Ossian, Chaucer. Pindar. Fragments of Pindar. Herald of Freedom.

In the Democratic Review, 1843. — The Landlord. Paradise (to be) Regained.

In Graham's Magazine, 1847. — Thomas Carlyle and his Works.

In the Union Magazine. — Ktaadn and the Maine Woods.

In Æsthetic Papers. — Resistance to Civil Government.

A Week on the Concord and Merrimac Rivers. Boston: James Monroe and Company, 1849.

In Putnam's Magazine. — Excursion to Canada (in part). Cape Cod (in part).

Walden. Boston: Ticknor and Company, 1854.

In the Liberator. — Speech at Framingham, July 4th, 1854. Reminiscences of John Brown (read at North Elba, July 4th, 1860).

In "Echoes from Harper's Ferry." — 1860. Lecture on John Brown, and Remarks at Concord on the day of his execution.

In the Atlantic Monthly, 1859. — Chesuncook, 1862. Walking. Autumnal Tints. Wild Apples.

In the N. Y. Tribune. — The Succession of Forest Trees (also printed in the Middlesex Agricultural Transactions). 1860.

"Nihil mihi rescribas, attamen ipse veni."

CHAPTER XIII.

PERSONALITIES.

"If great men wrong me, I will spare myself;
If mean, I will spare them." — DONNE.

"As soon as generals are dismembered and distributed into parts, they become so much attenuated as in a manner to disappear; wherefore the terms by which they are expressed undergo the same attenuation, and seem to vanish and fall." — SWEDENBORG.

"The art of overturning states is to discredit established customs, by looking into their origin, and pointing out that it was defective in authority and justice." — PASCAL.

"Adspice murorum moles, præruptque saxa,
Obrutaque horrenti vasta theatra situ,
Haec sunt Roma.   Viden' velut ipsa cadavera tantæ
Urbis adhuc spirent imperiosa minas." — JANUS VITALIS.

OUR author's life can be divided in three parts: first, to the year 1837, when he left college; next, to the publishing of his "Week," in 1849 (ten years after his excursion up the Merrimac River, of which that work treats); and the remainder of his doings makes the third. It was after he had graduated from Alma Mater that he began to embalm his thoughts in a diary, and not till many years' practice did they assume a systematic shape. This same year (1837) brought him into relation

11   P

with a literary man, by which his mind may have
been first soberly impregnated with that love of
letters that after accompanied him, but of whom
he was no servile copyist. He had so wisely been
nourished at the collegiate fount as to come forth
undissipated ; not digging his grave in tobacco and
coffee, — those two perfect causes of paralysis.
"I have a faint recollection of pleasure derived
from smoking dried lily-stems before I was a man.
I have never smoked any thing more noxious."
His school-keeping was a nominal occupancy of his
time for a couple of years ; and he soon began to
serve the mistress to whom he was afterward
bound, and to sing the immunity of Pan. Some
long-anticipated excursion set the date upon the
year, and furnished its materials for the journal.
And at length, in 1842, he printed in a fabulous
quarterly, "The Dial," a paper ; and again, in
1843, came out "The Walk to Wachusett," a
bracing revival of exhilarating thoughts caught
from the mountain atmosphere. In this same
came the poems before commented upon, and it
afforded him sufficient space to record his pious
hopes and sing the glories of the world he habitually admired. With the actual publication of the
"Week," at his own expense, and which cost him
his labor for several years to defray, begins a new
era, — he is introduced to a larger circle and

launches forth his paper nautilus, well pleased to eye its thin and many-colored ribs shining in the watery sunshine. His early friends and readers never failed, and others increased ; thus was he rising in literary fame, —

> " That like a wounded snake drags its slow length along."

Then came the log-book of his woodland cruise at Walden, his critical articles upon Thomas Carlyle and others ; and he began to appear as a lecturer, with a theory, as near as he could have one. He was not to try to suit his audience, but consult the prompting of his genius and suit himself. If a demand was made for a lecture, he would gratify it so far as in him lay, but he could not descend from the poetry of insight to the incubation of prose. Lecture committees at times failed to see the prophetic god, and also the statute-putty. " Walden " increased his repute as a writer, if some great men thought him bean-dieted, with an owl for his minister, and who milked creation, not the cow. It is in vain for the angels to contend against stupidity.

He began to take more part in affairs, the Anti-slavery crisis coming to the boil in 1857. Captain John Brown, after of Harper's Ferry, was in Con-cord that year, and had talk with Thoreau, who knew nothing of his revolutionary plans. He shot off plenty of coruscating abolition rockets at Framingham and elsewhere, and took his chance in preaching at those animated free-churches which pushed from the rotting compost of the Southern hot-bed. At Worcester he is said to have read a damaging-institution lecture upon "Beans," that has never got to print. He carried more guns at these irritable reform meetings, which served as a discharge-pipe for the virus of all the regular scolds, as he did not spatter by the job. At the time of Sims's rendition he offered to his townsmen that the revolutionary monument should be thickly coated with black paint as a symbol of that dismal treason. He, too, had the glory of speaking the first public good word for Captain John Brown after his attack upon the beast run for the American plate,—that Moloch entered by Jeff. Davis and backers. In three years more the United States, that killed instead of protecting bold Ossawatomie, was enlisting North Carolina slaves to fight against Virginia slaveholders.

It must be considered the superior and divine event of his human experience when that famed hero of liberty forced the serpent of slavery from its death-grasp on the American Constitution. John Brown "expected to endure hardness;" and this was the expectation and fruition of Thoreau, naturally and by his culture. His was a more sour

and saturnine hatred of injustice, his life was more
passive, and he lost the glory of action which fell
to the lot of Brown. He had nought in his
thoughts of which a plot could spin; neither did he
believe in civil government, or that form of police
against the Catiline or Cæsar who has ready a
coup d'état, such as the speckled Napoleonic egg,
now addled, that was laid in Paris. Thoreau
worshipped a hero in a mortal disguise, under the
shape of that homely son of justice: his pulses
thrilled and his hands involuntarily clenched together at the mention of Captain Brown, at whose
funeral in Concord he said a few words, and prepared a version of Tacitus upon Agricola, some
lines of which are furnished: —

" You, Agricola, are fortunate, not only because
your life was glorious, but because your death was
timely. As they tell us who heard your last words,
unchanged and willing you accepted your fate.
. . . Let us honor you by our admiration, rather
than by short-lived praises; and, if Nature aid us,
by our emulation of you." He had before said:
" When I now look over my common-place book of
poetry, I find that the best of it is oftenest appli-
cable, in part or wholly, to the case of Captain
Brown. The sense of grand poetry, read by the
light of this event, is brought out distinctly like
an invisible writing held to the fire. As Marvell
wrote: —

> 'When the sword glitters o'er the judge's head,
>   And fear has coward churchmen silenced,
>   Then is the poet's time ; 'tis then he draws,
>   And single fights forsaken virtue's cause :
>   Sings still of ancient rights and better times,
>   Seeks suffering good, arraigns successful crimes.'

"And George Chapman : —

> 'There is no danger to a man who knows
>   What life and death is ; there 's not any law
>   Exceeds his knowledge.'

"And Wotton : —

> 'Who hath his life from rumors freed,
>   Of hope to rise or fear to fall ;
>   Lord of himself, though not of lands,
>   And having nothing, yet hath all.' "

The foundation of his well-chosen attainment in Modern and Classic authors dates from the origin of his literary life. In college he studied only what was best, and made it the rule. He could say to young students : " *Begin with the best !* start with what is so, never deviate." That part of American history he studied was pre-pilgrim : the Jesuit relations, early New England authors, Wood, Smith, or Josselyn, afforded him cordial entertainment. Henry's Travels, Lewis and Clark, and such books, he knew remarkably well, and thought no one had written better accounts of things and made them more living than Goethe in his letters from Italy.

Alpine and sea-side plants he admired, besides

those of his own village : of the latter, he mostly
attended willows, golden-rods, asters, polygonums,
sedges, and grasses ; fungi and lichens he somewhat affected.   He was accustomed to date the
day of the month by the appearance of certain flowers, and thus visited special plants for a series of
years, in order to form an average ; as his white-
thorn by Tarbell's Spring, " good for to-morrow, if
not for to-day."   The bigness of noted trees, the
number of rings, the degree of branching by which
their age may be drawn, the larger forests, such as
that princely " Inches Oak-wood " in West Acton,
or Wetherbee's patch, he paid attentions to.   Here
he made his cards, and left more than a pack ; his
friends were surely disengaged, unless they had cut
off.   He could sink down in the specific history
of a woodland by learning what trees now occupied the soil.   In some seasons he bored a variety of forest trees, when the sap was amiable, and
made his black-birch and other light wines.   He
tucked plants away in his soft hat in place of a bot-
any-box.   His study (a place in the garret) held its
dry miscellany of botanical specimens ; its corner of
canes, its cases of eggs and lichens, and a weight
of Indian arrow-heads and hatchets, besides a store
of nuts, of which he was as fond as squirrels.
" Man comes out of his winter quarters in March
as lean as a woodchuck."

In the varieties of tracks he was a philologist, and read that-primeval language, and studied the snow for them, as well as for its wonderful blue and pink colors, and its floccular deposits as it melts. He saw that hunter's track who always steps *before* you come. Ice in all its lines and polish he peculiarly admired. From Billerica Falls to Saxonville ox-bow, thirty miles or more, he sounded the deeps and shallows of the Concord River, and put down in his tablets that he had such a feeling. Gossamer was a shifting problem, beautifully vague: —

> " A ceaseless glimmering near the ground betrays
> The gossamer, its tiny thread is waving past,
> Borne on the wind's faint breath, and to yon branch,
> Tangled and trembling, clings like snowy silk."

Insects were fascinating, from the first gray little moth, the *perla*, born in February's deceitful glare, and the "fuzzy gnats" that people the gay sunbeams, to the last luxuriating *Vanessa antiope*, that gorgeous purple-velvet butterfly somewhat wrecked amid November's champaign breakers. He sought for and had honey-bees in the close spathe of the marsh-cabbage, when the eye could detect no opening of the same; water-bugs, skaters, carrion beetles, devil's-needles ("the French call them *demoiselles*, the artist loves to paint them, and paint must be cheap"); the sap-green, glittering, irridescent cicindelas, those lively darlings of Newbury sandbanks and Professor Peck, he lingered over as heaven's never-to-be-repainted Golconda. Hornets, wasps, bees, and spiders, and their several nests, he carefully attended. The worms and caterpillars, washed in the spring-freshets from the meadow-grass, filled his soul with hope at the profuse vermicular expansion of Nature. The somersaults of the caracoling stream were his vital pursuit, which, slow as it appears, now and then jumps up three feet in the sacred ash-barrel of the peaceful cellar. Hawks, ducks, sparrows, thrushes, and migrating warblers, in all their variety, he carefully perused with his field-glass,— an instrument purchased with toilsome discretion, and carried in its own strong case and pocket. Thoreau named all the birds without a gun, a weapon he never used in mature years. He neither killed nor imprisoned any animal, unless driven by acute needs. He brought home a flying squirrel, to study its mode of flight, but quickly carried it back to the wood.

He possessed true instincts of topography, and could conceal choice things in the brush and find them again, unlike Gall, who commonly lost his locality and himself, as he tells us, when in the wood, master as he was in playing on the organ. If he needed a box on his walk, he would strip a piece of birch-bark off the tree, fold it when cut straightly together, and put his tender lichen or

11*

brittle creature therein. In those irritable thunder-claps which come, he says, "with tender, graceful violence," he sometimes erected a transitory house by means of his pocket-knife, rapidly paring away the white-pine and oak, taking the lower limbs of a large tree and pitching on the cut brush for a roof. Here he sat, pleased with the minute drops from off the eaves, not questioning the love of electricity for trees. If out on the river, haul up your boat, turn it upside-down, and yourself under it. Once he was thus doubled up, when Jove let drop a pattern thunderbolt in the river in front of his boat, while he whistled a lively air as accompaniment. This is noted, as he was much distressed by storms when young, and used to go whining to his father's room, and say, "I don't feel well," and then take shelter in the paternal arms, when his health improved.

> "His little son into his bosom creeps,
>   The lovely image of his father's face."

. While walking in the woods, he delighted to give the falling leaves as much noise and rustle as he could, all the while singing some cheerful stave, thus celebrating the pedestrian's service to Pan as well as to the nymphs and dryads, who never live in a dumb asylum.

> " The squirrel chatters merrily,
>   The nut falls ripe and brown,

> And, gem-like, from the jewelled tree
> The leaf comes fluttering down ;
> And, restless in his plumage gay,
> From bush to bush loud screams the jay."

Nothing pleased him better than our native vintage days, when the border of the meadows becomes a rich plantation, whose gathering has been described in the lines that follow : —

WILD GRAPES.

"Bring me some grapes," she cried, "some clusters
     bring,
Herbert, with large flat leaves, the purple founts."
Then answering he, — "Ellen, if in the days
When on the river's bank hang ripely o'er
The tempting bunches red, and fragrance fills
The clear September air, if then" — "Ah! then,"
Broke in the girl, — "then" —

                    September coming,
Herbert, the day of all those sun-spoiled days
Quite petted by him most, wishing to choose,
Alone set off for the familiar bank
Of the blue river, nor to Ellen spake ;
That thing of moods long since forgetting all
Request or promise floating o'er the year.
On his right arm a white ash basket swung,
Its depth a promise of its coming stores ;
While the fair boy, o'ertaking in his thought
Those tinted bubbles, the best lover's game,
Sped joyous on through the clear mellowing day.
At length he passed Fairhaven's cliff, whose front

Shuts in this curve of shore, and soon he sees
The harvest-laden vine.

                        Large hopes were his,
And with a bounding step he leaped along
O'er the close cranberry-beds, his trusty foot
Oft lighting on the high elastic tufts
Of the promiscuous sedge.   Alas, for hope,
As some deliberate hand those vines had picked
By most subtracting rule! yet on the youth
More eager sprang, dreaming of prizes rare.
To the blue river's floor fell the green marsh,
And a white mountain cloud-range slowly touched
The infinite zenith of September's heaven.
" I have you now!" cried Herbert, tearing through
The envious thorny thicket to the vines,
Crushing the alder sticks, where rustling leaves
Conceal the rolling stones and wild-rose stems,
And always in the cynic cat-briar pricked.
" I have you now!"

                        And rarely on the scope
Of bold adventurer, British or Spaniard,
Loomed Indian coasts till then a poet's dream,
More glad to them than this Etruscan vase
On his rash eyes, reward of hope deferred.
There swum before him in the magic veil
Of that soft shimmering autumn afternoon,
On the black speckled alders, on the ground,
On leaf and pebble flat or round, the light
Of purple grapes, purple or bloomed,
And the few saintly bunches Muscat-white!

Nor Herbert paused, nor looked at half his wealth,
As in his wild delight he grasped a bunch,
And till his fingers burst still grasped a bunch,
Heaping the great ash basket till its cave
No further globe could hold.   And then he stopped,
And from a shrivelled stub picked off three grapes,
Those which he ate.

                        'Tis right he wreathe about
This heaped and purple spoil that he has robbed
Those fresh unfrosted leaves green in the shade,
And then he weighs upon his hand the prize
And springs, — the Atlas on his nervous arm.
Now buried 'neath the basket Herbert sunk,
Or seemed, and showers of drops tickled his cheeks,
Yet with inhuman nerve he struggles on.
At times the boy, half fainting in his march,
Saw twirl in coils the river at his feet,
Reflecting madly the still woods and hills,
The quiet cattle painted on the pool
In far-off pastures, and the musing clouds
That scarcely sailed, or seemed to sail, at all.
Till the strong shadows soothed the ruby trees
To one autumnal black, how hot the toil,
With glowing cheeks coursed by the exacted tide,
Aching yet eager, resolute to win,
Nor leave a berry though his shoulder snap.

Within the well-known door his tribute placed,
A fragrance of Italian vineyards leagued
The dear New English farm-house with sweet shores
In spicy archipelagoes of gold,

Where the sun cannot set, but fades to moonlight,
And tall maids support amphoras on their brows.

And Ellen ran, all Hebe, down the stair
Almost at one long step, and while the youth still stood,
And wonder stricken how he reached that door,
She cried, "Dear mother, fly and see this world of
  grapes."
Then Herbert puffed two seconds, and went in.

And much fresh enjoyment he would have felt in the observing wisdom of that admirably endowed flower-writer, Annie S. Downs, a child of Concord (the naturalist's heaven), full of useful knowledge, and with an out-of-doors heart like his; a constant friend to flowers, ferns, and mosses, with an affectionate sympathy, and a taste fine and unerring reflected by the exquisite beings she justly celebrates. Must she not possess a portion of the snowdrop's prophecy herself as to her writings and this world's winter? when she says: —

> 'The tender Snowdrop, erect and brave,
>   Gayly sprang from her snow-strewn bed.
> She doubted not there was sunshine warm
>   To welcome her shrinking head;
> The graceful curves of her slender stem,
>   The sheen of her petals white,
> As looking across the bank of snow
>   She shone like a gleam of light."

Annie S. Downs and Alfred B. Street, *native American* writers in the original packages, not extended by the critics,— writers, under the providence of God, to be a blessing to those who love His works, like Thoreau!

On being asked of a future world and its rewards and punishments, by a bore, he said, " Those were voluntaries I did not take," and he did not bite at a clergyman's skilfully baited hook of immortality, of which he said could be *no* doubt. He spoke of the reserved meaning in the insect metamorphosis of the moth, painted like the summer sunrise, that makes its escape from a loathsome worm, and cheats the wintry shroud, its chrysalis. One sweet hour of spring, gazing into a grassy-bottomed pool, where the insect youth were disporting, the *gyrinæ* (boat flies) darting, and tadpoles beginning, like magazine writers, to drop their tails, he said : " Yes, I feel positive beyond a doubt, I *must* pass through *all* these conditions, one day and another ; I must go the whole round of life, and come full circle."

If he had reason to borrow an axe or plane, his habit was to return it more sharply. In a walk, his companion, a citizen, said, " I do not see where you find your Indian arrowheads." Stooping to the ground, Henry picked one up, and presented it to him, crying, " Here is one." After reading and dreaming on the Truro shore about the deeds of Captain Kidd and wrecks of old pirate ships, he walked out after dinner on the beach, and found a five-franc piece of old France, saying, " I thought it was a button, it was so black; but it is *cob-money* " (the name given there to stolen treasure). He said of early New English writers, like old Josselyn, " They give you one piece of nature, at any rate, and that is themselves, smacking their lips like a coach-whip, — none of those emasculated modern histories, such as Prescott's, cursed with a style."

> " As dead low earth eclipses and controls
> The quick high moon, so doth the body souls."

His titles, if given by himself, are descriptive enough. His " Week," with its chapters of days, is agglutinative, and chains the whole agreeably in one, —

> "Much like the corals which thy wrist enfold,
> Laced up together in congruity."

" Autumnal Tints " and " Wild Apples " are fair country invitations to a hospitable house : the platter adapts itself to its red-cheeked shining fruit. In his volume called, without *his* sensitiveness, " Excursions," the contents look like essays, but are really descriptions drawn from his journals. Thoreau, like some of his neighbors, could not *mosaic* an essay ; but he loved, like the steady shooting gossip, to tell a good story. He lacked the starch and buckram that vamps the Addison and Johnson mimes. His letters — of which more might have been printed — are abominably didactic, fitted to deepen the heroic drain. He wasted none of his precious jewels, his moments, upon epistles to the class of Rosa Matilda invalids, some of whom like leeches fastened upon his horny cuticle, but did not draw. Of this gilt vermoulu, the sugar-gingerbread of Sympathy, Hawthorne had as much. There was a blank simper, an insufficient sort of affliction, at your petted sorrow, in the story-teller, — more consoling than the boiled maccaroni of pathos. Hawthorne — swallowed up in the wretchedness of life, in that sardonic puritan element that drips from the elms of his birthplace — thought it inexpressibly ridiculous that any one should notice man's miseries, these being his staple product. Thoreau looked upon it as equally non-sense, because men had no miseries at all except those of indigestion and laziness, manufactured to their own order. The writer of fiction could not read the naturalist probably; and Thoreau had no more love or sympathy for fiction in books than in character. " Robinson Crusoe " and " Sandford and Merton," it is to be feared, were lost on him, such was his abhorrence of lies. Yet in the stoical *fond* of their characters they were alike; and it is believed that Hawthorne truly admired Thoreau. A vein of humor had they both; and when they

laughed, like Shelley, the operation was sufficient
to split a pitcher. Hawthorne could have said:
" People live as long in Pepper Alley as on Salis-
bury Plain ; and they live so much happier that an
inhabitant of the first would, if he turned cottager,
starve his understanding for want of conversation,
and perish in a state of mental inferiority." Henry
would never believe it.

As the important consequence from his gradua-
tion at Harvard, he urged upon that fading luminary, Jared Sparks, the need he had of books in the
library; and by badgering got them out. His per-
sistence became traditional. His incarceration for
one night in Concord jail, because he refused the
payment of his poll-tax, is described in his tract,
" Civil Disobedience," in the volume, " A Yankee
in Canada." In this is his signing-off: " I, H. D. T.,
have signed off, and do not hold myself responsible
to your multifarious, uncivil chaos, named Civil
Government." He never went to nor voted at a
town meeting, — the instrument for operating upon
a New England village, — nor to " meeting " or
church ; nor often did things he could not understand. In these respects Hawthorne mimicked
him. The Concord novelist was a handsome, bulky
character, with a soft rolling gait. A wit said he
seemed like a *boned pirate.* Shy and awkward,
he dreaded the stranger in his gates ; while, as

inspector, **he was employed to** swear **the oaths** *versus* **English** colliers. **When surveyor, finding** rum sent **to the African** coast **was** watered, he vowed he **would not ship** another **gill if** it was any thing but **pure proof spirit. Such was his** justice to the oppressed. **One of the things he** most dreaded was **to** be looked **at after he** was dead. Being at **a friend's demise, of whose** extinction **he had** the care, he enjoyed — as if it had been a **scene in some old** Spanish novel — his success in **keeping the waiters** from stealing the costly wines sent **in** for the **sick.** Careless of heat and cold in-doors, he lived in an Æolian-harp house, that could not be warmed : that he entered it **by a trap-door** from a rope-ladder is false. **Lovely, amiable, and** charming, his absent-mindedness passed **for un-**social when he was hatching a new tragedy. **As a writer, he** loves the morbid and the lame. The " Gentle **Boy " and** " Scarlet Letter " eloped with the girls' boarding-schools. His reputation is mas-**ter of his** literary **taste.** His characters are not drawn from life ; his **plots and** thoughts are often dreary, as he was **himself in** some lights. His favor-ite writers were " the English novelists," Boccaccio, Horace, and Johnson.

A few lines have been given from some **of Tho-**reau's accepted authors : he loved Homer for his na-**ture ;** Virgil **for his finish ;** Chaucer for his health ;

the Robin Hood ballads for their out-door blooming life ; Ossian for his grandeur ; Persius for his crabbed philosophy ; Milton for his neatness and swing. He never loved, nor did any thing but what was good, yet he sometimes got no bargain in buying books, as in " Wright's Provincial Dictionary ; " but he prized " Loudon's Arboretum," of which, after thinking of its purchase and saving up the money for years, he became a master. It was an affair with him to dispense his hardly earned pistareen. He lacked the suspicious generosity, the disguise of egoism: on him peeling or appealing were wasted ; he was as close to his aim as the bark on a tree. " Virtue is its own reward," " A fool and his money are soon parted." His property was packed like seeds in a sunflower. There was not much of it, but *that* remained. He had not the mirage of sympathies, such as Gorchakoff describes as wasted upon bare Poles. He squeezed the sandbanks of the Marlboro' road with the soles of his feet to obtain relief for his head, but did not throw away upon unskilled idleness his wage of living. No one was freer of his means in what he thought a good cause. " His principal and primary business was to be a poet : he was a natural man without design, who spoke what he thought, and just as he thought it." Antiquities, Montfaucon, or Grose, bibliomania, trifles instead of value,

dead men's shoes or fancies, he lay not up. At
Walden he flung out of the window his only ornament, — a paper weight, — because it needed dust-
ing. At a city eating-house his usual order was
" boiled apple" (a manual of alum with shortening),
seduced by its title. He could spoil an hour and
the shopman's patience in his search after a knife,
never buying till he got the short, stout blade with
the like handle. He tied his shoes in a hard lover's-
knot, and was intensely nice in his personal, —

"Life without thee is loose and spills."

He faintly piqued his curiosity with pithy *bon-
mots*, such as: " Cows in the pasture are good
milkers. You cannot travel four roads at one
time. If you wish the meat, crack the nut. If it
does not happen soon, it will late. Take time as it
comes, people for what they are worth, and money
for what it buys. As the bill, so goes the song ; as
the bird, such the nest. Time runs before men.
A good dog never finds good bones. Cherries
taste sour to single birds. No black milk, no white
crows. Foul weather and false women are always
expected. Occasion wears front-hair. No fish nor
salt when a fool holds the line. A poor man's
cow — a rich man's child — dies. Sleep is half a
dinner. A wit sleeps in the middle of a narrow
bed. Good heart, weak head. Cocks crow as for-

tune brightens. A fool is always starting. At a
small spring you can drink at your ease. Fire
is like an old maid the best company. Long talk
and little time. Better days, a bankrupt's purchase. What men do, not what they promise."

> " The poor man's childe invited was to dine,
>   With flesh of oxen, sheep, and fatted swine,
>   (Far. better cheer than he at home could finde,)
>   And yet this childe to stay had little minde.
>   You have, quoth he, no apple, froise, nor pie,
>   Stew'd pears, with bread and milk and walnuts by."

CHAPTER XIV.

FIELD SPORTS.

"At length I hailed him, seeing that his hat
Was moist with water-drops, as if the brim
Had newly scooped a running stream." — WORDSWORTH.

"I, to my soft still walk." — DONNE.

"Scire est nescire, nisi id me scire alius scierit." — LUCILIUS.

"Unus homo, nullus homo." — THEMISTIUS.

"What beauty would have lovely styled;
What manners pretty, nature mild,
What wonder perfect, all were til'd
Upon record in this blest child." — BEN JONSON.

AS an honorary member, Thoreau appertained to the Boston Society of Natural History, adding to its reports, besides comparing notes with the care-takers or curators of the *mise en scène*. To this body he left his collections of plants, Indian tools, and the like. His latest traffic with it refers to the number of bars or fins upon a pike, which had more or less than was decent. He sat upon his eggs with theirs. His city visit was to their books, and there he made his call, not upon the swift ladies of Spruce Street; and more than once he entered by the window before the janitor had digested his omelet, —

" How kind is Heaven to men ! "

When he found a wonder, he sent it, as in the case of the *ne plus ultra* balls from Flint's Pond, in Lincoln, made of grass, reeds, and leaves, triturated by washing upon the sandy beach, and rolled into polished reddish globes, about the bigness of an orange. A new species of mouse, three Blanding cistudas, and several box-turtles (rare here) were among his prizes. Of the *Cistuda Blandingii*, the herpetologist Holbrook says that its *sole* locality is the Illinois and Wisconsin prairies, and the one he *saw* came from the Fox *River*.

" Striving to save the whole, by parcells die."

On the Andromeda Ponds, between Walden and Fairhaven, he found the red snow; for things tropic or polar can be found if looked for. " There is no power to see in the eye itself, any more than in any other jelly : we cannot see any thing till we are possessed with the idea of it. The sportsman had the meadow-hens half-way into his bag when he started, and has only to shove them down. First, the idea or image of a plant occupies my thoughts, and at length I surely see it, though it may seem as foreign to this locality as Hudson's Bay is." Thus he clutched the Labrador *Ledum* and *Kalmia glauca.* His docility was great, and as the newest botanies changed the name of Andromeda to Cassandra, he accepted it, and became an accomplice to this tragic deed. Macbeth and Catiline are spared for the roses. His annual interest was paid, his banks did not fail; the lampreys' nests on the river yet surviving, built of small stones and sometimes two feet high. It is of this *petromyzon* our fishermen have the funereal idea, as they are never seen coming back after going up stream, that they all die. The dead suckers seen floating in the river each spring inspired his muse. He admired the otters' tracks, the remains of their scaly dinners, and the places on the river where they amused themselves sliding like boys. He had chased and caught woodchucks, but failed in this experiment on a fox; and caught, instead of him, a bronchial cold that did him great harm. He was in the habit of examining the squirrels' nests in the trees: the gray makes his of leaves; the red, of grass and fibres of bark. He has climbed successively four pines after hawks' nests, and was much stuck up; and once he gathered the brilliant flowers of the white-pine from the very tops of the tallest pines, when he was pitched on the highest scale. By such imprudent exertion, being strained, and that of wheeling heavy loads of driftwood, it was feared he impaired his health, always doing ideal work. Fishes' nests and spawn — more especially of the horn-pout and bream — were often

12

studied; and he carried to the entomologist Harris the first lively snow-flea he enjoyed.

> "In earth's wide thoroughfare below,
>   Two only men contented go, —
>   Who knows what 's right and what 's forbid,
>   And he from whom is knowledge hid."

Turtles were his pride and consolation. He has piloted a snapping-turtle, *Emysaurus serpentina*, to his house from the river, that could easily carry him on his back; and would sometimes hatch a brood of these Herculean monsters in his yard. They waited for information, or listened to their instinct, before setting off for the water. "If Iliads are not composed in our day, snapping-turtles are hatched and arrive at maturity. It already thrusts forth its tremendous head for the first time in this sphere, and slowly moves from side to side, opening its small glistening eyes for the first time to the light, expressive of dull rage as if it had endured the trials of this world for a century. They not only live after they are dead, but begin to live before they are alive. When I behold this monster thus steadily advancing to maturity, all nature abetting, I am convinced that there must be an irresistible necessity for mud-turtles. With what unshaking tenacity Nature sticks to one idea. These eggs, not warm to the touch, buried in the ground, so slow to hatch, are like the seeds of vegetable life. I am affected by the thought that the earth nurses these eggs. They are planted in the earth, and the earth takes care of them; she is genial to them, and does not kill them. This mother is not merely inanimate and inorganic. Though the immediate mother-turtle abandons her offspring, the earth and sun are kind to them. The old turtle, on which the earth rests, takes care of them, while the other waddles off. Earth was not made poisonous and deadly to them. The earth has some virtue in it: when seeds are put into it, they germinate; when turtles' eggs, they hatch in due time. Though the mother-turtle remained and boarded them, it would still be the universal World-turtle which through her cared for them as now. Thus the earth is the maker of all creatures. Talk of Hercules, — his feats in the cradle! what kind of nursery has this one had?"

"Life lock't in death, heav'n in a shell."

The wood-tortoise, *Emys insculpta*, was another annual favorite. It is heard in early spring, after the mud from the freshets has dried on the fallen leaves in swamps that border the stream, slowly rustling the leaves in its cautious advances, and then mysteriously tumbling down the steep bank into the river, — a slightly startling operation. He patiently speculates upon its shingled, pectinately engraved **roof or back, and its** perennial secrets in **that** indelible hierogram. **The** mud-turtle, **he** thought, only gained its peculiar odors after spring **had** come, **like** other **flowers;** and alludes to **the** high-backed, elliptical **shell of** the stink-pot covered with leeches. **Of the** trim painted tortoise he **asks:** "He **who painted** the tortoise thus, what **were his designs? The gold-bead turtle** glides **anxiously amid the** spreading calla-leaves **near** the **warm depths of the black** brook. **I have** seen **signs of** spring : I have seen a frog swiftly sinking **in a pool, or** where he dimpled the surface **as** he leapt in ; I have seen the brilliant spots of **the tor-**toises stirring **at** the bottom **of ditches; I** have seen the clear sap trickling from **the red** maple. The first pleasant days of spring **come** out like a squirrel, **and go in** again. I **do not** know at first what charms me."

THE COMING OF SPRING.

With the red leaves its floor was carpeted, —
Floor of that Forest-brook across whose weeds
A trembling tree was thrown, — those leaves so red
Shed from the grassy bank when Autumn bleeds
In **all the** maples; here the Spring first feeds
Her pulsing heart with the specked turtle's gold,
Half-seen emerging from the last year's reeds, —
Spring that is joyous and grows never old,
Soft in aerial hope, sweet yet controlled.

Gently the blue-bird warbled his sad song,
Shrill came the robin's whistle from the hill,
The sparrows twittering all the hedge along,
While darting trout clouded the reed-born rill,
And generous elm-trees budded o'er the mill,
Weaving a flower-wreath on the fragrant air;
And the soft-moving skies seemed never still,
And all was calm with peace and void from care,
Both heaven and earth, and life and all things there.

The early willows launched their catkins forth
To catch the first kind glances of the sun,
Their larger brethren smiled with golden mirth,
And alder tassels dropt, and birches spun
Their glittering rings, and maple buds begun
To cloud again their rubies down the glen,
And diving ducks shook sparkling in the run,
While in the old year's leaves the tiny wren
Peeped at the tiny titmouse, come to life again.

Frogs held his contrite admiration. " The same
starry geometry looks down on their active and
their torpid state." The little peeping hyla winds
his shrill, mellow, miniature flageolet in the warm
overflowed pools, and suggests to him this stupen-
dous image : " It was like the light reflected from
the mountain ridges, within the shaded portion of the
moon, forerunner and herald of the spring." He
made a regular business of studying frogs, — waded
for them with freezing calves in the early freshet,
caught them, and carried them home to hear their

sage songs. "I paddle up the river to see the moonlight and hear the bull-frog." He loved to be present at the instant when the springing grass at the bottoms of ditches lifts its spear above the surface and bathes in the spring air. "The grass-green tufts at the spring were like a green fire. Then the willow-catkins looked like small pearl buttons on a waistcoat. Then the bluebird is like a speck of clear blue sky seen near the end of a storm, reminding us of an ethereal region and a heaven which we had forgotten. With his warble he drills the ice, and his little rill of melody flows a short way down the concave of the sky. The sharp whistle of the blackbird, too, is heard, like single sparks, or a shower of them, shot up from the swamp, and seen against the dark winter in the rear. Here, again, in the flight of the goldfinch, in its ricochet motion, is that undulation observed in so many materials, as in the mackerel-sky." He doubts if the season will be long enough for such oriental and luxurious slowness as the croaking of the first wood-frog. Ah, how weatherwise he must be! Now he loses sight completely of those November days, in which you must hold on to life by your teeth. About May 22d, he hears the willowy music of frogs, and notices the pads on the river, with often a scolloped edge like those tin platters on which country people sometimes bake turnovers. The earth is all fragrant as one flower, and life perfectly fresh and uncankered. He says of the wood-frog, *Rana sylvatica:* "It had four or five dusky bars, which matched exactly when the legs were folded, showing that the painter applied his brush to the animal when in that position." The leopard-frog, the marsh-frog, the bull-frog, and that best of all earthly singers, the toad, he never could do enough for. It was, he says, a great discovery, when first he found the ineffable trilling concerto of early summer after sunset was arranged by the toads, — when the very earth seems to steam with the sound. He makes up his mind reluctantly, as if somebody had blundered about that time. "It would seem then that snakes undertake to swallow toads that are too big for them. I saw a snake by the roadside, and touched him with my foot to see if he were dead. He had a toad in his jaws which he was preparing to swallow, with the latter distended to three times his width; but he relinquished his prey, and fled. And I thought, as the toad jumped leisurely away, with his slime-covered hind-quarters glistening in the sun (as if I, his deliverer, wished to interrupt his meditations), without a shriek or fainting, — I thought, 'What a healthy indifference is manifested!' 'Is not this the broad earth still?' he said." He thinks the

yellow, swelling throat of the bull-frog comes
with the water-lilies. It is of this faultless singer
the good young English lord courteously asked, on
hearing it warble in the marsh one day, " What
Birds are those ? "

> " **Dear,** harmless age ! the short, swift span,
> When weeping virtue parts **with man.**"

In his **view, the squirrel** has the key to the
pitch-pine cone, **that** conical and spiry nest of
many apartments; and he is so pleased with the
flat top of the muskrat's head in swimming, and
his **back even with it, and the ludicrous way he**
shows his **curved tail when he dives, that he can-**
not fail to draw **them** on the **page. Many an** hour
he spent **in** watching the **evolutions of the** minnows **and the turtle laying its eggs,** running his
own patience **against that of the** shell, and at last
concludes the stink-pot laid its eggs in the dark,
having watched **it as long as** he could see without
their appearance. " **As soon as** these reptile eggs
are laid, the skunk comes and gobbles up the nest."
Such is a provision of Nature, who keeps that uni-
versal eating-house where guest, table, and keeper
are on the bill.

His near relation to flowers, their importance in
his landscape and his sensibility to their colors,
have been joyfully reiterated. He criticised his
floral children : " **Nature made ferns for** pure

leaves to show what she could do in that line. The
oaks are in the gray, or a little more; and the deciduous trees invest the woods like a permanent
mist. What a glorious crimson fire as you look up
to the sunlight through the thin edge of the scales
of the black spruce ! the *cones* so intensely glowing in their cool green buds, while the purplish
sterile blossoms shed pollen upon you. . . . It
seemed like a fairy fruit as I sat looking towards
the sun, and saw the red maple-keys, made all
transparent and glowing by the sun, between me
and the body of the squirrel." The excessively
minute thread-like stigmas of the hazel seen against
the light pleased him with their ruby glow, and
were almost as brilliant as the jewels of an ice-
glaze. It is like a crimson star first detected in the
twilight. These facts and similar ones, observed
afresh each year, verify his criticism, that he observes with the risk of *endless* *iteration*, he milks
the sky and the earth. He alludes to a bayberry bush without fruit, probably a male one, — " it
made me realize that this was only a more distant
and elevated sea-beach, and that we were within the
reach of marine influences," — and he sees " banks
sugared with the aster Tradescanti. I am detained
by the very bright red blackberry-leaves strewn
along the sod, the vine being inconspicuous, — how
they spot it ! I can see the anthers plainly on the

great, rusty, fusty globular buds of the slippery
elm. The leaves in July are the dark eyelash of
summer; in May the houstonias are like a sugaring
of snow. These little timid wayfaring flowers were
dried and eaten by the Indians,—a delicate meal,—

Speechless and calm as infant's sleep.

"The most interesting domes I behold are not
those of oriental temples and palaces, but of the
toadstools. On this knoll in the swamp they are
little pyramids of Cheops or Cholula, which also
stand on the plain, very delicately shaded off.
They have burst their brown tunics as they expanded, leaving only a clear brown apex, and on
every side these swelling roofs or domes are patched
and shingled with the fragments, delicately shaded
off thus into every tint of brown to the edge, as if
this creation of a night would thus emulate the
weather-stains of centuries; toads' temples, — so
charming is gradation. I hear the steady (not
intermittent) shrilling of apparently the alder-
cricket, — hear it! but see it not, clear and autumnal, a season round. It reminds me of past
autumns and the lapse of time, suggests a pleasing,
thoughtful melancholy, like the sound of the flail.
Such preparations, **such an** *outfit has our life, and
so little brought to pass.* Having found the *Calla
palustris* in one place, I soon found it in another."

He notes the dark-blue domes of the soap-wort gentian. " The beech-trunks impress you as full of health and vigor, so that the bark can hardly contain their spirits, but lies in folds or wrinkles about their ankles like a sock, with the *embonpoint* of infancy, — a wrinkle of fat. The fever-bush is betrayed by its little spherical buds, in January. Yellow is the color of spring ; red, that of mid-summer : through pale golden and green we arrive at the yellow of the buttercup ; through scarlet to the fiery July red, the red lily." He finds treasures in the golden basins of the cistus. The water-target leaves in mid-June at Walden are scored as by some literal characters. Some dewy cobwebs arrange themselves before his happy eyes, like little napkins of the fairies spread on the grass. The scent of the partridge-berry is between that of the rum-cherry and the Mayflower, or like peach-stone meats.

" How hard a man must work in order to acquire his language, — words by which to express himself. I have known a particular rush by sight for the past twenty years, but have been prevented from describing some of its peculiarities, because I did not know its name. With the knowledge of the name comes a distincter knowledge of the thing. That shore is now describable, and poetic even. My knowledge was cramped and confused before, and grew rusty because not used : it becomes communicable, and grows by communication. I can now learn what *others* know about the same thing. In earliest spring you may explore, — go looking for *radical* leaves. What a dim and shadowy existence have now to our memories the fair flowers whose localities *they* mark! How hard to find any trace of the stem now after it has been flatted under the snow of the winter! I go feeling with wet and freezing fingers amid the withered grass and the snow for their prostrate stems, that I may reconstruct the plant:—

> ' Who hath the upright heart, the single eye,
> The clean, pure hand ? '

It as sweet a mystery to me as ever what this world is. The hickories putting out young, fresh, yellowish leaves, and the oaks light-grayish ones, while the oven-bird thrums his sawyer-like strains, and the chewink rustles through the dry leaves, or repeats his jingle on a tree-top, and the wood-thrush, the genius of the wood, whistles for the first time his clear and thrilling strain. It sounds as it did the first time I heard it. I see the strong-colored pine, the grass of trees, in the midst of which other trees are but as weeds or flowers, a little exotic. The variously colored blossoms of the shrub-oaks, now in May hanging gracefully like

ear-drops, the frequent causeways and the hedge-
rows, jutting out into the meadows, and the islands,
have an appearance full of life and light. There
is a sweet, wild world which lies along the strain
of the wood-thrush, the rich intervales which border the stream of its song, more thoroughly genial
to my nature than any other."

> I heard the Spring tap at the door of Winter;
> Silently she drew herself within his house;
> Softly she with sun undraped its lights,
> And made her cottage gay.   With buds, with flowers,
> With her frail flowers, she painted the soft floors
> Of the romantic woods, and then the trees
> She broke into their clouds of foliage.
> The humming flies came forth, the turtles' gold
> Shone o'er the red-floored brook, the thrasher sang
> His singular song near by.
>
>   O Thou! the life
> That flames in all the maples, and whose hand
> Touches the chords of the mute fields until
> They sing a colored chorus, thou, my God,
> Let mortals kneel until thou callest them!

The neottia and the rattle-snake plantain are
the little things which make one pause in the wood,
— take captive the eye. The morning-glory by
Hubbard's bridge is a goblet full of purest morning air, and sparkling with dew, showing the dew-
point. He scents the perfume of the penny-royal
which his feet have bruised; the *Clethra alnifolia*
is the sweet-smelling queen of the swamp. The

white waxen berries of the white-berried or panicled cornel are beautiful, both when full of fruit
and when its cymes are naked, — delicate red
cymes or stems of berries, spreading their little
fairy fingers to the skies, their little palms ; *fairy
palms* they may be called. "I saw a delicate
flower had grown up two feet high between the
horses' path and the wheel-track. An inch more
to right or left had sealed its fate, or an inch
higher, and yet it lived to flourish as much as if it
had a thousand acres of untrodden space around it,
and never knew the danger it incurred. It did
not borrow trouble, nor invite an evil fate by
apprehending it."

"I think of what times there are, such as when
they begin to drive cows to pasture, and when the
boys go after the cows in July. There is that time
about the first of June, the beginning of summer,
when the buttercups blossom in the now luxuriant
grass, and I am first reminded of mowing and the
daisy ; when the lady's slipper and the wild-pink
have come out on the hill-sides amid the goodly
company of the blue lupines : Then has its summer-
hour fairly struck upon the clock of the seasons.
In distant groves the partridge is sitting on her
eggs. When the fresh grass waves rank, and the
toads dream, and the buttercups toss their heads,
and the heat disposes to bathe in the ponds and

streams, then is the summer begun. I saw how he fed his fish, they swimming in the dark nether atmosphere of the river rose easily to swallow such swimmers (June-bugs) of the light upper atmosphere, and sank to its bottom." He notices the *Datura stramonium* (thorn-apple) as he is crossing the beach of Hull, and felt as if he was on the highway of the world at the sight of this veteran and cosmopolite traveller. Nature in July seems like a hen with open mouth panting in the grass. He hears then, as it were, the mellow sounds of distant horns in the hollow mansions of the upper air, and he thinks more than the road-full. " While I am abroad the ovipositors plant their seeds in me ; I am fly-blown with thoughts, and go home to hatch and brood over them. It is now the royal month of August. When I hear the sound of the cricket, I am as dry as the rye which is everywhere cut and housed, though I am drunk with the season's pain. The swallow goes over with a watery twittering. The farmer has driven in his cows, and is cutting an armful of green corn-fodder for them. The loads of meadow-hay pass, which the oxen draw indifferently. The creak of the cricket and the sight of the prunella and the autumnal dandelion say: 'Work while it is day, for the night cometh in which no man can work.' "

" Both the common largest and the smallest hy-

pericums and the pin-weeds were very rich browns
at a little distance (in the middle of March), col-
oring whole fields, and also withered and falling
ferns reeking wet. It was a prospect to excite a
reindeer: these tints of brown were as softly and
richly fair and sufficing as the most brilliant autumnal tints. There **are now** respectable billows
on our vernal seas; the water is very high, and
smooth as ever it is. It is very warm; I wear but
one coat. On the water, the town and the land it
is built on seems to rise but little above the flood.
I realize how water predominates on the surface of
the globe; I am surprised to see new and unex-
pected water-lines drawn by the level edge of the
flood about knolls in the meadows and in the
woods, — waving lines which mark the boundary
of a possible or probable freshet any spring. In
September we see the ferns after the frost, like so
many brown fires they light up the meadows. In
March, when the browns culminated, the sun being
concealed, I was drawn toward and worshipped
the brownish light in the sod and the withered
grass on barren hills; I felt as if I could eat the
very crust of the earth, — I never felt so terrene,
never sympathized so with the surface of the earth.
At the same date comes the arrow-head crop, humanity patent to my eyes as soon as the snow goes
off. Not hidden away in some crypt or grave, or

under **a** pyramid, **no disgusting** mummery, but **a clean** stone ; the best symbol that could have **been, transmitted** to me, **the Red Man, his mark.   They** are not fossil bones, but, as it were, **fossil thoughts.** When I see these signs, I know that **the maker is** not far **off,** into whatever form transmuted.   **This arrow - headed** character **promises to outlast all** others.   Myriads **of** arrow-points lie sleeping **in the** skin of **the revolving** earth while meteors revolve in space.   **The footprint,** the mind-print of the oldest men, for they have camped on the plains of Mesopotamia and Marathon **too.   I** heard lately the voice of a hound **hunting by itself.   What an** awful sound to the denizens **of the wood, that re-**lentless, voracious, demonic cry, like the **voice of** a fiend ! at the hearing of which **the** fox, hare, and **marmot** tremble for their young and themselves, imagining the worst.   This, however, is the sound which the **lords** of creation love, and accompany with their bugles and *mellow* **horns,** conveying a singular dread to the **hearer, instead of** whispering peace to the hare's palpitating **breast."**

> " And their **sun does** never shine,
> And their fields are bleak and bare,
> And their ways are filled with thorns :
> It is eternal winter there."

" As the pine-tree bends and waves like a feather **in** the **gale, I see it** alternately dark and light, as the sides of the needles which reflect the cool sheen are alternately withdrawn from and restored to the proper angle. I feel something like the young Astyanax at the sight of his father's flashing crest. A peculiarity of these days (the last week of May) is the first hearing the cricket's creak, suggesting philosophy and thought. No greater event transpires now. It is the most interesting piece of news to be communicated, yet it is not in any newspaper. I went by Temple's, — for rural interest give me the houses of the poor. The creak of the mole cricket has a very afternoon sound. The heron uses these shallows on the river, as I cannot, — I give them up to him. I saw a gold-finch eating the seeds of the coarse barnyard grass, perched on it: it then goes off with a cool twitter. No tarts that I ever tasted at any table possessed such a refreshing, cheering, encouraging acid that literally put the heart in you and an edge for this world's experiences, bracing the spirit, as the cranberries I have plucked in the meadows in the spring. They cut the winter's phlegm, and now I can swallow another year of this world without other sauce. These are the warm, west-wind, dream-toad, leafing-out, willowy, haze days (May 9). No instrumental music should be heard in the streets more youthful and innocent than willow whistles. Children are digging dandelions by the

roadside with a pan and a case knife.   This re-
calls that paradisiacal condition, —

COUNTRY-LIVING.

Our reputation is not great,
Come! we can omit the date;
And the sermon, — truce to it;
Of the judge buy not a writ,
But collect the grains of wit,
And sound knowledge sure to hit.
Living in the country then,
Half remote from towns and men,
With a modest income, not
More than amputates the scot;
Lacking vestures rich and rare,
Those we have the worse for wear,
Economic of the hat,
And in fulness like the rat,
Let us just conclude we *are*,
Monarchs of a rolling star!
Fortune is to live on little,
Happily the chip to whittle,
He who can consume his ill,
Daintily his platters fill.
What 's the good of hoarding gold?
Virtue is not bought and sold.
He who has his peace of mind
Fears no tempest, seas, nor wind:
He may let the world boil on,
Dumpling that is quickly done,
And can drain *his* cup so pleasing,

> Not the ear of Saturn teasing;
> Thus defended in his state,
> Pass its laws without debate,
> And not wasting friends or fortune,
> Yet no distant stars importune.

He thus describes the last moments of an unfortunate minister: " Then this musky lagune had put forth in the erection of his ventral fins, expanding suddenly under the influence of a more than vernal heat, and his tender white belly where he kept no sight, and the minister squeaked his last! Oh, what an eye was there, my countrymen, — buried in mud up to the lids, meditating on what? Sleepless at the bottom of the pool, at the top of the bottom, directed heavenward, in no danger from motes! Pouts expect not snapping-turtles from below. Suddenly a mud volcano swallowed him up, — seized his midriff. He fell into those relentless jaws which relax not even in death. . . . I saw the cat studying ornithology between the corn-rows. She is full of sparrows, and wants no more breakfast this morning, unless it be a saucer of milk, — the dear beast! No tree has so fair a bole and so handsome an instep as the beech. The botanists have a phrase, *mantissa*, an additional matter about something, that is convenient." He uses " crichicroches, zigzagging, brattling, tussucky, trembles, flavid, z-ing;" and says of a farmer, that he keeps twenty-eight cows, which are milked at four and a half o'clock, A.M.; but he gives his hired men none of the milk with their coffee. " Frogs still sound round Callitriche Pool, where the tin is cast; no doubt the Romans and Ninevites had such places: to what a perfect system this world is reduced! I see some of those little cells, perhaps of a wasp or bee, made of clay: it suggests that these insects were the first potters. They look somewhat like small stone jugs. Evergreens would be a good title for my things, or **Gill-go-over-the-ground**, or **Winter Green,** or Checkerberry, or Usnea lichens. Methinks the scent is a more oracular and trustworthy inquisition than the eye. When, I criticise my own writing, I go to the scent, as it were. It reveals, of course, what is concealed from the other senses; by it, I detect earthiness. How did these beautiful rainbow tints get into the shell of the fresh-water clam, buried in the mud at the bottom of our dark river?

" When my eyes first rested on Walden, the striped bream rested on it though I did not see it, and when Tahatawan paddled his canoe there. How wild it makes the pond and the township to find a new fish in it! America renews her youth here. The bream *appreciated* floats in the pond as the centre of the system, a new image of God.

Its life no man can explain more than he can his own. I want you to perceive the mystery of the bream: I have a contemporary in Walden. How was it when the youth first discovered fishes? was it the number of the fin-rays or their arrangement? No! but the faint recognition of a living and new acquaintance, a friend among the fishes, a provoking mystery. I see some feathers of a blue jay scattered along a wood-path, and at length come to the body of the bird. What a neat and delicately ornamented creature! finer than any work of art in a lady's boudoir, with its soft, light purplish-blue crest, and its dark blue or purplish secondaries (the narrow half) finely barred with dusky. It is the more glorious to live in Concord because the jay is so splendidly painted. . . . In vain were the brown spotted eggs laid [of a hen-hawk killed], in vain were ye cradled in the loftiest pine of the swamp! Where are your father and mother? will they hear of your early death, before ye had acquired your full plumage? They who nursed and defended ye so faithfully!" "It is already fall (August 4) in low swampy woods where the cinnamon-fern prevails. So do the seasons revolve, and every chink is filled. While the waves toss this bright day, the ducks asleep are drifting before it across the ponds; snow-buntings are only winged snow-balls (where do they pass the night?) This (April 3) might be called the Day of the Snoring Frogs, or the Awakening of the Meadows; and toad-spawn is like *sun-squawl*, relating our marshes to Provincetown Beach. We love to wade through the shallows to the Bedford shore; it is delicious to let our legs drink air. The *palustris* frog has a hard, dry, unmusical, fine, watchman's-rattle-like stertoration; he knows no winter. . . . Nature works by contraries: that which in summer was most fluid and unresting is now, in February, most solid and motionless. Such is the cold skill of the artist, he carves a statue out of a material which is as fluid as water to the ordinary workman, — his sentiments are a quarry with which he works. I see great bubbles under the ice as I settle it down, three or four feet wide, go waddling or wabbling away, like a scared lady impeded by her train. So Nature condenses her matter: she is a thousand thick."

"Some circumstantial evidence is very strong, as when you find a trout in the milk. 'Says I to Myself,' — should be the motto to my journal. . . . They think they love God! It is truly his old clothes of which they make scarecrows for the children. When will they come nearer to God than in those very children? Hard are the times when the infants' shoes are second-foot, — truncated at the toes. There is one side of Abner's house painted as if with the pumpkin pies left over after Thanksgiving, it is so singular a yellow : —

> " And foul records
> Which thaw my kind eyes still."

—" I saw the seal of evening on the river. After bathing, even at noonday, a man realizes a morning or evening life, — a condition for perceiving beauty. How ample and generous was Nature! My inheritance is not narrow. The water, indeed, reflects heaven because my mind does. The trivialness of the day is past; the greater stillness, the serenity of the air, its coolness and transparency, are favorable to thought (the pensive eve). The shadow of evening comes to condense the haze of noon, the outlines of objects are firm and distinct (chaste eve). The sun's rays fell at right angles on the pads and willow-stems, I sitting on the old brown geologic rocks, their feet submerged and covered with weedy moss. There was a quiet beauty on the landscape at that hour which my senses were prepared to appreciate. I am made more vigorous by my bath, more continent of thought. Every sound is music now in view of the sunset and the rising stars, as if there were two persons whose pulses beat together."

CHAPTER **XV.**

CHARACTERS.

"Without misfortunes, what calamity!
And what hostility without a foe?"

YOUNG.

"O thou quick **heart,** which pantest to possess
All that anticipation feigneth fair!
Thou vainly curious mind which wouldest guess
Whence thou didst come, and whither thou mayst **go,**
And that which never yet was known would know."

SHELLEY.

"How seldom, Friend! **a good** great man inherits
Honor or wealth, with all his worth **and pains?**
Greatness and goodness are not means, but ends,—
Hath he not always treasures, always friends,
The great good man? three treasures, **love and light**
And calm thoughts, regular as infant's breath."

COLERIDGE.

"**The very dust of** his writings **is gold.**" — BENTLEY OF BISHOP PEARSON.

RECOURSE can **once more** be had to **the** note-**books of** Thoreau's conversations, **as** giving his opinions in a familiar **sort as well** as to afford in some measure **a shelter from the blasts of** fate. "Here **is** news **for a poor man, in the** raw of a September morning, **by way of breakfast** to him."

SOCIETY.

The house looks shut **up.**

Oh, yes! the owner is gone; he is absolutely out.

We can then explore the grounds, certain not to interrupt the studies of a philosopher famed for his hospitality.

How like you the aspect of the place now we have passed the gate ?

It seems well designed, albeit the fences are dropping away, the arbors getting ready for a decent fall, and the bolts and pins lacking in the machinery of the gardens. I think mostly of the owner, whom you, however, know so much better than I can.

I know him as I know old fables and Grecian mythologies. Further from all this modern life, this juggling activity, this surperfluous and untamable mediocrity, seems he to remove with each season. Dear Eidolon dwelleth in the rainbow vistas in skies of his own creating. No man in history reminds me of him, nor has there been a portrait left us of so majestic a creature, who certainly hath more a fabled and half-divine aspect than most of those so liberally worshipped by the populace. Born in the palmy days of old Greece, and under the auspices of Plato, he would have founded a school of his own, and his fame had then descended to posterity by his wise sayings, his lovely manners, his beautiful person, and the pure austerities of a blameless and temperate life. Gladly had the more eminent sculptors of the Athenian metropolis chiselled in stone his mild and serene countenance, his venerable locks, and **in the** free and majestic garb of those picturesque eras he would have ap**peared as** the most graceful **and noble of** all their popular figures. He would **have** founded their best institutions especially chosen by the **youth of** both sexes, and all who loved purity, sanctity, and the culture of the moral sentiment had flocked **about this** convenient **and** natural leader. Nor should his posthumous writings have been left ined**ited ;** for the worthiest **of his** scholars, seizing upon these happy proofs of his indefatigable industry, **and** such evidences of **his** uninterrupted communications with higher **natures,** would have **made it the** most chosen pleasure of his life to have **prepared** them in an orderly and beautiful design for coming ages. **I** know not but **he** had been worshipped formally **in** some peculiar temple set apart for his particular religion, for there inevitably springs out of him a perfect *cultus,* which a wise and imaginative age could have shaped **into its** practical advantage. **Born upon a** platform of sordid and mechanical aims, he **has** somewhat eclipsed and atrophied, and, if detected critically, blurred with scorn or ridicule, so **that** perchance he **had** been more pleasantly omitted from **all observation.**

Thou hast drawn, O Musophilus ! the portrait of

a null imaginary paragon. I have not seen the Phœnix of whom thou hast been discoursing.

No: there is not much of the worshipping kind in thee, though thou shouldst pass well for being worshipped. Thou art, I fear, among the scoffers. Be certain that the truth is so; that our ancient Eidolon does represent those aspects of the worthier ages, and yet shall his memory be respected for these properties.

I admire not thy notices and puffs of a better age, of a happier time: Don Quixote's oration to the goat-herds should have despatched that figment. I like better Jarno's opinion, — "our America is here or nowhere." Beneath our eyes grow the flowers of love, religion, sentiment, and valor. To-day is of all days the one to be admired. Alas for the sentimental tenderness of Jean Paul, that amusing madman with a remnant of brains! he has flung up his Indian ocean with the peacock-circle of its illuminated waves before our island, and Thomas Carlyle with his bilious howls and bankrupt draughts on hope distracts us. Give this class of unhappy people a little more room and less gloom. What canker has crept into so many kind-hearted creatures to deride our respectable times? I believe, too, in the value of Eidolon, but it is as good company. There are no milestones, no guide-posts, set up in that great listener's waste. His ears are open spaces, **abysses of air into** which you **may pour** all day **your wisest and** best, your moonshine **and yo**ur dreams, **and** still he stands like one ready to hear. All other men seem to **me** obstructions. Their minds are full of their **own** thoughts,— things **of** Egypt, as Mr. Borrow's gypsy Antonio calls them,— but Eidolon **has reached this** planet for no purpose but **to** hear patiently, smoothly, and *in toto* **the doings of** your muse ; and if he replies, **it is in a soft, sweet, and** floating fashion, in a sea **of** soap-bubbles that puts your dull phlegmatism going, loosens the rusty anchor of your cupidity, and away sails your sloop.

What we **so** loosely **name a** community should have been the appropriate sphere for this excellent genius. Even in these flatulent attempts **they** demand what they call **a** practical man, a desperate experimenter, sure **to** run the communal bank under **the** water. **A few** gravelly acres, some dry cows **and** pea-hens **to saw** up the sunny noons, with our good Eidolon **at the head,** behold a possible community. **In his pocket lies the** practical man's notions of communing,— **I** mean his purse.

I have fancied Cervantes shadows **in** his **novel the** history **of** our socialists.

Not of the whole : **ere** long the community must be **the** idea and the practice of American society. Each year more clearly sets forth the difficulties under which we labor to conduct the simplest social operations, like mere household service. Such a rough grindstone is your Christian American family to the hard-worked Irish girl, and wild is the reaction of the strong-tempered blade on the whirling stone, — to make coffee and bake bread. Not to do the thing for yourself constitutes the person who does it at once the possessor of your moneys, goods, and estate ; and, from the lack of sympathy and equality in the contract, Bridget slides out of your kitchen the victor in this unequal contest, when you have made her by your lessons valuable to others. And what better is your relation with the gentleman you send to Washington by means of your votes and good wishes, having his eye bent on the main chance. Cities are malignant with crime ; paupers are classed and studied like shrimps ; the railroad massacres its hundreds at a smash ; steamboats go down, and blow up ; and these evils are increasing steadily, till the social crisis comes. Nothing for all these cases but the community, no more selfish agents, no corporations fighting each other, no irresponsible actors, — all must be bound as one for the good of each, labor organized for the whole equally.

We have sat too long in this crazy arbor: it is contagious. Let us walk amid last year's stalks. " Little joy has he who has no garden," says Saadi.

"He who sees my garden sees my heart," said the prince to Bettine. I prefer the names of pears to those of most men and women. Our little gentleman, with his gaseous inflamed soul, can never be satisfied with that little which he needs and not for long. Satisfied! No, Faintheart, you are as unsatisfied as the toper without his glass, the maid without her lover, or the student without his book. I can allow thee, mortal as I am, but six minutes to tell thy story. What needest thou, then, added to that thou hast? Community, indeed! a mere artifice of the do-nothings to profit by the labors of industry. There thou art, with thy five feet eight in thy shoes, and a certain degree of bodily vigor and constitution. I have not heard thee complain of the headache or the gout; thou hast never St. Anthony's fire; thy corns, if thou hast, are limited; and thou canst, on occasion, plod thy dozen of miles and not expire. Let us agree that middle-age has come, and one half the vital candle has been burnt and snuffed away. Some kind of shed, with a moderate appurtenance of shingle, belongs to your covering, on the outskirts of yonder village; some little table-linen, not damask I grant; maybe a cup of coffee to your breakfast, and some crust of haddock, or soured residuum of starch, called bread, to thy meal. Of clothing thou hast not cloth of gold, — we are plain country people and decline it. **A few** friends remain, as many or more than thou **hast deserved. Having all** this, some **liberty** and hope of Marston's immortality (that depends **on** personal value), I seriously demand, what more could you have? **Can** nothing appease the ever **disorderly** cravings of that adamantine contradiction, thy imbecile soul? Buy **him up or flatter him into quiet;** or could you not give **him** away or sell **him into splendid** exile? **at least, expunge him!**

Whichever way we choose in the fields, **or down the** locomotive **spine that bands with yellow the** else green meadow, you will observe the hay-maker. Now **is** the high holiday and the festival of that gramineous sect ; now are the cattle kneeled to by humanity; and all these long baking days there they **toil and** drudge, collating the winter **hay-mow of** cow and ox, determined by some secret fate **to** labor for an inferior race.

They are so serious in such matters, one **might** suppose they never speculate on the final **cause of** pitching hay.

Just as seriously this excellent society contemplates the butcher, the grocer, or the clergyman. As if, given time and the human race, at once follows absurd consequence. **Spring to** your pitch, **jolly** haymakers! you **fancy you are** putting time **to good** advantage in chopping away so many innocent spires of grass, drying them, and laying **them** industriously **in** the mow. **In** spite of that official serenity which nothing can disturb, **if you would** forego the **cow and horse** from your contemplations you might leave the grass unmown for **ever** and a day. Organize an idea **among the brethren of** spending their **hours after a certain fashion, and** then woe be to the lunatics who **discern its imper-** fections. In history, haymaking may figure **as an** amazing bit of the antique, and pitchforks **be ex-** hibited in museums for curiosities.

I understand your jest : it is your old notion **to** abbreviate human **work. You** would **fain** intro duce the study of botany or metaphysics **for these** vigorous games of our sunburnt **swains, and con-** vert them into sedentary pedants, **to be fed on** huckleberries and mast. In the sweat of **thy** face shalt thou earn thy bread. Labor comes out of human existence, like the butterfly out **of** the caterpillar. How tremendously that vigorous Hibernian pokes aloft his vast pitchfork of blue timothy! May I never be **seated on the** prong! And his brogue is as thick as **his hay-mow.** No law ever made such a police as labor. **Early to bed and** early to rise grows by farming. Tire him, says Destiny; wear **him out,** arms, legs, and back; secure his mischievous wild energy; get him under, **the** dangerous cartridge **he** is of exploding un-

13*

licensed sense; and whether it be good for cow or horse, whatever the means, the end is delightful. Nature must have made the human race, like most of her things, when she had the chance, and without consideration of the next step. She drove along the business, and so invented mankind as rapidly as possible; and observing the redskin, cousin to the alligator, — living on the mud of rivers, the sap of trees, with a bit of flat stone for his hatchet, and a bit of pointed stone for his cannon, — redskin, a wild fellow, savage and to the manner born, — leaving the woods and fields, the flowers, insects, and minerals untouched, she was thus far content. This imperfect redskin was surely some improvement upon the woodchuck and the musquash. But after coming to the age of bronze, the Danish Kitchen-möddings, and the Swiss lake-dwellings, some million centuries, and a certain development, the aboriginal began to develop a new series of faculties that Nature in eliminating him never thought nor dreamed of; for we must carefully confess Nature misses imagination. Our redskin had fenced himself from bears and deer with their own skins, lit a perennial fire, (was it not hard, yet to be expected in the Greeks, that they had never a temple of Prometheus?) dug out some stones and melted them, burnt the trunks of trees into boats, at length built houses, and all the while with his arts, fine or coarse, grew up his passions. Our whiteskin — for now the color of him, by shelter and clothing, had turned white — became a cultivated savage, and still luxuriating in his old cannibal propensities hacked and hewed, fought and killed his kind, much to the surprise of his sleepy mother; and not after the honest primeval fashions that she liked well enough, being of her own invention, but after every excruciating device of artist-demonism. Now what could she do for him, how keep him in place, circumvent his trucidating mania, and make him somewhat helpless? It was the work of a moment (Nature's moments being somewhat extended), an accident. She not only taught whiteskin how to work, but he came to be just a mere laboring machine; the savage had his *insouciance*, the civilizee has his competitive industry, — "dearest, choose between the two?" This new toy is the true Danaïdes sieve, the rock of Tantalus, which is christened industry, economy, or money, like the boy's toad in the well, whose position his master set him to make out as a task, — the toad jumping one step up and falling two steps back, how long would it require for him to get to the top? The boy ciphered a long time and filled his slate, went through recess, and noon and afternoon: at last his instructor asked him, after keeping him at it all day, as to his progress and how far he had got the toad. "What?" said the boy, — "that toad, that nasty little toad? Why, to be sure, he's half way down into —— by this time." That is where the great mother, blessings on her comfort, has located our brother-man, with his pitchfork, plough-tail, and savings-bank. It is the consequence of a quandary, this *boasted civilization*, as Fourier terms it, when Nature, having hurried her poor plucked creature into existence (even if Darwin thinks he rubbed off his wool climbing bread-fruit trees and flinging down cocoa-nuts to his offspring), was compelled for safety to set up this golden calf, this lovely mermaid-civilization, with a woman's head and a fish's tail, clipper-ships, and daily papers. Expediency is Nature's mucilage, her styptic. Never shall we see the terminus of this hastily built railroad, no station. But there must be a race that will, when the mind shall be considered before the belly, and when raising food for cows, other things being possible, may not be to every human being just an inscrutable penalty. Cows may get postponed after a time for mere men and women ; but even milking a beast is a better course of policy than cutting holes in your brother's skull with a bushwhack. Our mythology hath in it a great counterpoise of ethics and compensation, while the Greeks hung aloft their theoretical people, where at least they could do no harm if they did not any benefit, while some of our goodies to-day seem to be, like the spider, spinning an immortal coil of ear-wax.

I strive to be courtesy itself, yet I may not accept thy fact nor thy conclusion. That redskin was nearer nature, was truer than this pale-face; his religion of the winds, the waters and the skies, was clearer and fresher than your dry and desiccated theologies, dug out of Egyptian tombs and Numidian sandbanks. He properly worshipped the devil, the evil spirit, wisely agreeing that if the good spirit was of that ilk he was harmless, like the Latins, whom I look upon as the best type of Indians that ever lived. As Tiberius says, who made his Latin rhyme (no doubt they had as much rhyme as they wanted), "*deorum injuriæ, dis curæ*," — "the gods may cut their own corns for all me." Or what old Ennius thinks: —

> "Ego deum genus dixi et dicam cœlitum,
>   Sed eos **non** curare, opinor, quid agat humanum genus;
>   Nam, si curent, bene bonis sit, male malis, quod nunc abest."

In other words, "I know all about your race of gods, but little they trouble their heads about your folks; if they cared a snap, they would see the good well off and the bad punished, which is just the opposite to the fact." Is not that good Indian? Or what Lucan says in his Pharsalia (vii. 447): —

> " Mentimur regnare Jovem . . . mortalia nulli
>   Sunt curata Deo."

" Every fool knows it 's a lie that Jove reigns, — the gods don't busy their brains about such nobodies as men." I try to give you the ideas of these solemn **Latin** savages, who had **neither** hats to their heads, shirts to their bodies, **nor shoes to** their feet. **Why** might not some **learned professor** derive us **from the Romans?** I **believe a** return **to** the savage state would be a good thing, interpolating what is really **worthy in our arts and sciences and** thousand appliances, —

> " That the wind blows,
>   Is all that anybody knows."

I believe in having things as they **are not?** **Ay,** down **to the dust** with **them, slaves as** they *are !* **Down** with your towns, governments, tricks and **trades, that seem like the boy** who was building the model of a **church** in dirt as the minister was **passing !** " Why, my little lad," said **he,** " why, making a meeting-house of that **stuff?** Why, why !" " Yes," **answered the youth,** " yes, I am ; and I expect to have enough left over to make a Methodist minister besides." There is always some new fatality attending your civility. Here is our town, six miles square, with so many dogs and cats, so many men and women upon it, a town library and a bar-room, taxes, prisons, churches, railroads, — and always more and more to come. And I must be taxed as well as the others; as if I am ripe for chains or the gibbet, because the drunkard, poisoned with his own rum while selling it for the good of his neighbors, dies of cerebral congestion or a pistol. Society has no definitions, and of course no distinctions; accepts no honesties, believes too much in going to the bad.

You are over-critical. The true art of life consists in accepting things as they are, and not endeavoring vainly to better them. It is but a drawing of lots. I am melted when I see how finely things come out, and pin-pricks decide grave affairs. A certain man (I will not name him here, as personalities must be avoided) determined to keep house on a better plan: no flies, no bills, — even the cry of offspring at night cancelled. This was enough evil for that day: the next all the doors were open, flies abounded, children cried in swarms, cash for bills was needed. Our friend began again with it all, put his reforms in practice, and serenity came from his efforts for the time being; but there is another relapse as soon as his hand leaves the crank of the household. So he consults Mrs. Trip, — she has experience as a housekeeper, — details his wretchedness: life is at such a pass, expense vast, little to be had for it and nothiug to defray it; a ream of German fly-paper has

produced double the number of flies that it kills;
as for his babies, there seems to have been a com-
bination among them to blow their lungs out with
squalls. Mrs. Trip heard the social horrors, and
said, "Mr. Twichett, excuse me, there is a little
matter." "Yes, mum, I know it," says our gentleman, supposing it the latest infant or the bill for
salt-fish. "It appears, Mr. Twichett, that you
keep your eyes open. Yes, sir! you keep your
eyes open."

CHRYSOSTOM.

I lately paid a visit upon an ingenious gentleman, and found him mopping up a topic which had
a singular importance in his eyes, and that was
New England. "Indeed," I thought, "a fine
subject for the dead of winter!" You must
know, sir, that friend Chrysostom presents the
aspect of man talking, as dear Eidolon thinking.
And, as the honey-lipped philosopher is about to
embark on a voyage to the provinces, he is resolved
to enlighten them there on this his favorite problem. "Indeed," I thought to myself, "this man,
like Curtius, is also a hero in his way: he is a man
of parts; and, next to beating carpets on the Common, I must say he chooses delightful subjects."
I fell upon him with my modern flail, to see what
grain I could find amid his glittering straws.

And how did you prosper? **Was there much** sediment in the husk?

Chrysostom is too learned a master of his weapon to abandon all his treasure to the unreserved gaze of each incredulous worldling. He has, however, attained proximately to something that might **be** termed a criticism of New England. Good, bad, or indifferent, 'tis not a pure vacuity that one finds in this pitiful corner of **a** continent, with Cape Cod for a seacoast and Wachusett for a mountain. Chrysostom has picked his men as specimens of the mass; his persons **on** which he so much insists, the merchant, the scholar, the reformer, the **proser,** and what not,—along the dusty high-roads of life, but you may no**t** greatly expand the list,— lead flats. A few serenities stand sentinel **on the** watch-towers of thought, not as stars to the mass, but as burnt-out tar-barrels. Materialism carves turkeys and cuts tunnels. Be bright, my dear talker, shine and go along; as Dante says, " Hurry on your words." I deemed not so much of his topics as of the man himself, greater far than all his topics, the ultimate product of all the philosophies, with an Academe of Types. He has caught the universe on his thumbnail, and cracked it; he has been at the banquet of the gods, and borrowed the spoons. Most other men have some superstitious drawback **to** them, some want of confidence in their universal wholes. But our great friend, with his muscular **habit of** thought, grasps **hold** of infinity and breaks it across his arm, as Gustavus Adolphus, that hero of Captain Dalgetty's, a horse-shoe. " Never," said he, " can you get a good brain until all the people of the earth are poured into one, and when the swarthy Asiatic thinks in the same skull with the ghostly Swede. And soon I see that this railroad speed of the age shall transmigrate into **the** brain. Then shall **we** make the swiftness **of the** **locomotive into the** swiftness of the thought ; **and the** great abolition society shall come, not of slavery alone, — in **dress and diet, in social relations** and religion. It may not prevail **for a pair of** hermits to go out together **and make a** community ; for so shall they be the more **solitary.** You think the men are too near that I should draw their portraits **truly, but** you know not that I am living as **one** dead, and that my age is like one walking far **off in a** dream to me. That golden steed, the Pegasus, on which I am mounted, has shot with me **far** beyond the thoughts and the men of to-day." **As he** said this, I looked up at the window, certainly expecting to see some **sort of** strange apparition in the air, some descent of **a** sign from heaven upon this glorious expanding beyond time ; but all I could see was a fat serving-maid, in a back case**ment,** arranging some furniture with a vacillating rag. **Types of the ideal** and the real, I thought **to** myself, " Man should never for an instant blame the animals," he continued, " **for** showing their apparent inferiorities : they **do simply formalize our** sins; and Agorax **should beware of pork, as he is** feasting upon **his** ancestry. **The** tail **of the** dog is **the type of the** affections." **No** matter how dry **the** topic, it seems as **if** Chrysostom had plunged down **into the** cellar of the **gods,** and moistened **his** intellectual clay **at** every golden cider-bung. " Nature is a fine setting **for** man; and when **I speak of the** New English, how can I forget the departure **from** their **old abbeys,** green fields, and populated wheat-lands for this sour fish-skin? **Three** degrees **of elevation towards the pole overturn all** jurisprudence, and virtue **faints in the city of the** pilgrims. **The** handsome **youth** fires the **tragic** pistol, **the handsome girl** seeks **her** swift **revenge on prose in her** opium. And in these architectures **cold,** still, **and locked, in** these flat, red-brick **surfaces, and the** plate-glass windows **that try to flatten your nose when you** think **to** look **in, — do you not behold** something **typical? This prismatic nucleus of** trade, deducting **its tolls** from the country through **its roads,** drawing **Vermont and New** Hampshire and floating them **away** o'er **yon** glittering blue **sea** between **those** icy islands! **Some smaller German orchestra** leads off

the musical ear, and the **shops are** cracking with
French pictures **that** would **not be sold in** Paris.
The merchant has **his** villa, his park, and **his *ca-
lèche :*** it is the recoil of the passions ; **it is** fate,
and no **star of** heaven is visible. The oak in the
flower-pot might serve as a symbol ; or, as Jugur-
tha said, when he was thrust **into** his prison,
'Heavens, how cold is this bath **of** yours!' **If
the All-Father** had said to our metaphysical North-
man, to this Brain-berserkir : Come and sit **thee
beneath** the fluttering palms, **and listen** to the flow
of lordly rivers ; thee will I **feed** on orient pearls of
dew, thy bed shall be **of sun-flowers, thy** dress
of the gossamer twilight!"

> Light **from the** spirit-land,
> Fire **from a** burning brand,
> If in this cold sepulchral clime,
> Chained to an unmelodious rhyme,
>   **Thou** slowly **moulderest,** —
> **Yet cheer** that great **and humble heart,**
> Prophetic eye **and sovereign part,**
> And be thy future greatly **blest,**
> And by some richer gods impressed,
>   And a sublimer art.
>
> Strike on ! **nor** still **the** golden **lyre,**
> That sparkles with Olympian **fire,**
> And be thy words the soul's **desire**
>   Of this dark savage land ;

Nor shall thy sea of glory fail
Whereon thou sweepest, — spread thy sail,
And blow and fill the heaviest gale,
　　It shall not swerve thy hand.

Born for a fate whose secrets none
Shall gaze upon beneath earth's sun,
Child of the high, the only One,
　　Thy glories sleep secure ;
Yet on the coast of heaven thy wave
Shall dash beyond an unknown grave,
And cast its spray to light and save
　　Some other barks that moor !

CHAPTER XVI.

MORAL.

" Exactissima norma Romanæ frugalitatis."
Said of Mannius Curius.

" Laborers that have no land
To lyve on but hire handes."
PIERS PLOWMAN.

"Les gros bataillons ont toujours raison."
JOMINI.

" The day that dawns in **fire will die in storms,**
Even though the noon be calm."
SHELLEY.

" When thou dost shine, darkness looks white and fair,
Frowns turn to music, clouds to smiles and air."
VAUGHAN.

" Dum in Prœlio non procul hinc
Inclinatam suorum aciem
Mente manu voce et exemplo
Restituebat
Pugnans ut heroas decet
Occubuit."
MARSHAL KEITH'S EPITAPH.

WHAT a life is the soldier's, — like other
men's! what a master is the world! Heaven
help those who have no destiny to fulfil, balked of
every chance or change, of all save the certainty of
death! Thoreau had a manifest reason for living.
He used to say, "I do not know how to entertain

those who can't take long walks. A night and a
forenoon is as much confinement to those wards
(the house) as I can stand." And although the
rich and domestic could "beat him in frames,"
like that Edinburgh artist whom Turner thus com-
plimented, he was their match in the open. Men
affected him more naturally. "How earthy old
people become, — mouldy as the grave. Their
wisdom smacks of the earth : there is no foretaste
of immortality in it. They remind one of earth-
worms and mole-crickets." Seeing the negro barber
sailing alone up the river on a very cold Sunday,
he thinks he must have experienced religion ; a
man bathing from a boat in Fairhaven Pond suggests: " Who knows but he is a poet in his yet
obscure and golden youth?" And he loved to go
unmolested. He would not be followed by a dog
nor cane. He said the last was too much company. When asked whether he knew a young
miss, celebrated for her beauty, he inquired, " Is
she the one with the goggles?" He thought he
never noticed any one in the street; yet his contemporaries may have known as much of him while
living as of Shakespeare when dead. His mental
appearance at times almost betrayed irritability ;
his words were like quills on the fretful porcupine
(a libel on the creature, which is patience *ab ovo*).
One of his friends complained of him : " He is so

pugnacious I can love, but I can **never** like him."
And he had a strong aversion to **the Scribes and**
Pharisees. Those cracked potsherds, traditionary
institutions, served him **as butts,** against whose
sides he discharged the arrows of his wit, echoing
against their massive hollowness. Yet, **truly,** the
worship of beauty, of the fine things in nature, **of**
all good **and** friendly pursuits, was his staple ; **he**
enjoyed **common people ; he relished strong, acrid**
characters.

When with **temperaments** radically opposed **to**
his, he **drew in the head of his** pugnacity like
that portion **of one of his beloved** turtles, **and**
could hiss and snap with **any** ancient of **them all.**
The measured, conservative class, **dried-up** Puritan
families, who fancy **the** Almighty Giver of all good
things has fitted **their** exquisite brain precisely to
his evangelic nightcap ; prosers with their uni-
verse of meanness and conceit to change square
with you against **gold** and diamonds ; folks of
easy manners, polished and oiled to run sharply on
the track of lies and compliments, — of *such* he was
no great admirer. Neither did he go with Goethe, that other people are wig-blocks on which we
must fit **our own** false heads of hair to fetch them
out. Like **a cat he would** curl up his spine and
spit **at a** fop **or** monkey, and despised those who
were running well down **hill to damnation. His**

advice to a drunkard as the **wisest plan for him to** reform, **" You had** better **cut** your throat," — that **was** his idea of moral suasion, **and** corresponded with his pleasure at John **Brown's** remark of a **bor**-der ruffian he had despatched, rapidly paring away his words, — " He had a perfect right to be hung." To this his question points, — " If it were not for virtuous, brave, generous natures, would there be any sweet fragrance ? Genius rises above nature in spite **of heat, in** spite **of cold,** works and lives." **Persons with whom he had** no sympathy were to him more removed than stocks and stones : " Look-**ing** at the latter, I feel comparatively **as if I** were with my kindred. **Men may** talk about **measures** till all is blue and smells of brimstone, **and then go** home and expect their measures to do their duty for them : the only measure is integrity and man-hood. **W**e seem to have used up all our inherited freedom **like** the young bird the albumen in the shell. **Ah, how** I have thriven on solitude and pov-erty ! **I** cannot overstate this advantage, I am per-haps more wilful than others. Common life is hasty, coarse, and trivial, as if you were a spindle in a fac-tory. No exercise implies more manhood and vigor than joining thought to thought. How few men can tell **what** they have thought ! I hardly know half a dozen **who** are not too lazy for this. You conquer fate by thought. **If you think** the fatal thought of

14

men and institutions, you need never pull the trigger. The consequences of thinking inevitably follow. There is no more Herculean task than to think a thought about this life, and then get it expressed. There are those who never do or say any thing, whose life merely excites expectation. Their excellence reaches no further than a gesture or mode of carrying themselves; they are a sash dangling from the waist, or a sculptured war-club over the shoulder. They are like fine-edged tools gradually becoming rusty in a shop-window. I like as well, if not better, to see a piece of iron or steel out of which such tools will be made, or the bushwhack in a man's hand. . . . The watchmaker finds the oil from the porpoise's jaw the best thing for oiling his watches. Man has a million eyes, and the race knows infinitely more than the individual. Consent to be wise through your race. We are never prepared to believe that our ancestors lifted large stones or built thick walls. . . . There is always some accident in the best things, whether thoughts, or expressions, or deeds. The memorable thought, the happy expression, the admirable deed are only partly ours. The thought came to us because we were in a fit mood, also we were unconscious and did not know that we had said or done a good thing. We must walk consciously only part way toward our goal, and then leap in the dark to our success. What we do best or most perfectly is what we most thoroughly learned by the longest practice, and at length it fell from us without our notice as a leaf from a tree. It is the *last* time we shall do it, — our unconscious leavings : —

> 'Man is a summer's day, whose youth and fire
> Cool to a glorious evening and expire.'

"It is remarkable how little we attend to what is constantly passing before us, unless our genius directs our attention that way. In the course of ages the rivers wriggle in their beds until it feels comfortable under them. Time is cheap and rather insignificant. It matters not whether it is a river which changes from side to side in a geological period, or an eel that wriggles past in an instant. A man's body must be rasped down exactly to a shaving. The mass of men are very unpoetic, yet that Adam that names things is always a poet. No man is rich enough to keep a poet in his pay, yet what a significant comment on our life is the least strain of music. This poor, timid, unenlightened, thick-skinned creature, what can it believe ? When I hear music, I fear no danger ; I am invulnerable ; I see no foe ; I am related to the earliest times, and to the latest. I hear music below ; it washes the dust off my life and every thing I look at. The field of my life becomes a boundless plain, glorious to tread, with no death or disappointment at the end of it. In the light of this strain there is no Thou nor I. How inspiring and elysian it is to hear when the traveller or the laborer, from a call to his horse or the murmur of ordinary conversation, rises into song! It paints the landscape suddenly; it is at once another land,—the abode of poetry. Why do we make so little ado about echoes? they are almost the only kind of kindred voices that we hear:—

' Scattering the myrrhe and incense of thy prayer.' "

A coxcomb was railed at for his conceit: he said, " It is so common every one has it; why notice it specially in him?" He gets up a water-color sketch of an acquaintance. "He is the moodiest person perhaps I ever saw. As naturally whimsical as a cow is brindled, both in his tenderness and in his roughness he belies himself. He can be incredibly selfish and unexpectedly generous. He is conceited, and yet there is in him far more than usual to ground conceit upon. He will not stoop to rise. He wants something for which he will not pay the going price. He will only learn slowly by failure, not a noble but a disgraceful failure, and writes poetry in a sublime slip-shod style." But despite his *caveats*, his acceptance was large, he took nearly every bill. The no-money men, butter-egg folks; women who are talking-machines and work the tbreads of scandal ; paupers, walkers, drunk or dry, poor-house poets, no matter, the saying of Tacitus abided, — "I am a man, and nothing human but what can go down with me." Of such a one he says, "His face expressed no more curiosity or relationship to me than a custard pudding." Of such is the kingdom of poor relations.

No man had a better unfinished life. His anticipations were vastly rich: more reading was to be done over Shakespeare and the Bible; more choice apple-trees to be set in uncounted springs, — for his chief principle was faith in all things, thoughts, and times, and he expected, as he said, "to live for forty years." He loved hard manual work, and did not mean to move every year, like certain literary brethren. In his business of surveying he was measurably diligent, and having entered on a plan would grind his vest away over the desk to have done with it. He laid out every molecule of fidelity upon his employer's interests, and in setting a pine-lot for one says, "*I set every tree with my own hands.*" Yet like moralists, though he tried to pay every debt as if God wrote the bill, he takes himself to task: "I remember with a pang the past spring and summer thus far. I have not been an early riser: society seems to have invaded and overrun me."

Thus intensely he endeavored to live, but living

is not all. He had now more than attained the middle age, his health sound to all appearance, his plans growing more complete, more cherished ; new lists of birds and flowers projected, new details to be gathered upon trees and plants, now embarking more closely in the details of this human enterprise which *had* been something miscellaneous ; the time had fairly come to take an account of stock, and to know how we really stood on *terra firma.* Here was a great beginning in a condition of matchless incompleteness to be adjusted by no one but the owner. In November, 1860, he took a severe cold by exposing himself while counting the rings on trees and when there was snow on the ground. This brought on a bronchial affection, which he much increased by lecturing at Waterbury ; and although he used prudence after this, and indeed went a-journeying with his friend, Horace Mann, Jr., into Minnesota, this trouble with the bronchiæ continued. With an unfaltering trust in God's mercies and never deserted by his good genius, he most bravely and unsparingly passed down the inclined plane of a terrible malady, pulmonary consumption, working steadily at the completing of his papers to his last hours, or so long as he could hold the pencil in his trembling fingers. Yet, if he did get a little sleep to comfort him in this year's campaign of sleepless affliction, he was sure to interest those about him with his singular dreams, more than usually fantastic: he said once that, having got a few moments of repose, " sleep seemed to hang round my bed in festoons." The last sentence he incompletely spoke contained but two distinct words, " moose," and " Indians," showing how fixed in his mind was that relation. Then the world he had so long sung and delighted in faded tranquilly away from his eyes and hearing, till on that beautiful spring morning of May 6th, 1862, it closed on him.

> " **In** this roadstead I have ridden,
> In this covert I have hidden,
> Friendly thoughts were cliffs to me,
> And I was beneath their **lea.**
>
> This true people **took the stranger,**
> **And** warm-hearted housed **the ranger;**
> **They** received their roving guest,
> **And** have fed **him** with the best;
>
> Whatsoe'er the land afforded
> To **the stranger's** wish accorded,
> Shook **the olive, stripped the** vine,
> And expressed **the** strengthening wine.
>
> And by night they did spread o'er **him**
> What by day they spread before **him,**
> That good-will which was repast
> **Was his** covering at last."

His state of mind during this, his only decided illness, deserves notice as in part an idiosyncrasy. He accepted it heroically, but in no wise after the traditional manner. He experienced that form of living death when the very body refuses sleep, such is its deplorable dependence on the lungs now slowly consumed by atoms; in its utmost terrors refusing aid from any opiate in causing slumber, and declaring uniformly that he preferred to endure with a clear mind the worst penalties of suffering, rather than be plunged in a turbid dream by narcotics. He ineffably retired into his inner mind, into that unknown, unconscious, profound world of existence where he excelled; there he held inscrutable converse with just men made perfect, or what else, absorbed in himself. " The night of time far surpasses the day ; and who knows when was the equinox ? Every hour adds unto the current arithmetic, which scarce stands one moment. And since death must be the Lucina of life ; since our longest sun sets on right declensions, and makes but winter arches, therefore it cannot be long before we lie down in darkness and have our light in ashes. Sense endureth no extremities, and sorrows destroy us or themselves : our delivered senses not relapsing into cutting remembrances, our sorrows are not kept raw by the edge of repetitions." An ineffable reserve shrouded this to him unforeseen fatality: he had never reason to believe in what he could not appreciate, nor accepted formulas of mere opinions; the special vitalization of all his beliefs, self-consciously, lying in the marrow of his theology.

As noticed, he had that forecast of life which by no means fulfils its prediction deliberately; else why are these mortal roads on which we so predictively travel strewn with the ashes of the young and fair, — this Appian Way devised in its tombs, from the confidence of the forty years to come? "*Quisque suos patimur manes,* — we have all our infirmities first or last, more or less. There will be, peradventure, in an age, or one of a thousand, a Pollio Romulus, that can preserve himself with wine and oil; a man as healthy as Otto Hervardus, a senator of Augsburg in Germany, whom Leovitius, the astrologer, brings in for an example and instance of certainty in his art; who, because he had the significators in his geniture fortunate, and free from the hostile aspects of Saturn and Mars, — being a very cold man, — could not remember that ever he was sick." The wasting away of his body, the going forth and exit of his lungs, which, like a steady lamp, give heat to the frame, was to Henry an inexplicably foreign event, the labors of another party in which he had no hand; though he still credited the fact to a lofty inspiration. He would often say that we could look on ourselves as a third person, and that he could perceive at times that he was out of his mind. Words could no longer express these inexplicable conditions of his existence, this sickness which reminded him of nothing that went before : such as that dream he had of being a railroad cut, where they were digging through and laying down the rails, — the place being in his lungs. His habit of engrossing his thoughts in a journal, which had lasted for a quarter of a century ; his out-of-door life, of which he used to say, if he omitted that, all his living ceased, — all this now became so incontrovertibly a thing of the past that he said once, standing at the window, " I cannot see on the outside at all. We thought ourselves great philosophers in those wet days, when he used to go out and sit down by the wall-sides." This was absolutely all he was ever heard to say of that outward world during his illness ; neither could a stranger in the least infer that he had ever a friend in field or wood. Meanwhile, what was the consciousness in him, — what came to the surface ? Nothing save duty, duty, work, work ! As Goethe said at the loss of his son, " It is now alone the idea of duty that must sustain us," Thoreau now concentrated all his force, caught the shreds of his fleeting physical strength the moment when the destinies accorded to him a long breath, **to** complete **his stories of the** Maine **Woods, then in press ; endeavor** vainly to finish his lists of Birds and Flowers, **and** arrange his papers on Night and Moonlight. **Never** at any time **at** all communicative **as** to **his own** physical condition, having caught that **Indian trick of** superlative reticence, he calmly bore the fatal torture, this **dying** at the stake, **and was torn limb from limb in silence : —**

> " When **all** this frame
> **Is** but one dramme, and what thou now **descriest**
> In sev'rall parts shall want a name."

His patience was **unfailing :** assuredly he **knew** not aught save resignation **; he did** mightily **cheer** and **console** those whose strength was less. **His every** instant now, his least thought **and** work, sacredly belonged to them, dearer **than his** rapidly perishing **life, whom he** should **so** quickly leave behind. **As** long **he could** possibly sit up, he **insisted** on his **chair at the family-table,** and **said,** " It would not **be social to take** my **meals** alone." And on hearing **an** organ **in the** streets, playing **some old** tune of his childhood he should never hear again, the tears fell from his eyes, and he **said,** " Give him some money ! give him some **money ! "**

> " He was retired as noontide dew,
> Or fountain in a noon-day grove ;

> And you must love him, ere to you
> He would seem worthy of your love.
>
> The outward shows of sky and earth,
> Of hill and valley, he has viewed ;
> And impulses of deeper birth
> Have come to him in solitude."

His mortal ashes are laid in the Concord burying-ground. A lady on seeing this tranquil spot, and the humble stone under the pitch-pine tree, replied to one who wished for him a starry-pointing monument, " This village is his monument, covered with suitable inscriptions by himself."

Truth, audacity, force, were among Thoreau's mental characteristics, devoted to humble uses. His thoughts burned like flame, so earnest was his conviction. He was transported infinitely beyond the regions of self when pursuing his objects, single-hearted, doing one thing at a time and doing that in the best way ! Self-reliance shall serve for his motto, —

> " His cold eye truth and conduct scanned."

His faith in wildness was intrinsic. Whatever sport it was of nature, this child of an old civilization, this Norman boy with the blue eyes and brown hair, held the Indian's creed, and believed that plant and animal were a religion unto themselves and unto him. He spoke with that deeper than

self-conscious conviction which must animate nature. It required, literally, an unquestioning
obedience to that sphere and rule of life he kept;
his means to his ends, — Thoreau, the Poet-
Naturalist.

MEMORIAL VERSES,

ILLUSTRATING CHIEFLY—

SCENES OF THOREAU'S LIFE.

———◆———

I.

To Henry.

Hearest thou the sobbing breeze complain
  How faint the sunbeams light **the** shore?—
His heart more fixed than earth or main,
  Henry! thy faithful **heart is** o'er.

Oh, weep not thou thus **vast a soul,**
  Oh, do not mourn **this lordly man,**
As long as Walden's **waters roll,**
  And Concord river fills a span.

For thoughtful minds in Henry's page
  Large welcome **find,** and bless his **verse,**
Drawn from **the** poet's heritage,
  From wells of right and nature's **source.**

Fountains **of hope and** faith! inspire
  Most stricken hearts to lift this cross,
His perfect trust shall keep the fire,
  His **glorious peace** disarm **the loss!**

II.

WHITE POND.

GEM of the wood and playmate of the sky,
How glad on thee we rest a weary eye,
When the late ploughman from the field goes home,
And leaves us free thy solitudes to roam!

Thy sand the naiad gracefully had pressed,
Thy proud majestic grove the nymph caressed,
Who with cold Dian roamed thy virgin shade,
And, clothed in chastity, the chase delayed,
To the close ambush hastening at high noon,
When the hot locust spins his Zendic rune.

Here might Apollo touch the soothing lyre,
As through the darkening pines the day's low fire
Sadly burns out, and Venus nigh delay
With young Adonis, while the moon's still ray
Mellows the fading foliage, as the sky
Throws her blue veil of twilight mystery.

No Greece to-day, no dryad haunts the road
Where sun-burned farmers their poor cattle goad;
The black crow caws above yon steadfast pine,
And soft Mitchella's odorous blooms entwine

These mossy rocks, and piteous catbirds scream,
And redskins flicker through the white man's
  dream.

Who haunts thy wood-path? — ne'er in summer
  pressed
Save by the rabbit's foot, its winding best
Kept a sure secret, till the tracks, in snow
Dressed for their sleds, the lumbering woodmen
  plough.
How soft yon sunbeam paints the hoary trunk,
How fine the glimmering leaves to shadow sunk!
Then streams across our grassy road the line
Drawn firmly on the sward by the straight pine;
And curving swells in front our feet allure,
While far behind the curving swells endure;
Silent, if half pervaded by the hum
Of the contented cricket. Nature's sum
Is infinite devotion. Days nor time
She emulates, — nurse of a perfect prime.
Herself the spell, free to all hearts; the spring
Of multiplied contentment, if the ring
With which we're darkly bound.
                    The pleasant road
Winds as if Beauty here familiar trode,
Her touch the devious curve persuasive laid,
Her tranquil forethought each bright primrose
  stayed
In its right nook. And where the glorious sky
Shines in, and bathes the verdant canopy,
The prospect smiles delighted, while the day
Contemns the village street and white highway.

Creature all beauteous!   In thy future state
Let beauteous Thought a just contrivance date;
Her altars glance along thy lonely shore,
Relumed; and on thy leafy forest floor
Tributes be strewn to some divinity
Of cheerful mien and rural sanctity.
Pilgrims might dancing troop their souls to heal;
Cordials, that now the shady coves conceal,
Reft from thy crystal shelves, we should behold,
And by their uses be thy charms controlled.

Naught save the sallow herdsboy tempts the shore,
His charge neglecting, while his feet explore
Thy shallow margins, when the August flame
Burns on thy edge and makes existence tame;
Naught save the blue king-fisher rattling past,
Or leaping fry that breaks his lengthened fast;
Naught save the falling hues when Autumn's sigh
Beguiles the maple to a sad reply;
Or some peculiar air a sapless leaf
Guides o'er thy ocean by its compass brief.

Save one, whom often here glad Nature found
Seated beneath yon thorn, or on the ground
Poring content, when frosty Autumn bore
Of wilding fruit to earth that bitter store;
And when the building winter spanned in ice
Thy trembling limbs, soft lake! then each device
Traced in white figures on thy seamed expanse
This child of problems caught in gleeful trance.
Oh, welcome he to thrush and various jay,
And echoing veery, period of the day!

To each clear hyla trilling the new spring,
And late gray goose buoyed on his icy wing ;
Bold walnut-buds admire the gentle hand,
While the shy sassafras their rings expand
On his approach, and thy green forest wave,
White Pond! to him fraternal greetings gave.
The far white clouds that fringe the topmost pine
For his delight their fleecy folds decline ;
The sunset worlds melted their ores for him,
And lightning touched his thought to seraphim.
Clear wave, thou wert not vainly made, I know,
Since this sweet man of Nature thee could owe
A genial hour, and hope that flies afar,
And revelations from thy guiding star.
Oh, may that muse, of purer ray, recount,
White Pond! thy glory, and, while anthems mount.
In strains of splendor, rich as sky and air,
Thy praise, my Henry, might those verses share.
For He who made the lake made it for thee,
So good and great, so humble yet so free ;
And waves and woods we cannot fairly prove,
Like souls descended from celestial Jove,
Men that defraud the pathos of the race
By cheerful aims, and raise their dwelling-place
On safe Olympus ; hopes that swell untold,
Too far for language, honesty ne'er sold.

With thee he is associate.   Hence I love
Thy gleams, White Pond! thy dark, familiar grove ;
Thy deep green shadows, clefts of pasture ground ;
Mayhap a distant bleat the single sound,
One distant cloud, the sailor of the sky,
One voice, to which my inmost thoughts reply.

III.

A Lament.

A WAIL for the dead and the dying!
They fall in the wind through the Gilead tree,
Off the sunset's gold, off hill and sea;
    They fall on the grave where thou art lying,
    Like a voice of woe, like a woman sighing,
Moaning her buried, her broken love,
Never more joys, — never on earth, never in heaven
        above!

Ah, me! was it for this I came here?
Christ! didst thou die that for this I might live?
    An anguish, a grief like the heart o'er the bier —
Grief that I cannot bury, nor against it can strive —
Life-long to haunt me, while breath brings to-morrow,
Falling in spring and in winter, rain and sleet sorrow,
Prest from my fate that its future ne'er telleth,
Spring from the unknown that ever more welleth.

Fair, O my fields! soft, too, your hours!
Mother of earth, thou art pleasant to see!
    I walk o'er thy sands, and I bend o'er thy flowers.
There is nothing, O nothing, thou givest me,
Nothing, O nothing, I take from thee.

What are thy heavens, so blue and so fleeting?
(Storms, if I reck not), no echo meeting
In this cold heart, that is dead to its beating,
Caring for nothing, parting or greeting!

IV.

MORRICE LAKE.

ON Morrice Lake I saw the **heron flit**
And the wild wood-duck **from her** summer perch
Scale painted by, trim in **her plumes, all** joy;
And the old **mottled** frog **repeat his bass,**
Song of our **mother earth, the child so dear.**
There, in **the stillness of the forest's night,**
Naught **but the interrupted sigh of the breeze,**
Or the far panther's **cry, that, o'er the** lake,
Touched with its sudden irony and woke
The sleeping shore; and then I hear its crash,
Its deep **alarm-gun on the** speechless night, —
A falling **tree, hymn** of the **centuries.**

No sadness haunts **the** happy **lover's mind,**
On thy lone **shores,** thou anthem of **the woods,**
Singing her calm reflections; the tall pines,
The sleeping **hill-side** and the distant sky,
And thou! the sweetest figure in the scene,
Truest and best, **the** darling **of my** heart.

O Thou, the ruler of **these** forest shades,
.And by thy **inspiration who controll'st**

The wild tornado in its **narrow path,**
And deck'st with fairy **wavelets the small breeze,**
That like some lover's sigh entreats the **lake ;**
O Thou, who in the shelter of these groves
Build'st up the life of nature, as a **truth**
Taught to dim shepherds on their **star-lit** plains,
Outwatching midnight ; who in **these deep shades**
Secur'st the bear and catamount a place,
Safe from the **glare of the infernal gun,**
And leav'st the finny **race their** pebbled home,
Domed with **thy watery sunshine,** as a mosque ;
God of the solitudes ! **kind to** each thing
That creeps or flies, **or launches** forth its webs, —
Lord ! in thy mercies, **Father !** in thy **heart,**
Cherish thy wanderer **in these** sacred **groves ;**
Thy spirit send **as erst o'er** Jordan's **stream,**
Spirit and love and mercy **for his needs.**
Console him with thy seasons as they **pass,**
And with an unspent joy attune his soul
To endless rapture. Be to him, — thyself
Beyond **all** sensual things that **please** the eye,
Locked **in his inmost** being ; let no dread,
Nor **storm with** its wild splendors, nor the tomb,
Nor all that **human hearts can sear or** scar,
Or cold forgetfulness **that** withers hope,
Or base undoing **of** all human love,
Or those faint sneers that pride and riches cast
On unrewarded merit, — **be, to** him,
Save as **the echo** from uncounted depths
Of an unfathomable past, **burying**
All present griefs.

Be merciful, be **kind** !

Has he not **striven,** true **and** pure **of** heart,
Trusting in thee ?   Oh, falter **not,** my child !
Great store of recompense thy **future holds,**
Thy love's sweet councils and those faithful hearts
Never to be estranged, that **know thy worth.**

V.

TEARS IN SPRING.

THE swallow is flying over,
But he will *not* come to me;
He flits, my daring rover,
From land to land, from sea to sea;
Where hot Bermuda's reef
Its barrier lifts to fortify the shore,
Above the surf's wild roar
He darts as swiftly o'er, —
But he who heard his cry of spring
Hears that no more, heeds not his wing.

How bright the skies that dally
Along day's cheerful arch,
And paint the sunset valley!
How redly buds the larch!
Blackbirds are singing,
Clear hylas ringing,
Over the meadow the frogs proclaim
The coming of Spring to boy and dame,
But not to me, —
Nor thee!

And golden crowfoot 's shining near,
Spring everywhere that shoots 'tis clear,

A wail in the wind is all I hear;
A voice of woe for a lover's loss,
A motto for a travelling cross, —
And yet it is mean to mourn for thee,
In the form of bird or blossom or bee.

Cold are the sods of the valley to-day
Where thou art sleeping,
That took thee back to thy native clay;
Cold, — if above thee the grass is peeping
And the patient sunlight creeping,
While the bluebird sits on the locust-bough
Whose shadow is painted across thy brow,
And carols his welcome so sad and sweet
To the Spring that comes and kisses his feet.

VI.

The Mill Brook.

THE cobwebs close are pencils of meal,
   Painting the beams unsound,
And the bubbles varnish the glittering wheel
   As **it** rumbles round and round.
Then the Brook began to talk
   And the water found **a** tongue,
We have danced a long dance, said **the gossip,**
   A long way have we danced and sung.

Rocked in a cradle of sanded **stone**
Our waters wavered ages alone,
Then glittered at **the** spring
On whose banks **the** feather-ferns **cling,**
And **down** jagged ravines
We fled tortured,
And our wild eddies **nurtured**
Their black **hemlock screens ;**
And o'er the soft **meadows we** rippled along,
And soothed their lone hours with a sweet pensive
    song, —
Now at this mill **we're plagued to** stop,
To let our miller **grind the crop.**

So the clumsy farmers come
With their jolting wagons far **from home.**

We grind their grist, —
It wearied a season to raise,
Weeks of sunlight and weeks of mist,
Days for the drudge and Holydays.
To me fatal it seems,
Thus to kill a splendid summer,
And cover a landscape of dreams
In the acre of work and not murmur.
I could lead them where berries grew,
And sweet flag-root and gentian blue,
And they will not come and laugh with me,
Where my water sings in its joyful glee;
Yet small the profit, and short lived for them,
Blown from Fate's whistle like flecks of steam.

The old mill counts a few short years, —
Ever my rushing water steers!
It glazed the starving Indian's red,
On despair or pumpkin fed,
And oceans of turtle notched ere he came,
Species consumptive to Latin and fame,
(Molluscous dear or orphan fry,
Sweet to Nature, I know not why).

Thoughtful critics say that I
From yon mill-dam draw supply. —
I cap the scornful Alpine heads,
Amazons and seas have beds,
But I am their trust and lord.
Me ye quaff by bank and board,
Me ye pledge the iron-horse,
I float Lowells in my source.

The farmers lug **their bags and say,** —
"**Neighbor,** wilt **thou grind the grist to-day?**"
Grind it with his **nervous** thumbs,
Clap his aching shells behind it,
Crush it into crumbs?

No! his dashboards from the **wood**
Hum the dark pine's solitude;
Fractious teeth are **of the quarry**
That I crumble in **a hurry,** —
Far-fetched duty is to me
To turn this old wheel carved of a **tree.**

I like the maples in my side,
Dead leaves, the darting trout;
Laconic rocks (they sometime put me **out)**
And moon or stars that ramble with **my tide,**
The polished air, I think **I could abide.**

This selfish race **to prove me,**
Who use, but do not love me!
Their undigested **meal**
Pays not my labor **on** the **wheel.**
I like better the sparrow
Who sips up **a drop** at morn,
Than the men who vex my marrow,
To grind their cobs and corn.

Then said I to my brook, "**Thy** manners **mend,**
Thou art a tax on earth for me to spend."

VII.

STILLRIVER, THE WINTER WALK.

The busy city or the heated car,
The unthinking crowd, the depot's deafening jar,
These me befit not, but the snow-clad hill
From whose white steeps the rushing torrents fill
Their pebbly beds, and as I look content
At the red Farm-house to the summit lent,
There, — underneath the hospitable elm,
That broad ancestral tree, that is the helm
To sheltered hearts, — not idly ask in vain,
Why was I born, — the heritage of pain?

The gliding trains desert the slippery road,
The weary drovers wade to their abode;
I hear the factory bell, the cheerful peal
That drags cheap toil from many a hurried meal.
How dazzling on the hill-side shines the crust,
A sheen of glory unprofaned by dust!
And where thy wave, Stillriver, glides along,
A stream of Helicon unknown in song,
The pensive rocks are wreathed in snow-drifts high
That glance through thy soft tones like witchery.

To Fancy we are sometimes company,
And solitude's the friendliest face we see.

Some serious village slowly through to pace,
No form of all its life thine own to trace;
Where the cross mastiff growls with blood-shot eye,
And barks and growls and waits courageously;
Its peaceful mansions my desire allure
Not each to enter and its fate endure, —
But fancy fills the window with its guest;
The laughing maid, — her swain who breaks the jest;
The solemn spinster staring at the fire,
Slow fumbling for his pipe, her solemn sire;
The loud-voiced parson, fat with holy cheer,
The butcher ruddy as the atmosphere;
The shopboy loitering with his parcels dull,
The rosy school-girls of enchantment full.

Away from these the solitary farm
Has for the mind a strange domestic charm,
On some keen winter morning when the snow
Heaps roof and casement, lane and meadow through.
Yet in those walls how many a heart is beating,
What spells of joy, of sorrow, there are meeting!
One dreads the post, as much the next, delay,
Lest precious tidings perish on their way.
The graceful Julia sorrows to refuse
Her teacher's mandate, while the boy let loose
Drags out his sled to coast the tumbling hill,
Whence from the topmost height to the low rill,
Shot like an arrow from the Indian's bow,
Downward he bursts, life, limb, and all below
The maddening joy his dangerous impulse gives;
In age, how slow the crazy fact revives!

15*

Afar I track the railroad's gradual bend,
I feel the distance, feel the silence lend
A far romantic charm, the Farm-house still
And spurn the road that plods the weary hill, —
When like an avalanche the thundering car
Whirls past, while bank and rail deplore the jar.
The wildly piercing whistle through my ear
Tells me I fright the anxious engineer;
I turn, — the distant train and hurrying bell
Of the far crossing and its dangers tell.
And yet upon the hill-side sleeps the farm,
Nor maid or man or boy to break the charm.

Delightful Girl! youth in that farm-house old,
The tender darling in the tender fold, —
Thy promised hopes fulfilled as Nature sought
With days and years the income of thy thought;
Sweet and ne'er cloying, beautiful yet free,
Of truth the best, of utter constancy;
Thy cheek whose blush the mountain wind laid on,
Thy mouth whose lips were rosebuds in the sun;
Thy bending neck, the graces of thy form,
Where art could heighten, but ne'er spoil the charm;
Pride of the village school for thy pure word,
Thy pearls alone those glistening sounds afford;
Sure in devotion, guileless and content,
The old farm-house is thy right element.
Constance! such maids as thou delight the eye,
In all the Nashua's vales that round me lie!

And thus thy brother was the man no less, —
Bred of the fields and with the wind's impress.

With hand as open as his heart was free,
Of strength half-fabled mixed with dignity.
Kind as a boy, he petted dog and hen,
Coaxed his slow steers, nor scared the crested wren.
And not far off the spicy farming sage,
Twisted with heat and cold, and cramped with age,
Who grunts at all the sunlight through the year
And springs from bed each morning with a cheer.
Of all his neighbors he can *something* tell, —
'Tis bad, whate'er, we know, and like it well!—
The bluebird's song he hears the first in spring,
Shoots the last goose bound South on freezing wing.

Ploughed and unploughed the fields look all the same,
White as the youth's first love or ancient's fame ;
Alone the chopper's axe awakes the hills,
And echoing snaps the ice-encumbered rills,
Deep in the snow he wields the shining tool,
Nor dreads the icy blast, himself as cool.
Seek not the parlor, nor the den of state
For heroes brave, make up thy estimate
From these tough bumpkins clad in country mail,
Free as their air and full without detail.

No gothic arch *our* shingle Pæstum boasts, —
Its pine cathedral is the style of posts, —
No crumbling abbey draws the tourist here
To trace through ivied windows pictures rare,
Not the first village squire allows his name
From aught illustrious or debauched by fame.

That sponge profane who drains away the bar
Of yon poor inn extracts the mob's huzza ;

Conscious of-morals lofty as their own,
The glorious Democrat, — his life a loan.
And mark the preacher nodding o'er the creed,
With wooden text, his heart too soft to bleed.
The Æsculapius of the little State,
A typhus sage, sugars his pills in fate,
Buries three patients to adorn his gig,
Buys foundered dobbins or consumptive pig;
His wealthy pets he kindly thins away,
Gets in their wills, — and ends them in a day.
Nor shall the strong schoolmaster be forgot,
With fatal eye who boils the grammar pot:
Blessed with large arms he deals contusions round,
While even himself his awful hits confound.

Pregnant the hour when at the tailor's store,
Some dusty Bob a mail bangs through the door.
Sleek with good living, virtuous as the Jews,
The village squires look wise, desire the news.
The paper come, one reads the falsehood there,
A trial lawyer, lank-jawed as despair.
Here, too, the small oblivious deacon sits,
Once gross with proverbs, now devoid of wits,
And still by courtesy he feebly moans,
Threadbare injunctions in more threadbare tones.
Sly yet demure, the eager babes crowd in,
Pretty as angels, ripe in pretty sin.
And the postmaster, suction-hose from birth,
The hardest and the tightest screw on earth,
His price as pungent as his hyson green,
His measure heavy on the scale of lean.

A truce to these reflections, as I see
The winter's orb burn through yon leafless tree,
Where far beneath the track Stillriver runs,
And the vast hill-side makes a thousand suns.
This crystal air, this soothing orange sky,
Possess our lives with their rich sorcery.
We thankful muse on that superior Power
That with his splendor loads the sunset hour,
And by the glimmering streams and solemn woods
In glory walks and charms our solitudes.

VIII.

T R U R O.

I.

Ten steps it lies from off the sea,
　Whose angry breakers score the sand,
　A valley of the sleeping land,
Where chirps the cricket quietly.

The aster's bloom, the copses green,
　Grow darker in the softened sun,
　And silent here day's course is run,
A sheltered spot that smiles serene.

It reaches far from shore to shore,
　Nor house in sight, nor ship or wave,
　A silent valley sweet and grave,
A refuge from the sea's wild roar.

Nor gaze from yonder gravelly height, —
　Beneath, the crashing billows beat,
　The rolling surge of tempests meet
The breakers in their awful might.

And inland birds soft warble here,
　Where golden-rods and yarrow shine,

And cattle pasture — sparest kine!
A rural place for homestead dear.

Go not then, traveller, nigh the shore,
  In this soft valley muse content,
  Nor brave the cruel element,
That thunders at the valley's door.

And bless the little human dell,
  The sheltered copsewood snug and warm, —
  Retreat from yon funereal form,
Nor tempt the booming surges' knell.

II.

THE OLD WRECKER.

He muses slow along the shore,
  A stooping form, his wrinkled face
  Bronzed dark with storm, no softer grace
Of hope; old, even to the core.

He heeds not ocean's wild lament,
  No breaking seas that sight appall, —
  The storms he likes, and as they fall
His gaze grows eager, seaward bent.

He grasps at all, e'en scraps of twine,
  None is too small, and if some ship
  Her bones beneath the breakers dip,
He loiters on his sandy line.

Lonely as ocean is his mien,
  He sorrows not, nor questions fate,
  Unsought, is never desolate,
Nor feels his lot, nor shifts the scene.

Weary he drags the sinking beach,
  Undaunted by the cruel strife,
  Alive, yet not the thing of life,
A shipwrecked ghost that haunts the reach.

He breathes the spoil of wreck and sea,
  No longer to himself belongs,
  Always within his ear thy songs,
Unresting Ocean! bound yet free.

In hut and garden all the same,
  Cheerless and slow, beneath content,
  The miser of an element
Without a heart, — that none can claim.

Born for thy friend, O sullen wave,
  Clasping the earth where none may stand!
  He clutches with a trembling hand
The headstones from the sailor's grave.

III.

Unceasing roll the deep green waves,
  And crash their cannon down the sand,
  The tyrants of the patient land,
Where mariners hope not for graves.

The purple kelp waves to and fro,
  The white gulls, curving, scream along;
  They fear not thy funereal song,
Nor the long surf that combs to snow.

The hurrying foam deserts the sand,
  Afar the low clouds sadly hang,
  But the high sea with sullen clang,
Still rages for the silent land.

No human hope or love hast thou,
  Unfeeling Ocean, in thy might,
  Away — I fly the awful sight,
The working of that moody brow.

The placid sun of autumn shines, —
  The hurrying knell marks no decline,
  The rush of waves, the war of brine,
Force all, and grandeur, in thy lines.

Could the lone sand-bird once enjoy
  Some mossy dell, some rippling brooks,
  The fruitful scent of orchard nooks,
The loved retreat of maid or boy.

No, no; the curling billows green,
  The cruel surf, the drifting sand,
  No flowers or grassy meadow-land,
No kiss of seasons linked between.

The mighty roar, the burdened soul,
  The war of waters more and more,
  The waves, with crested foam-wreaths hoar,
Rolling to-day, and on to roll.

w

IV.

WINDMILL ON THE COAST.

With wreck of ships, and drifting plank,
  Uncouth and cumbrous, wert thou built,
  Spoil of the sea's unfathomed guilt,
Whose dark revenges thou hast drank.

And loads thy sail the lonely wind,
  That wafts the sailor o'er the deep,
  Compels thy rushing arms to sweep,
And earth's dull harvesting to grind.

Here strides the fisher lass and brings
  Her heavy sack, while creatures small,
  Loaded with bags and pail, recall
The youthful joy that works in things.

The winds grind out the bread of life,
  The ceaseless breeze torments the stone,
  The mill yet hears the ocean's moan,
Her beams the refuse of that strife.

V.

I hear the distant tolling bell,
  The echo of the breathless sea;
  Bound in a human sympathy
Those sullen strokes no tidings tell.

The spotted sea-bird skims along,
  And fisher-boats dash proudly by ;
  I hear alone that savage cry,
That endless and unfeeling song.

Within thee beats no answering heart,
  Cold and deceitful to my race,
  The skies alone adorn with grace
Thy freezing waves, or touch with art.

And man must fade, but thou shalt roll
  Deserted, vast, and yet more grand ;
  While thy cold surges beat the strand,
Thy funeral bells ne'er cease to toll.

VI.

MICHEL ANGELO — AN INCIDENT.

Hard by the shore the cottage stands,
  A desert spot, a fisher's house,
  Where could a hermit keep carouse
On turnip-sprouts from barren sands.

No church or statue greets the view,
  Not Pisa's tower or Rome's high wall,
  And connoisseurs may vainly call
For Berghem's goat, or Breughel's hue.

Yet meets the eye along a shed,
  Blazing with golden splendors rare,
  A name to many souls like prayer,
Robbed from a hero of the dead.

It glittered far, the splendid name,
  Thy letters, Michel Angelo, —
  In this lone spot none e'er can know
The thrills of joy that o'er me came.

Some bark that slid along the main
  Dropped off her headboard, and the sea
  Plunging it landwards, in the lee
Of these high cliffs it took the lane.

But ne'er that famous Florentine
  Had dreamed of such a fate as this,
  Where tolling seas his name may kiss,
And curls the lonely sand-strewn brine.

These fearless waves, this mighty sea,
  Old Michel, bravely bear thy name!
  Like thee, no rules can render tame,
Fatal and grand and sure like thee.

VII.

Of what thou dost, I think, not art,
  Thy sparkling air and matchless force,
  Untouched in thy own wild resource,
The tide of a superior heart.

No human love beats warm below,
  Great monarch of the weltering waste, —
  The fisher-boats make sail and haste,
Thou art their savior and their foe.

Alone the breeze thy rival proves,
　Smoothing o'er thee his graceful hand,
　Lord of that empire over land,
He moves thy hatred and thy loves.

Yet thy unwearied plunging swell,
　Still breaking, charms the sandy reach,
　No dweller on the shifting beach,
No auditor of thy deep knell ; —

The sunny wave, a soft caress ;
　The gleaming ebb, the parting day ;
　The waves like tender buds in May,
A fit retreat for blessedness.

And breathed a sigh like children's prayers,
　Across thy light aerial blue,
　That might have softened wretches too,
Until they dallied with these airs.

Was there no flitting to thy mood ?
　Was all this bliss and love to last ?
　No lighthouse by thy stormy past,
No graveyard in thy solitude !

Cambridge : Press of John Wilson and Son.